Laced with Magic

Titles by Barbara Bretton

LACED WITH MAGIC
CASTING SPELLS
JUST DESSERTS
JUST LIKE HEAVEN
SOMEONE LIKE YOU
CHANCES ARE
GIRLS OF SUMMER
SHORE LIGHTS
A SOFT PLACE TO FALL
AT LAST
THE DAY WE MET
ONCE AROUND
SLEEPING ALONE
MAYBE THIS TIME
ONE AND ONLY

Anthologies

THE CHRISTMAS CAT
**(with Julie Beard, Jo Beverly,
and Lynn Kurland)**

Laced with Magic

BARBARA BRETTON

**Doubleday Large Print
Home Library Edition**

BERKLEY BOOKS, NEW YORK

This Large Print Edition, prepared especially for Doubleday Large Print Home Library, contains the complete, unabridged text of the original Publisher's Edition.

THE BERKLEY PUBLISHING GROUP
Published by the Penguin Group
Penguin Group (USA) Inc.
375 Hudson Street, New York, New York 10014, USA
Penguin Group (Canada), 90 Eglinton Avenue East, Suite 700, Toronto, Ontario M4P 2Y3, Canada
(a division of Pearson Penguin Canada Inc.)
Penguin Books Ltd., 80 Strand, London WC2R 0RL, England
Penguin Group Ireland, 25 St. Stephen's Green, Dublin 2, Ireland
(a division of Penguin Books Ltd.)
Penguin Group (Australia), 250 Camberwell Road, Camberwell, Victoria 3124, Australia
(a division of Pearson Australia Group Pty. Ltd.)
Penguin Books India Pvt. Ltd., 11 Community Centre, Panchsheel Park, New Delhi—110 017, India
Penguin Group (NZ), 67 Apollo Drive, Rosedale, North Shore 0632, New Zealand
(a division of Pearson New Zealand Ltd.)
Penguin Books (South Africa) (Pty.) Ltd., 24 Sturdee Avenue, Rosebank, Johannesburg 2196,
South Africa

Penguin Books Ltd., Registered Offices: 80 Strand, London WC2R 0RL, England

This book is an original publication of The Berkley Publishing Group.

This Large Print Book carries the Seal of Approval of N.A.V.H.

For Bertrice Small, who was right

1

Chloe

Did you ever have the feeling that you were exactly where you were meant to be, that the fates had finally got it right and the rest of your life was going to be clear sailing? That was how I felt the first time Luke MacKenzie and I kissed: like I was seeing the world through new eyes.

The first time our hands touched over a basket of alpaca roving, sparks flew. Bright silver-white sparks that shot from our fingertips and lit up the night. It was every love story I had ever read, every romantic movie I had ever wept over, all my hopes and dreams wrapped up into one tall, dark, and handsome package. It didn't even matter that he was one hundred percent human and I was the daughter of a sorceress. I believed that now that I had finally found love, the rest would fall into place like magick.

Crazy? I wouldn't bet against it. Despite all the evidence to the contrary, I still believed I was on my way to the storybook happy ending none of the women in my family had ever managed to achieve.

I mean, I even made a sweater for him, and every knitter on the planet knows you *never* knit a sweater for the one you love until you have the ring on your finger.

What was I thinking?

I guess the truth is I wasn't thinking at all. All those romantic movies and novels I had devoured over the years hadn't prepared me for the real thing. Luke and I had gone from zero to sixty in a nanosecond, from strangers to lovers to living together in less time than it took most people to shake hands.

But then, this wasn't the real world. It just looked like it.

By the way, I'm Chloe Hobbs, knit shop owner and de facto mayor of Sugar Maple, a tiny little town tucked between two mountains in the northwest corner of Vermont. We're a classic New England hamlet, famous for scenic views and great shopping, but trust me, there's more going on in Sugar Maple than meets the eye.

Up until Luke, a former police detective from Boston, showed up in early December to investigate the drowning death of his friend Suzanne Marsden, I had been the only resident human. Well, half human, to be precise, but without magick, the sorceress side of my lineage hardly mattered.

Remember the old TV show *The Munsters*? Marilyn was the all-American blonde who stuck out like a sore thumb in her family of irregulars. I guess you could say that was the part I played here in Sugar Maple. When the real world came calling, I was the one who answered.

And even I had to admit I was the logical choice.

A tenth-generation witch owns the Cut & Curl across the street from my knit shop. The hardware store is run by the sweetest family of werewolves you'll ever meet. The Sugar Maple Arts Playhouse is under the direction of shapeshifters who serve as their own repertory company. Faeries keep the Inn's restaurant fully booked, and I guess it wouldn't surprise you to learn that the town funeral parlor belongs to a happily married couple who happen to be vampire.

And that doesn't count the trolls, selkies, goblins, sprites, spirits, and mountain giants who call our town home.

The unexpected success of my yarn shop had brought even more attention to Sugar Maple than our white picket fences and picturesque village green. My shop had been rated New England's number one knitting destination two years running, and if the blogosphere had anything to do with it, we were about to make it three for three. A protective spell cast over our town by one of my ancestors made it possible for us to hide in plain sight, but when that spell started wearing down last year—well, that was when the troubles really started.

My ancestor Aerynn had fled Salem during the infamous witch hunts and found sanctuary here with other outcasts in search of a home. Aerynn was a sorceress, and she expressed her gratitude by casting a protective charm over Sugar Maple designed to keep the village safe from the sharp eyes of the real world as long as one of her female descendants walked the earth.

I was the last descendant of Aerynn and, in the eyes of almost everyone in town, pretty much a loser. Oh, they loved me, but I don't think even my closest friends believed I would ever come through for Sugar Maple. I mean, I was almost thirty years old with no husband, no kid, and no magick. Even worse, I had no prospects of any kind. The only thing I had going for me was the ability to knit and spin like my foremothers, but even I didn't think I could stockinette my way out of the mess the town was in.

And then Luke showed up and everything changed.

Who would have guessed that love would trigger my inner sorceress and awaken powers I didn't know existed? Suddenly I had everything I had ever dreamed about: magick and love and enough yarn to last ten lifetimes.

And who would have guessed it wouldn't be close to enough to save us?

⁓

It all began to fall apart on the day of our monthly town meeting. I'm not ashamed to admit I was grateful we moved it up two days so that it didn't fall on the night of the full moon. Town meetings were crazy enough; they didn't need any help from lunar forces on the loose. The snow had finally melted, and while much of the landscape was a giant trough of mud, the promise of spring was everywhere I looked.

The tourist trade had been quiet all week and I spent most of my time playing catch-up with the projects I'd let slide over the winter. (You don't want to know how many things I had on the needles. It's too embarrassing.) I'd been working on the edging of an Orkney Pi for what seemed like three or four lifetimes and hoped to finish it off in time for the Weekend of Lace Workshop I had planned for early May.

Lace knitting has a way of taking over a knitter's brain. Sit down with a complicated lace pattern and I guarantee you won't think of anything else until you finally come up for air. But that day the front door to the shop was open and the air finally smelled of spring, and not even the lure of lace could hold me.

Okay. I admit it. It wasn't so much spring fever that made me close down the shop early and pull Luke away from his desk in the police station next door; it was more the sense that something was slipping away from us and I didn't know exactly what it was, much less how to stop it.

Actually it felt more like a certainty. The knowledge that the first part of our journey was over and now the hard part was about to begin.

My surrogate mother, Sorcha, had warned me that there would be trouble ahead. "Let him go, daughter," she had said. "I'm too late to keep you from falling in love with him but not too late to keep you from ruining his life."

I refused to believe that loving me could ruin Luke's life. I wasn't blind to all he would be giving up if he decided to stay in Sugar Maple permanently. His family and friends were down in Boston. His normal warm-blooded human family who loved him and missed him and wanted him to marry another normal warm-blooded human and have kids and settle in one of the nearby suburbs.

Luke's contract with the state would expire in a little over a month and we still hadn't talked about whether he would sign on as Sugar Maple's permanent chief of police. Last week the powers-that-be in Montpelier contacted me about a few of their own candidates that had literally made my blood run cold. I guess it was naïve of me, but I'd assumed that since we were a couple, Luke would want the job. I mean, it wasn't like there was much call for police chiefs in our part of the state. If he wanted to be an alpha cop, we were pretty much his best bet.

I knew I should talk to him about it. The villagers had been asking about his plans since the day he drove into town. It would be nice to finally have an answer for them.

Which, of course, was a total lie. I wanted the answer for myself and I wanted it to be yes.

And it would be yes. I knew it would be. Except for the whole magick/human problem, we were perfect for each other. We made each other laugh. We listened to each other's stories. I loved the way he looked and smelled and sounded. I loved the feel of his hands on me when we made love, the look in his eyes just before he kissed me.

And yes, I loved the fact that he was a mortal man. I had never been attracted to men with magick. Over the years my friends had set me up with selkies and shapeshifters and wizards, but none had ever come close to catching my eye.

I loved that Luke was full-blooded human. I loved that there was nothing for him here in Sugar Maple. He didn't want to pull the town beyond the mist or make a grab for power. He was still here for only one reason, because he loved me, and that one reason made me the happiest woman in this realm or any other.

My plan was simple: drive out to the waterfall, dazzle Luke with our local scenery, and then casually ask him how he'd feel about signing a three-year contract with the county to become our official chief of police. Three years may not sound like much to you, but from where I stood, it was a major commitment. That meant three years of happiness. Three years of basking in his human warmth. Three wonderful years to hold on to in case the future didn't work out the way I hoped it would.

And it would give me time to knit him some more sweaters . . .

"Must be serious," Luke said as he climbed into the passenger seat of my gigantic eighties-era Buick. "You're actually driving."

"I have to," I said. "You're going to be blindfolded."

The gleam in his eyes made my toes curl. "I like the sound of this."

I gestured toward the glove box. "It's in there. Put it on."

His left eyebrow lifted. "You keep a blindfold in the glove box?"

I gave him a wide-eyed look. "Something wrong with that?"

"Not a damn thing." He pulled the black satin eye covering from beneath a stack of expired insurance cards, registration documents, and an owner's manual so old it had actually yellowed. "Am I going to turn into a frog or something when I put this on?"

"That only happened once and it was an accident," I said. "Now put it on or we're not going anywhere."

The possibility of kinky sex in broad daylight bent him to my will faster than any spell I could conjure up. Apparently a girl could get just as far with a blindfold and a dream.

My aversion to driving is legendary. I'm not just a reluctant driver; I'm also a bad driver and a slow one.

"Where are you taking me?" he asked as I approached the township limits. "Afghanistan?"

"We're still in Sugar Maple," I said, laughing. "Be patient."

"What are you doing, driving backward?"

"I'm obeying the speed limit," I said, "something that should have special significance to you, *Chief* MacKenzie."

"How come I never realized your voice was so hot?" he said. "Talk dirty to me. It'll help pass the time."

"I have to concentrate on my driving."

"I thought you were a power multitasker."

"It rained last night. You don't want to get stuck in the mud, do you?"

He reached to pull off the blindfold. I swatted him with the back of my right hand. The car swerved toward the shoulder but I quickly straightened it out.

"Don't look so scared," I said. "Everything's okay."

"I'm not scared."

"You were praying."

"I figured we needed all the help we could get."

No argument there.

I made it to the edge of the clearing and found a nonmuddy area where I could leave the car without worrying about it sinking into the mire.

"Can I take the blindfold off now," Luke asked, "or is it part of the fun?"

"Keep it on," I said, trying to get into a dominatrix groove. "Put your hands on my waist and follow me."

"You're good at this," he said as I carefully led him deeper into the woods. "What other talents have you been hiding?"

"You'll find out soon enough."

His hands slipped from my waist to my hips. His broad fingers splayed down over my belly and then reached lower. I stumbled, then caught myself. His chuckle was deliciously dirty.

"Okay," I said. "Now you can take off the blindfold."

"You'd better be naked."

"Take off the blindfold and see."

He did and the look of wonder in his eyes made me laugh out loud. "What the hell—?" He glanced over at me. "Is this some kind of magic trick?"

I raised my hands in the air. "No tricks. Nothing up my sleeve."

"Where the hell have you been hiding this?"

"Three miles east of my cottage as the crow flies but you'd never find it if you didn't know where to look."

He whistled low. "Sugar Maple knows how to keep its secrets."

Which, of course, was an understatement. Nature had done a good job of hiding the Sinzibukwud Falls from nosy tourists and other interlopers, and over the centuries the residents of Sugar Maple had managed to keep it that way. Jagged slashes of granite, darkened almost black with time, provided the backdrop for the sixty-foot plunge of water.

"Sinziwhat?" Luke asked.

"*Sinzibukwud* was the Indian name for 'maple sugar,'" I told Luke as we walked closer to the falling water. "The native people believed they were closer to their ancestors here than anywhere else. Bet you don't have anything like this in Boston."

"Not even close," he said.

During Sugar Maple's early years, local artists and needleworkers and craftsmen had immortalized the Falls, but interest had waned over the years. Now we kept the tumbling waters as an attraction known only to villagers. We had enough on our collective plate trying to control tourists who came to Sugar Maple for the shopping.

There was no denying the power of the place. I don't know if it was all that tumbling water, the lush vegetation, the craggy rocks, or something else, but my entire body was tingling with anticipation. I have to admit I'd never been a big fan of the Falls. Sure, I could see they'd be a huge attraction if we ever went public, but there was something too overwhelming about the place for my taste, as if the power unleashed by the force of the water was about to break free and take us all with it. When the sun hit the Falls from a certain angle, they took on a living quality that got under my skin and made me want to be anywhere else.

But Luke loved it, as I'd hoped he would, and I was all about anything that would keep him here with me forever. He crouched down in front of an outcropping of rock, staring intently at the formation. I watched, fascinated, as he drew his forefinger along the vertical cleft.

"So you're an outdoors boy," I said as he examined another odd formation. "Who knew?"

"These rocks have faces," he said with a slightly sheepish grin. "I thought the damn thing was going to bite me."

"You're probably one of those kids who saw elephants and angels in the clouds."

"You weren't?" he asked.

"I grew up in Sugar Maple," I reminded him. "There really *were* elephants and angels in the clouds."

"Look at that formation." He pointed to an imposing outcropping. "I wouldn't be surprised if it slid open and revealed a whole other world."

"Too many video games," I said with a laugh. "I know it's hard to believe, considering this is Sugar Maple and all, but those are just rocks."

Human males are fascinating creatures. No matter how old they get, the little boy never goes away. "This place is incredible."

"I thought you'd like it." I angled him a smile. "Legend has it this was a busy lover's lane way back when."

He drew me close and I nuzzled against his neck, drinking in his warmth and human essence. "Did you ever come up here with anyone?"

I knew this was one of those times when a lie was the right way to go, but I was only half human and opted for the truth instead.

"Once," I said, watching his expression. "With Gunnar."

"I thought you two never—"

"We didn't," I broke in quickly, "but we hung out together in high school." And gave love a try a few times over the years of our friendship but never made it past exploratory kissing.

A little muscle in his jaw twitched. It might as well have been a neon sign flashing overhead. Gunnar's death continued to haunt us in so many ways. My dear friend had loved me enough to save Luke's life at the cost of his own, and that selfless act was the five-hundred-pound gorilla we pretended wasn't sitting there next to us every single day.

I felt guilty that my happiness had come at the expense of a treasured friend's existence in this realm. Gunnar's friendship had been a constant in my life for as long as I could remember, and I had believed with my entire heart and soul that he would continue to be part of my life until it was my time to pierce the veil.

And Luke? I knew his feelings about Gunnar were all wrapped up with gratitude, jealousy, and the human male's need to be the hero of his own story. Not an easy mix for a man who was making his way in a very different world from the one he'd left behind.

I reached for the blindfold dangling from his hand. "Put it back on," I said, spinning it around my index finger. "I have another surprise."

The shadows lifted and he flashed me the grin I loved. "I have a better idea. You put it on."

My skin registered his heat and I couldn't hold back a sigh of pleasure. I loved his warm skin, his hot kisses. I had been drawn to his warmth from the beginning.

Excitement snaked up my spine, followed swiftly by a long, dark ripple of anticipation. My human blood ran hot for him.

"Slow down," he whispered in my ear as he slid the mask over my eyes. "We want this to last."

Forever sounded just about right.

Town Hall—Later That Evening

Maybe if I hadn't been in the sensual haze that followed great sex, I would have seen the signs, but a few hours after our blistering lovemaking at the waterfall, I still wasn't thinking straight.

See the pattern here? I wasn't thinking at all. I was still pure sensation.

"You look awfully smug for a Wednesday night," Janice said as she joined me near the snack table. She owned the hair salon across the street from Sticks & Strings and was one of my closest friends. "Does it have anything to do with that trip you and the human made to the waterfall?"

They say that in times of extreme danger your entire life passes in front of your eyes, and that was what happened to me, except in most of the scenes I was doing things that could get me arrested.

"Don't look so horrified!" Janice gave me a quick pat on the arm. "I didn't see anything. The spell you cast around the two of you worked too darn well."

I flashed back to some of the juicier moments, especially the one that included a big, hard rock, a blindfold, and both of us half-naked. "Sometimes I wish I lived somewhere normal like Philadelphia."

Janice threw back her head and laughed out loud. "Honey, you'd never make it through the day in Philly. Too many humans. You're one of us now."

Meaning my destiny was here in Sugar Maple and always would be. I guess she felt I needed to be reminded of that fact. My half-human blood would always mark me as different.

I poured myself another cup of coffee and debated whether or not this was a sugar-and-cream kind of night. Lynette Pendragon, whose shapeshifting family owned the Sugar Maple Arts Playhouse, popped up next to me. Before my powers kicked in, I would have sworn she was a ringer for Catherine Zeta-Jones. Now when

I looked at her, I saw a pretty, dark-haired, middle-aged woman and not a movie goddess. It was one of the trade-offs that came with the magick and it still required an adjustment on my part.

"Did you tell her?" she said to Janice.

"I thought we weren't—"

"You can't let her be blindsided by—"

I didn't like the sound of this. "Somebody tell me something and fast," I demanded. "The meeting's about to begin."

"We were sworn to secrecy," Lynette said, her voice little more than a whisper, "but Colm Weaver has been trying to put together a committee to find a candidate for chief of police."

"Luke is our candidate."

"Luke is *your* candidate," Janice pointed out, "which means he's not theirs."

Resentment from the Fae within the community had grown exponentially since I banished Isadora from this realm. I didn't have the power to end her existence since the Fae didn't die in the mortal sense. They moved from dimension to dimension over more human years than we can count until their essence finally faded and they were absorbed into the greater community of ancestors. They were mercurial, occasionally loving, frequently devious, and few beings in any dimension ever bested them. The fact that I had managed to ban Isadora from the human plane was a victory by anyone's standards. I probably shouldn't have been surprised to learn that the Weavers were working against me, but I'd hoped a lifetime of friendship would count for something.

"If you're going to install Luke as the permanent chief, you'd better do it fast," Lynette warned. "They're moving more quickly than anyone would have anticipated."

"Fine," I said. "I'll do it tonight."

They exchanged glances.

"I didn't mean that fast," Lynette said.

"Why not?" I shot back. "According to our town charter, I can appoint officials to key positions without putting it to a vote. Luke is here. He understands how to work with the bureaucrats. He already knows our secrets and he's proved himself trustworthy."

"Have you talked to him about staying on?" Janice asked.

"Not yet," I admitted, "but I'm sure he'll sign on again."

We were in love. We were happy. What more could he want?

"Watch out for Colm tonight," Lynette said *sotto voce*. "Cyrus heard him talking about Luke at Fully Caffeinated this morning and it wasn't good."

The truth is I'm not big on confrontation and I was starting to wonder if I was in for a major one tonight. I can hold my own in a fight, but for the most part when I sense trouble brewing, my natural inclination is to reach for the Chips Ahoy and wait for the storm to blow over. The vibes in the room were making me think longingly of the emergency bag I had stashed away at the yarn shop. That and a bucket of Ben & Jerry might get me through.

"The natives are getting restless," Janice observed. "You'd better start on time this month."

"I started on time last month but Simone was doing a Welcome to Spring pole dance on the lawn and nobody heard me."

Simone was a sultry spirit who had a way of attracting attention even when she was dematerialized.

"The Souderbushes are here," Lynette

observed. "And the Harrises. That will help. They love Luke."

As if on cue, we all turned to look across the room at him. He was standing near the open side door, talking animatedly with the Griggs boys. Judging by his hand gestures, he was probably saying something rude about the New York Yankees.

"Isn't that the sweater you knitted for him?" Lynette asked.

"That's the one."

"You're not afraid—"

"Not even a little bit. I can't believe you buy into those old knitter's superstitions."

"Firsthand experience," Janice said. "I made my first boyfriend a sweater. He broke up with me the next day."

"Handknits scare them more than 'I love you.'" Lynette shook her head. "Cyrus didn't call me for two months after I made him a cashmere raglan."

I didn't have the guts to tell them I had started an Aran for Luke and was thinking about a Cobblestone. Every time he slipped on that sweater or grabbed for a pair of socks I made for him, I totally melted like one of those girls in the romantic movies.

Believe me, you know you love a guy if you're willing to knit a pair of socks for his size-twelve feet.

On US0 needles, no less.

Why couldn't all of life be so simple, so clear?

Across the room Luke laughed.

"Poor human," Janice said without a touch of her trademark sarcasm. "He hasn't a clue what he's in for."

I knew she wasn't talking about sweaters.

"It will be fine," I said, hoping I sounded more confident than I was actually feeling. "He's a known quantity now. It's not like when he first came to town and we had to figure out how to live with an outsider around full-time."

Janice was known for her cynical perspective on life and she didn't disappoint. "There's plenty to worry about. Half the town doesn't like humans and the other half doesn't trust them."

We both waited for Lynette's traditional glass-half-full take on the matter, but she didn't say a word, and I chalked it up to the fact that she seemed to be occupied aiming daggers at her husband, Cyrus, who was engaged in animated conversation with one of the Weavers' beautiful Fae daughters.

Most of the villagers trusted Luke even if they didn't want their daughters to marry him. Hadn't he proven himself that terrible night in my knit shop when it seemed like Isadora had garnered the forces of hell in her attempt to destroy us?

He was a cop who knew all of our secrets. He could have made a fortune selling those secrets to the world beyond our township limits.

But he didn't.

He could have left Sugar Maple and never turned back.

But he hadn't.

That had to count for something.

Lynette and Janice took their seats as Luke joined me near the podium. Our fingers brushed, and as always, sparks flew.

"I don't think I'll ever get used to that," he said. "It's like the Fourth of July every time."

We couldn't have kept our love secret if we had wanted to.

My human father had lived among the villagers for more than six years, and they still hadn't totally accepted him as one of their own before he died. Even now, many years later, there were still flashes of resentment over the human who had lured my mother from her path.

But Luke hadn't lured me from my path. He was part of it, and I liked to think that would make a difference.

Then again, love makes you crazy. Love crawls into your brain and plays games with your neurons. All the things you thought you knew about yourself fly out the window when love flies in.

I mean, I was the mayor of a town that thrived on secrets so why was I so surprised when I found out Luke had a few of his own?

2

LUKE

The first time I observed a town hall meeting, I was on the outside looking in.

Literally.

It was one of those three-dog December nights they specialized in up here in northern Vermont and I'd ended up spending part of it hidden behind a frozen azalea bush, peering through the window at the woman I would spend the rest of my life with.

Not that I knew it then. That night the only thing I knew for sure was that freezing my ass off was a small price to pay to watch her smile.

Yeah, go ahead. Laugh. If anybody had told me I would fall in love at first sight with a tall skinny blonde who knitted for a living and moonlighted as mayor of a small Vermont town, I would have laughed too.

I was a burned-out detective, a hard case when it came to love or anything close to it. I had been looking to put as much distance between myself and my old life as I could, and when the opportunity to be the interim chief of police in a nowhere town presented itself, I jumped on it.

I wanted to disappear. I wanted to stop feeling. I wanted to stop thinking about the life I'd lost.

Sugar Maple sounded like the perfect place to do it: a Norman Rockwell painting come to life, a Christmas card of a town that boasted a zero crime rate and a healthy tourist economy based on nothing more than great-looking people and proximity to some pretty serious skiing. A place filled with happy people living happy lives. A place where nothing bad ever happened.

I had a lot to learn.

I've been here a few months now and

I'm still not sure I've managed to wrap my head around what really goes on here. Retired vampires. Gorgeous troll librarians. Hairstylist witches. And a girlfriend who happens to be a sorceress-in-training locked in mortal combat with a banished Fae queen.

See what I mean? It takes some getting used to.

This was my third monthly town hall meeting as temporary chief of police. Since Sugar Maple didn't register on the state crime meter, my presence was more ceremonial than anything else. I had signed on for six months or however long it took me to investigate my old friend Suzanne's drowning death in Snow Lake. The investigation had been completed quickly, but by then I had already fallen in love with Chloe and leaving Sugar Maple was the last thing on my mind.

Okay, so maybe it wasn't the last thing on my mind. I wouldn't have minded leaving the magic behind for a few days. I'm not sure humans are cut out for a steady diet of vampires, werewolves, and things that go bump in the night. Lately normal has been sounding pretty good to me and

I'd been trying to convince Chloe to let me schedule a getaway weekend for us, but she kept putting me off. Not even a day trip down to Boston and back. She claimed the knit shop as her excuse, and I couldn't argue that her every waking hour was claimed by Sticks & Strings.

Still, being the only resident human in town wasn't the easiest gig, and I'd found myself thinking a lot about the world beyond the township limits. A world I wanted to share with Chloe. I knew she was bound to Sugar Maple by a destiny I couldn't pretend to totally understand, but even cons got time off for good behavior.

It wasn't like she was trapped here by some kind of curse or anything. Hell, she'd put in a few semesters at BU not that long ago. My world wasn't totally unfamiliar to her.

I zoned out during the lilacs-versus-hydrangeas debate and tried hard not to scratch where my sweater itched. Chloe wisely tabled a discussion on Christmas displays until after Labor Day and then yielded the floor to an insistent Midge Stallworth, who demanded to know why, with all the magic flying around town, nobody had managed to repair the DANGEROUS CURVE AHEAD sign near her family's funeral home.

"I don't mind new business," she said, her eyes twinkling as she looked straight at me, "but I'd rather get it my way, if you know what I mean."

The crowd burst into laughter and I joined in. I still had trouble with vampire humor, and for a second I found myself wondering what in hell I thought I was doing, trying to build a new life in a place like this. Chloe was half-human and even she had trouble figuring out where she belonged in a magic town. What chance did I have?

But we were on the same wavelength. She must have known we needed to put some space between us and all of those prying, unseen watchers. Getting away from everyone for the afternoon, even if it was only as far as the waterfall, had been a good thing.

A damn good thing.

Chloe naked in the pale spring sunlight. The sounds she made when I spread her legs and found her with my mouth. Her wicked good hands on my body, turning me harder than the rock beneath us.

If you had asked me this afternoon if we had a future, I would have said hell yes. The second she put on the blindfold, the barriers between us vanished. Sugar Maple and all its history vanished. Sure it was erotic as hell, but there had been more going on there than getting off on each other. She had been more purely human in my arms than she'd ever been before and I liked it.

KAREN

"How far to Sugar Maple?" I asked the gas station attendant as I pushed two twenties across the counter toward him. I had been on the road since noon and it was now after dark. Either I was getting close or the next stop would be Canada.

He ignored the money and gestured toward the tote slung across my body. "Your bag's been ringing since you pulled in. Aren't you going to answer it? Somebody wants to talk to you wicked bad."

Not until I heard the right ringtone. "I guess my voice mail is full. So how far am I from Sugar Maple?"

"Four, five miles," he said, pushing two quarters' change in my direction, "but I wouldn't go there tonight if I was you. Not unless you got a place to stay."

"They have an inn," I said. "I saw it in the guidebook." It was mud season. Nobody sane went to Vermont during mud season. Even a five-star inn would have vacancies.

"They don't rent rooms."

"An inn that doesn't rent rooms?" And they said I was crazy . . .

"Eat at the restaurant, then go back where you came from. That's how they like it up that way." His brow furrowed like a worried shar-pei as he pointedly raised his voice over the bleat of my cell. "I'd grab myself a room at Motel 6. Save Sugar Maple for the morning."

Good, solid, well-meaning advice that I was going to ignore. I didn't care where I slept. I'd sleep in the car if I had to. I didn't care what I ate or if I ate at all. The only thing I cared about was finding my ex-husband before it was too late.

The phone went silent for a moment, then sprang to life again. But this time—

I ripped the phone from my bag and

flipped it open. "Steffie! Talk to me, honey! It's Mommy. Please talk to me—"

The line went dead.

"Steffie!"

I didn't mean to scream but her name tore from my throat, from my gut. The gas station attendant, who clearly thought I was a runaway mental patient, took three steps back.

"It's the mountains," he said slowly. "Busts up the signal. She'll call back."

"It's not the mountains," I said, struggling to rein in my emotions. "It's me. It's . . . everything."

I mean, what would he think if I told him that call was from my dead daughter? He would probably lock himself in his storeroom and call the cops.

That was Steffie on the line. I had no doubt. Two calls. One last week, one a few moments ago. Both signaled by the same ringtone: Steffie's lullaby. Our secret song, we called it. A tune we had made up together, a silly mix of nonsense words and sounds that made us both giggle. Not even her father had ever known about it. But somehow, some way, it had ended up as a ringtone.

Mommy . . . Mommy . . . can you hear me . . . ?

"Lady?" The poor cashier was looking at me like he was afraid I'd pull a gun on him. "Is something wrong? No offense but you look like you haven't eaten in a while. We've got some sandwiches in the vending machine."

I stared at him blankly, then started to laugh, a crazy out-of-control laugh that made my whole body shake. Had I eaten today? I hadn't a clue. I wasn't sure I ate yesterday or the day before. Or slept for that matter. He was looking at me with such compassion mixed with curiosity that I almost spilled my whole story onto the ground between us, but something—my last shred of sanity maybe—held me back.

Last week I'd told my friend Angela from work everything and the first thing she did was stage an intervention designed to force me into some kind of mental hospital where they would help me deal with my grief.

Grief. What a small nothing of a word to describe the ripping, clawing pain I had felt every day since Steffie died.

They said I was grieving too hard, mourning too long, that it was time to suck it up and get on with it. They were right. I knew they were right. I'd been trying to pull myself back from the edge and had actually managed to make some progress when I started having the dreams and then the visions and now the phone calls from Steffie, and I was in deeper than ever.

The attendant tossed a Twix in my direction. "On the house."

I smiled at him and pocketed the candy bar. Sometimes it was easier to say thanks and get on with it. At least one of us would be happy.

"Just keep driving along the state road," he said as I climbed back behind the wheel. "Check in at the motel. Sugar Maple'll be there in the morning."

I drove right on past.

WELCOME TO SUGAR MAPLE—EST. 1692
POPULATION 417

We had more than four hundred seventeen people in our high school graduating class. The thought of my ex-husband in a place like this was baffling, but Fran said he'd been here almost six months now, working as interim chief of police. Hard to imagine a big-city cop setting up shop in a town with only one traffic light, but then neither of us had ended up where we'd expected.

We had expected to grow old together. At least in the beginning, before life got the better of us, we'd believed that we were destined to spend our golden years scoping out the early bird specials between visits from our kids and grandkids.

I didn't have an address but it shouldn't be too hard to find the police station in a town this size. Except that I couldn't find it. I found everything else: a yarn shop, a bagel place, a bank, a library, but no police station. It wasn't even eight o'clock and the town was shut down tight.

I wasn't sure why but the place gave me the creeps. There was something too Stepford about it for my taste. I would have paid somebody to litter. It was hard to imagine real, live, messy human beings living there. The town was too pretty, too perfect, too empty. I know it sounds crazy, but I was starting to understand how a deer felt during hunting season. Just because you couldn't see the hunters didn't mean they weren't there.

The gas station attendant had been right. They didn't exactly roll out the welcome mat for visitors after dark. Suddenly I wanted to get back on the road as fast as possible, find that Motel 6, and wait for the goose bumps on the back of my neck to go down.

I made a U-turn on Osborne and aimed the car toward the township line and had managed to get about a half mile away when my cell phone on the seat next to me lit up and Steffie's song filled the cabin of the rental car.

I turned and grabbed for the phone at the same instant a deer leaped directly into the path of my rental car.

All I could do was hit the brakes and pray.

3

CHLOE

We managed to work our way to the end of the agenda without incident. So far the Weavers had kept almost unnaturally silent, not even offering a comment about the flower beds the Garden Club was offering to plant and maintain in front of local establishments, including the Inn. The back of my neck felt like it was being pinched by a giant monkey fist that probably wouldn't let go until I tackled one last issue.

"Looks like that's everything," Verna Griggs said, snapping shut her steno pad.

Verna was serving as township recording secretary. "If we adjourn now, I still have time to catch *CSI: Miami*."

If only there was some kind of magick to make my stomach stop doing backflips.

"There's one more piece of business," I said, ignoring the loud moans of disappointment from the crowd. "As you are all aware, Luke MacKenzie has been serving in a temporary capacity since December and—" I tilted my head in the direction of a rhythmic tapping coming from the center of the room. "Does anyone else hear that noise?"

"If you mean the appalling sound of nepotism, I certainly do." My former friend Renate Weaver was perched on the old-fashioned pencil sharpener attached to the desk beneath the window.

"Stop it, Mother," her eldest daughter, Bettina, snapped. "This isn't nepotism. Chloe and Luke aren't related."

"It's favoritism," Colm, *pater familias* of the Weaver clan, declared. "After what she did to Isadora, she shouldn't even be our mayor."

I knew it was ridiculous to be intimidated by a man the size of your average blue jay, but I was just the same.

When I banished Isadora from this realm, I had also unwittingly banished the Weavers from my life, a turn of events I regretted deeply.

"As I was saying, we have less than six weeks to name a permanent chief of police or Montpelier will do it for us." I grinned at the chorus of boos the mention of the state capitol always elicited. New Englanders were nothing if not independent. "I propose that Luke—" I stopped and glanced down at the floor. "Is it just me or did the earth move?"

"I'd say it's been moving every night since your sweetie came to town," Midge observed to more laughter.

I waited for everyone to settle down. "I'm proposing we offer Luke a three-year contract at a salary to be determined after review by our town treasurer." I turned to Luke, who was hiding behind what I called his cop face. He was better than a shapeshifter when it came to keeping his true self under wraps.

In my eagerness to keep from being blindsided by the Weavers, I had managed to totally blindside the man I loved with a public declaration of intent. It was too late now. All I could do was push forward and apologize later. "We'll present you with a formal offer tomorrow, as soon as I can get to my computer and print one out."

He nodded and I liked to think he was about to say something like "Where do I sign?" but he didn't. He didn't say anything, and his silence could be heard loud and clear in the last row.

Renate's smile was wide and triumphant. Colm's held more than a touch of malice. Janice and Lynette looked as uncomfortable as I felt. Lilith, her eyes brimming with compassion, pinched her husband Archie's leg. I didn't ask why. Archie was capable of saying just about anything.

I caught a ripple of laughter from the northeast corner of the room. Luke stood up and I swear to you my heart almost stopped beating. I didn't need powers to know it wasn't good.

"I have to leave."

"You can't!" Could this get any more humiliating?

He flashed his pager. "Minor one-car accident a half mile outside of town. Gotta go."

And he did.

About as quickly as any human could, short of an Olympic sprinter.

"I think we have our answer, people." Renate could barely keep the triumph from her voice. "That's hardly a man looking to stay in Sugar Maple."

"There was an accident," I snapped. "He had to leave."

"An accident?" Midge Stallworth piped up. "In town? That can't be! Did the charm stop working?"

"This is unacceptable. Four months and she still hasn't figured out how to keep things running smoothly," Colm said with a sad shake of his head. "I ask you, everyone, is this the way you want to continue?"

"And she's not even pregnant!" Mona was a mermaid currently land-enabled while she studied the healing arts with Lilith and Janice. "Isn't that what this is about? If Chloe doesn't get pregnant, you'll all lose."

"Precisely," Colm said with a satisfied nod in Mona's direction. "Without a descendant to fulfill Aerynn's blessing, we are doomed to the same fate as befell our Salem ancestors."

"He's right." Rose from Assisted Living

nodded her tightly coiffed head. "We'll be hounded like dogs, then driven from our homes! I'd rather go beyond the mist."

"You're all out of order," I said. "If you want to be recognized, please follow the accepted procedures."

"You might want to try that yourself," Colm shot back. "Next time you should ask your boyfriend how he feels before you offer him a job. He took off to keep from embarrassing you."

"Luke received an emergency call, Colm. He had to leave and you know it."

"Right," he said. "And you're not your mother's daughter."

"Take that back!"

"I offended you?" He feigned innocence. "Guinevere was a lovely woman. I meant it as a compliment. You're very much like your mother."

"Because I fell in love with a human?"

The mask of innocence dropped away, and I saw nothing but hatred in his eyes.

"Because we can't count on you any more than you could count on her."

I started to shake with rage. Even my teeth rattled. The power of my anger scared me until I realized that I was being shaken from the outside, not the inside, and so was everyone else in the room.

"Earthquake!" Manny bellowed. He aimed his motorized Scooter toward the exit, but his wheel locks were on and he started moving in lazy circles.

"Damn heating system!" Paul Griggs said, glancing around. "We're going to have to spring for a new boiler before the old one blows."

With all the magick afoot in Sugar Maple, you would think we could just conjure up a new heating system, but not even sorcery could replace a good plumber.

Lynette stood up and pointed toward one of the pillars on the bride's side of the old church. "I just saw a flash of light over there!"

"I didn't see anything," Janice said, "but it's definitely getting hot in here."

"I smell smoke," Archie said.

But it wasn't smoke he smelled. It was the smell the air got just before an electrical storm broke loose. Sharp, metallic, and frighteningly familiar.

Above my head the Souderbush family collectively dematerialized. You knew something bad was coming when even the dead were afraid to stick around.

The center of the room pulsated in time to a rhythmic pounding that sounded like a thousand battering rams slamming against a locked door. I felt the sound in my very bones and it was gaining power with every second.

"There's nothing to worry about," I called out. "We're safe. The spell's still in place. This is just a little blip. Nothing can harm us!"

I'd no sooner uttered the words than the room split in two from ceiling to floor with a sound like giant metal gears grinding together. If Hell had a sound, this would be it.

If Hell had an image, it would be the streaks of purple glitter I saw near the corner of the room.

Glitter was the Fae equivalent of fingerprints, the one thing even the cleverest among them couldn't disguise. Only one member of the Fae carried deep purple glitter within her, and that was Isadora.

Terror sprang to life inside my chest and clawed like a wild thing trying to get out. Isadora couldn't possibly be here. With help from the Book of Spells, I had banished her forever and then rebanished her twice more just to be on the safe side.

The pounding, thundering noise grew louder, faster, more insistent. The pressure in the room intensified until I thought my head would burst open like an overripe cantaloupe. Something terrible was about to happen, something—

"Everybody down!" I cried out, and the next thing I knew, I was flat on my back as the world exploded around me like a thousand Fourth of Julys.

A sickeningly sweet mist quickly filled the room, swirling up to the eaves, then snaking back down around our ankles. I knew that smell. I remembered that oily film on my skin just before—

Isadora . . . oh God, not Isadora . . .

I had banished the Fae leader three times. I had called upon every ancient charm and spell I could find in the Book and doubled their strength. She shouldn't have been able to get anywhere near Sugar Maple, much less the human realm.

The villagers were in a state of total meltdown, which would quickly turn into a full-scale riot if anyone else noticed Isadora's calling card. Now that I knew the Weavers weren't the only family in Sugar Maple who harbored resentment toward me for banishing Isadora, I wasn't ready to find out just how deep the opposition ran.

When it came to magick, I was better with the bigger brush strokes. The finer movements, like moving a quarter-ounce of faerie glitter from Point A to Point B, took a deeper level of concentration that I could tap into only rarely. And usually at the cost of a killer migraine that lasted for days.

Luckily tonight I was able to access my power almost immediately, and I watched as the glitter neatly slid itself under the podium and out of sight a split second before Renate swooped by, shrieking at the top of her tiny lungs like a demented budgie, leaving a trail of lemon yellow glitter in her wake.

I quickly scanned the area to see if anyone else had noticed. The crew from Fully Caffeinated were helping one another out from beneath a toppled bookcase while Lilith pulled a wooden bench off her husband, Archie, who was trapped between the watercooler and the photocopy machine. Paul Griggs was trying valiantly to help his wife, Verna, down from the transom while Manny and Frank had locked wheels on their Scooters and were yelling for their pal Rose to come pry them apart.

"Help us!" Caitlin from the bank cried out. "Do something, Chloe!"

I was a Hobbs woman, a descendant of Aerynn, and the future of Sugar Maple was my responsibility. It was time for me to step up to the plate and remind everyone in town that I would never let them down, no matter what.

And maybe it was time I reminded myself as well.

LUKE

The driver's side of the rented Nissan was sunk in the mud-filled ditch right up to the wheel wells. The passenger-side door was open. The dome light illuminated the cabin, and I quickly gauged that the driver had abandoned the vehicle and apparently gone in search of help.

Which was exactly what the GPS Help operator had instructed the driver not to do.

That was one of the problems with rural living. Events unfolded at their own pace, and that pace didn't often meet outsiders' expectations. It had taken me less than eight minutes to reach the site, but the car rental service's outsourced GPS Help system had taken fifteen to decide to route the call to Sugar Maple.

I hadn't noticed any pedestrians wandering the streets between here and town hall. Sugar Maple after dark was usually a ghost town, and yeah, I mean that literally. I couldn't see them but there was no mistaking that *you're-not-alone* sensation once the sun went down.

I searched the car for paperwork, receipts, anything that might provide a clue about the driver, but there was nothing but an unopened Twix candy bar on the floor near the brake pedal.

Shit. I glanced around, expecting to see muddy footprints that would lead me to the driver, but the small imprints ended at the blacktop. I knew where the driver wasn't. Now all I had to do was figure out whether he or she had followed the road out of town or cut across the open field and—

What the hell was going on? It was early April but that definitely sounded like Fourth of July fireworks coming from the center of town. I scanned the night sky and saw a thin plume of smoke rising from where the old church they used as a town hall was located.

Chloe . . .

CHLOE

In less than ten minutes I managed to take a head count, check everyone for broken bones and other injuries, and dispatch the healers among us to demonstrate their art. Paul and a group of men ventured down to the basement to check for damages while others milled around nervously, exchanging war stories about exploding hot water heaters and propane tanks. I didn't correct them.

It had been a close call. Clearly Isadora's powers were not at full intensity, or none of us would have been left standing. Which meant she was hobbled by her banishment, or she had meant this as a warning.

A piece of stained glass from the blown-out window of Saint George had done a number on my forearms, and I disappeared into the back to look for some hydrogen peroxide. Even though I had acquired some magickal healing abilities, my old human habits were hard to break.

I was looking for the Band-Aids when Luke's voice in the doorway made me jump.

"What the hell happened?"

"Nothing good," I said as I pushed aside a stack of towels. "We had an explosion."

"I heard it outside of town. I was—" His words died and he moved closer to me. His wonderful human warmth raised the temperature in the small space by at least a few degrees. "Paul said it was the hot water heater."

"I don't think so."

He grabbed my arms and inspected the fine scratches and blossoming bruises. "What do you mean, you don't think so?"

I lowered my voice. "Isadora." I told him about the telltale purple glitter.

"You banished her," he said. "I thought we didn't have to worry anymore."

"I guess we were wrong."

I started to tell him about the ugly confrontation with Colm and how sorry I was for springing the whole permanent police chief thing on him, but Midge Stallworth's sweet cartoonish voice sounded from the vestibule.

"People!" she called out. "We have an unconscious woman back here and she isn't one of us!"

Exactly what we didn't need. But I refused to panic. I loved Midge but she wouldn't necessarily be my go-to girl in an emergency. Without her glasses on, she wouldn't know her own daughters. I wasn't going to freak out until it was absolutely necessary.

Luke headed up the aisle at a run. I wasn't far behind him. Maybe she was a visitor from one of our sister communities. Hadn't a lovely selkie couple from the Orkney Islands passed through town last month? Or maybe she was a wayward knitter who had been attracted by the lights and the promise of some lace-weight mohair.

I quickly replayed the mental tape of the meeting. We hadn't discussed anything that could compromise our secret. At least, I didn't think we had. Except for the explosion in the center aisle, it had been a run-of-the-mill small-town meeting.

"She's out cold," Midge said, her round cheeks pink from either excitement or a recent feeding. "I don't think she's dead but you never know." I ignored the note of hopefulness in her voice. After all, in her world, death was the ultimate happy ending.

The woman was tiny, almost doll-like, with pale freckled skin and hair the color of a burnished copper penny. She wore jeans at least a size too big for her and a hand-knit peach-colored cardigan over a plain white cotton shirt. Veronik Avery's Salt Peanuts? I'd bet my Addis on it. My inner knitter made a quick assessment and gave the sweater high marks.

She was the kind of woman most men wanted to protect. Just by existing she made them feel big and strong by comparison. Just by existing she made me feel like an overgrown giraffe.

I glanced over at Luke. Except for a small muscle twitching along the right side of his jaw, he was motionless, and a sudden, almost sickening surge of adrenaline coursed through my bloodstream.

He crouched down next to the unconscious woman, and an odd ripple of something close to dread moved through me. It reminded me of the way I had felt seconds before the explosion. *This isn't going to be good . . .*

Please don't let her be dead, I thought. This was Sugar Maple. Things like that didn't happen here. Or at least they hadn't before I stepped up to the plate.

And they definitely didn't happen twice in less than six months.

If I had to explain another dead tourist to Joe Randazzo at the County Seat—

"Maybe we should go through her purse," Midge was saying. "Find out who she is." She paused for a respectful instant. "Her next of kin."

Luke's eyes met mine and the world stopped spinning.

"Don't bother," he said, not breaking his gaze. "Her name is Karen MacKenzie and she's still breathing."

"MacKenzie!" Midge exclaimed. "Is she your sister?"

"No," the man I loved said. "She's my wife."

4

CHLOE

"Your wife?" I sounded like I was from Mars. My voice was high and tight, and the only thing keeping me from a total meltdown was the fact that the entire town was waiting to see what came next.

"Ex-wife," Luke said with an emphasis on the *ex*. He looked terrible. His face had drained of color and the look in his eyes—

I wasn't going to think about the look in his eyes as he ran his powerful hands over his ex's delicate body searching for breaks or other injuries. I knew those hands. I knew that touch.

So does she, Chloe, a small voice whispered.

(I hate those small voices.)

"Are you okay?" Janice murmured into my right ear. "I have some erotianimus root with me. Takes the sting out of moments like this."

I found it hard to believe anyone on the planet had ever had a moment quite like this one.

"I'm fine."

"You're a lousy liar," Janice said, patting my shoulder.

I could hear the buzzing behind me, like a hive filled with angry bees.

"His wife? I didn't know he had a wife." Lilith sounded horrified.

"It just goes to show what I've always said is true." Renate sounded downright triumphant. "Nothing good comes from associating with humans."

"Poor thing." Frank from Assisted Living clicked his dentures for emphasis. "Looked like she was finally going to get herself knocked up and now this."

What I wanted to do was tell them all to shut up, but instead I gritted my teeth and ignored the clamor. In the excitement of seeing my romance blow up in my face like an exploding cigar, they had all but forgotten about the real explosion, which definitely worked in my favor.

I watched as he rubbed her wrists, then cradled her against his chest. It was one thing to know your lover had an ex-wife in his past. It was something else again to see her in his arms.

"She's coming around." The note of relief in his voice was unmistakable.

I reminded myself that this surprising capacity for tenderness was one of the things I first loved about him, but right now I wasn't too crazy about it.

The former Mrs. MacKenzie murmured something low and the place instantly fell silent. Five minutes ago I couldn't shut them up with a tranquilizer dart.

Not that they would limit themselves to auditory snooping. Thanks to my newly acquired powers, I was able to see dozens of glittering silver thought probes unspooling across the floor toward Luke and his ex.

"Come on, people," I said as they gathered closer. "Let's give the woman room to breathe."

The number of thought probes doubled.

Fortunately they were invisible to humans. I hadn't even known they existed until a few months ago when my powers began to kick in. I have to admit it gave me a creepy feeling to know that everyone in town had had access to my deepest feelings all those years. It was like seeing your diary plastered on the Internet. I drew a protective circle in the air, and in less than an instant the probes were bouncing off a giant mind shield with a soft ping and falling harmlessly to the floor.

The crowd backed off and Luke shot me a grateful look, but I wasn't feeling particularly warm or fuzzy at the moment.

The former Mrs. MacKenzie opened her eyes, screamed, then started to struggle against him.

"Karen." Luke's voice was gentle but firm as he held her close. "You're okay . . . Calm down . . . You're with me."

You're with me?

A triple bypass without anesthesia would have hurt less. I'm not proud of myself, but I was almost happy when she struggled even harder against him. At least she seemed to remember they weren't together any longer.

"Why is she yelling?" I heard one of the Griggs boys ask.

"Humans do that," Renate said with obvious disdain. "They're needy, helpless creatures who express their weakness through noise."

Not so needy and helpless that I didn't consider knocking Renate flat on her little faerie ass, but I controlled myself. I was proud of the human half of my lineage, but I wasn't sure it was worth going to war over. If Isadora really was trying to crash back into this realm, I didn't need to alienate other members of the Fae community any more than I already had.

Besides, I had more important things to worry about.

Luke's ex was conscious again, and this time she wasn't screaming. Her eyes darted from the scattered debris to the faces peering down at her, and I found myself praying Isadora's stunt hadn't somehow pierced the protective charm that enabled us to hide the truth in plain sight.

"Where am I?" she asked. "Madame Tussaud's?"

"The wax museum?" Lilith's husband,

Archie the troll, was outraged. "You scrawny little—"

"I think she means it as a compliment," Luke said, then looked down at the little woman. "All the movie stars and models, right?"

"I thought Ingrid Bergman was dead," she said, pointing toward Rose.

I stepped forward with my biggest professional smile on my face. After all, I had spent most of my life making sure Sugar Maple and the real world didn't rub each other the wrong way.

"Rose works for one of those celebrity look-alike agencies down in Nashua," I said with practiced ease as I crouched down to her level. "Are you okay? You were out cold."

She barely registered my presence. "Am I bleeding?" she asked Luke, touching a bony forefinger to her left temple.

"You're fine." Luke forced a smile. "Midge found you back here on the floor."

She glanced around her. "Here?"

"Right here, honey," Midge said with a thirsty smile. "I found you myself. I think you slipped and fell."

"No, I didn't. I crashed into a wall right

where you're standing. I went into it face-first."

Midge exchanged glances with me. "I don't think so, honey," she said in an almost singsong voice. "There is no wall."

I had the awful feeling that she really had bumped headfirst into a wall and that the wall was Isadora's force field.

I gave Luke a "do something" look. She was his ex-wife. Let him lie to her.

She touched her forehead and winced. "Are you sure I'm not bleeding?"

"Not a scratch," Luke said, all business. "Were you driving the rented Nissan?"

She groaned and rubbed her left temple. "If it's in a ditch, that's me. I waited forever for someone to show up, then decided to walk to town and see if I could find you."

Now that started up the buzz again. Luke and his perky ex-wife together again with poor Chloe out in the cold once again. I wanted to smack those looks of pity off their faces.

She looked over at me, then at Luke, and I could see the relationship wheel of fortune spinning. "Who *are* you?"

"Chloe Hobbs," I said, "acting mayor of Sugar Maple. If you need a doctor, I'd be happy to take you to the ER. You shouldn't fool around with a head injury." Even if it might mean an eight- or nine-hour wait to be seen.

"I don't have a head injury. The air bags worked just fine." She brushed my words aside with a wave of her hand and pinned her attentions on Luke again. "Is there someplace we can talk?"

What was I, a piece of lint on her shoulder? I felt my face turn fiery hot with embarrassment.

"Bitch," Janice murmured. "Want me to make her hair fall out?"

It was tempting but I shook my head. "I'm fine." Maybe if I said it often enough, I'd start to believe it.

"No, you're not," Lynette said. "Your aura is tangerine."

I hadn't reached the tangerine aura portion of the Book of Spells yet so its significance was lost on me. Clearly from the look on my friends' faces, it wasn't a good thing.

Midge Stallworth joined us. "Honey, why are you standing here? Get over there and stake your claim before that little red-headed string bean does."

I jumped as a thought probe nipped my ankle, then angled around me, heading straight for Luke's ex-wife, and I realized the shield had dissolved along with my confidence. I tried to redo the spell, stronger this time, but I kept bumping up against powerful resistance, as if the air itself had grown heavier, less yielding.

A strange prickling sensation traveled up my arms and made me shiver.

I'm not finished yet.

Isadora's voice filled my head with sound. I spun around but she was nowhere in sight. Only a telltale purple glow emanating from the glitter swept under the desk and the faintest vibration beneath my feet gave away her presence.

The former Mrs. MacKenzie was saying something to Luke, something he didn't want to hear if his body language was any indication. She was leaning forward, her delicate frame almost rigid with intensity, talking, talking, talking, but I knew Luke well enough to know he had stopped listening to her.

"People, we don't know whether or not the structure has sustained serious damage. Grab your belongings and head out-

side. We'll need to bring in an inspector."
Mostly I needed to get everyone out before they realized Isadora's glitterprints were all over the damage.

"What about my Tupperware?" Midge asked, her round face creased with worry. "I brought my best serving pieces."

"The place is gonna crash down around her and she's worried about her Tupperware," Manny from Assisted Living said to nervous laughter.

"Just go," I said to Midge. "I'll make sure you get your Tupperware." Even if it meant enduring another one of her sales parties.

"You heard her," Janice bellowed. "Everybody out! Now!"

You would have thought they'd been hit by a collective cattle prod. The church cleared in a matter of seconds.

"You're good at this," I said to my friend.

"Four kids. It comes with the territory."

"I'll erase the glitter," Lynette whispered in my ear. "I don't think anyone noticed."

Which meant she had. Could things get worse?

We could worry about the rest of the cleanup tomorrow when we didn't have an outsider watching our every move.

Luke helped his ex-wife to her feet. She was even tinier than I had imagined. The top of her head barely grazed the middle of his chest. He had to lean way down to hear her words.

I, however, had no trouble hearing every single one of them.

" . . . we can go to your place," she was saying to him.

Midge was right. It was time to stake my claim.

"We can take your car unless you're up for walking," I said to the ex–Mrs. MacKenzie. "My cottage isn't far from here."

From the look on her face, you would think I had suggested a threesome.

"My car is in a ravine," she said in a clipped tone of voice.

"My gracious!" Midge exclaimed. "I've lived here all my life. I didn't even know we *had* a ravine!"

"A ditch," Luke said, looking supremely uncomfortable. "Not a ravine."

"Whatever," said the ex. "I need to speak to Luke in private."

I had to hand it to the woman. She was very okay with confrontation.

I expected Luke to jump in and tell her

that she could say anything she wanted to in front of me because we had no secrets, but he didn't and in the end all I could manage was a weak nod of my head.

It wasn't like I didn't know he had been married before. He had mentioned it once and I had registered the fact somewhere deep inside my brain, but I hadn't pursued the issue. I guess with all the magick breaking loose in my life at the time, a failed marriage barely registered on my radar.

He didn't ask me about the men I had dated. I didn't ask him about the woman he had married.

Up until twenty minutes ago it had seemed like a perfect arrangement.

Now I ran the risk of everyone in the village divining the juicy details before I did.

They weren't even trying to be subtle about it. They were lined up on the stairs, eager to get a closer look at the newcomer and to see how I was taking this new development.

The ex didn't seem to notice anything, but I registered every look and heard every single pointed comment. This was the twenty-first century. Out there in the world of humans, women were no longer judged by their marital status. They were judged by their intellect and their accomplishments, not by whether some man loved them.

But here in Sugar Maple my life was defined by a spell cast by my ancestor Aerynn three hundred years ago. A spell that tied me to one man, one love, one chance to be happy.

Right now my prospects weren't looking too good.

We walked down the front steps in silence, across the muddy yard to the curb, where Luke's truck was parked.

She claimed the front passenger seat.

"Chloe sits there," Luke said.

She murmured something that sounded like "go to Hell" and didn't move.

I didn't think it was code for "I love you," but then again, you never know.

"Let it go," I said to Luke. "I'll sit in the back."

The five-minute drive to my cottage felt like a dozen lifetimes. I made one attempt at conversation but was met with hostile silence from the missus and a monosyllabic response from Luke. My cats were better conversationalists and they had no ex-spouses waiting to pounce.

Fine, I thought. Be that way. I didn't know what their issues were and I didn't want to know. I just wanted this night to be over before anything else exploded in my face.

After what seemed like a cross-country crawl, Luke made the turn into my driveway and came to a stop behind my Buick. I jumped out so fast you would have thought my hair was on fire.

"Give me five," I called over my shoulder as I hurried up the path to the front door. "I'd better make sure the felines are under control." And make sure no blue flame holographic phone messages were sitting on the couch reading this week's issue of *People*.

"She has cats?" I heard the ex ask with a note of horror in her voice. "You live with *cats*?"

I was smiling as I opened the door.

This might be more fun than I thought.

5

LUKE

"She looks like Uma Thurman," Karen said as Chloe disappeared inside the cottage. "How did you end up with a supermodel?"

"My office is next to her shop."

"My office was next to the bakery but I'm not living with Charlie Fetzler." She cut me a look that felt like outpatient surgery. "Is it serious?"

"Yes."

The word hung there for a moment, then faded as a dense dark silence settled between us. I knew that silence. It had been the soundtrack to the last few months of our marriage.

"That explains the sweater."

"What the hell does that mean?" I asked. The sweater might itch like crazy but even I knew it was a great piece of knitting.

"It means you always told me wool makes you itch."

"It still does."

"But you wear it because she knitted it for you."

I didn't see much reason to state the obvious.

I drummed the steering wheel with my thumbs. She watched as a small blue light flickered to life behind the front window, then grew into obvious flames the color of a cartoon version of a Caribbean sea.

It looked exactly the way Chloe had described blue light communication to me. Now I understood why it had been rendered invisible to us nonmagick types.

Except it wasn't invisible anymore. What was that about anyway? I'd been here four months and this was the first time I'd actually seen proof of blue light. Up until now I'd taken Chloe's word for it. Turned out she hadn't exaggerated. It definitely beat the hell out of my BlackBerry.

The flames filled the front window, then slipped out and began licking their way up toward the roof of Chloe's cottage.

"Your girlfriend's house is on fire."

The place looked like it was being attacked by a bottle of flaming Windex. "I don't see anything."

"You don't see those big blue flames wrapped around the house?"

"Nope."

She yanked her cell phone out of her bag and pressed a series of buttons.

My cell rang a half second later.

"You're 911?"

I nodded. "Guilty."

"This is crazy." She dropped her phone, then flung open the car door and jumped out. "Fire!" she yelled as she ran toward the house. "Fire!"

Hard to believe a night that included an explosion in a crowded church filled with werewolves, vampires, and trolls could get any worse, but I'd underestimated the potential.

She raced up the porch steps and into

the cottage. Seconds later I burst into the hallway and almost ran smack into her. She was standing there, frozen in place, staring into the living room with the widest eyes I'd ever seen short of one of those black velvet paintings.

Chloe was standing calmly at the desk near the front window. Pyewacket was sprawled on the back of the sofa while Lucy and Blot watched from the top of the bookcase in the corner. Dinah, the serious calico with an overbite, was draped across Chloe's shoulders.

Except for the fact that the calico's tail was on fire, everything looked normal to me.

Karen made a noise somewhere between a shriek and a hiccup, then started slithering to the ground like a melting candle. This time I was there to catch her before she crashed.

"What's her problem?" Chloe muttered as she unwrapped Dinah from around her neck and placed the cat on the ground. "So I haven't vacuumed in a week. Sue me."

"Dinah's tail is on fire." I swept Karen into my arms and carried her into the room, where I deposited her on the sofa with the cats.

"Don't be ridiculous."

"Blue flames are shooting out of her butt."

She frowned and looked at the calico sprawled at her feet. "You're crazy."

I checked Karen's pulse and respiration. Everything seemed normal. "When was the last time I told you one of your cats was shooting blue butt flames?"

"Point taken." She bent down next to us and took a long assessing look at Karen. "Neither one of you should have been able to see the blue flames."

"Yeah, but you should have."

Our eyes locked. We were in big trouble.

I motioned for her to stop talking as Karen's eyes fluttered open and she began pulling away from my grasp.

"The fire!" She struggled to a sitting position. "You have to do something."

Chloe crouched down next to her. "There's no fire. Everything's fine."

"I saw it," Karen protested. "The house was wrapped in flame." She pointed toward

Dinah, who was watching us from the windowsill. "That cat's tail was on fire."

Chloe and I exchanged looks.

"You passed out twice," Chloe said. "I think you might still be a little off-kilter."

"Is that a polite way of saying crazy?"

"No," Chloe said patiently. "It's a polite way of saying you were wrong."

"Your house was on fire," Karen said again. "So was your cat. I didn't imagine it. I don't go around imagining flaming cats."

Chloe spread her arms wide. "If there was a fire, where's the damage?"

Karen's gaze swept the room. It lingered on Dinah, who was patiently grooming her right foreleg. "I know what I saw."

"I don't think you do."

"You're telling me I'm hallucinating?"

"I'm telling you that if my cat's butt was on fire, I think the cat might be the first to know." She pointed toward Dinah, who had stopped grooming and was now entwining herself around Chloe's left ankle.

Chloe turned to me. "Maybe she'll listen to you. I have to make a few calls. I'll be in the bedroom if you need me."

"She thinks I'm crazy," Karen said as

Chloe's footsteps receded down the hall-way.

"She didn't say that."

"She didn't have to. She couldn't get away fast enough." She buried her face in her hands, and the sound of choked laughter filtered through her fingers.

I felt like a bastard for letting her believe she'd hallucinated the flames so I changed the subject.

"When was the last time you ate?"

She looked up at me. "Yesterday. The day before." She waved her hand in the air. "One of those days."

"There's your answer. Eat something and you'll quit seeing flaming cats."

"Will I stop seeing Steffie?"

I felt like I'd been gut shot. "What did you say?" Maybe it was my turn to halluci-nate.

"Two weeks ago," she said, stumbling over her words. "In the park behind the old house. She was sitting on her favorite swing near the duck pond." She dragged her sleeve across her eyes and kept going. "She was wearing the red sweater I made for her that last Christmas and she—"

Her words crashed against the inside of my head and something in me snapped.

"Shut up." My voice went harsh and ugly with emotion. "Don't talk about her. Don't say her name."

"She called me on the cell this morning." She gestured toward her tote bag on the floor. "I know that sounds crazy but—"

"Prove it."

"I can't prove it."

"Let me hear the message."

"She didn't leave one."

"Then show me the call-back number."

"There wasn't one."

"That's what I thought."

"I'm telling the truth, Luke. Just because I can't explain it doesn't mean it isn't real."

Which was analogous to my stay in Sugar Maple, but anger trumped logic hands down.

"You don't understand. It had to be Steffie because of the ringtone," she said. "She used our special song."

I whistled the first two bars from "Good Morning Starshine." "Not that unusual, Karen."

"That's not it. We made this one up." She leaned closer and I could feel the heat of desperation rising off her. "Steffie was the only other person who knew it."

The look in her eyes scared the shit out of me. I'd seen that look before on people in locked cells and psych wards. This wasn't the woman I'd been married to for ten years. This was a stranger.

"You probably dreamed it." I wondered if her friends back in Boston knew what was going on with her, because I sure as hell didn't have a clue.

"I was wide-awake."

"What do you want from me, Karen? You want me to say that I believe our daughter is making phone calls from the grave? Tell me what you want me to hear and I'll say it."

"She asked me to find you. That's why I'm here."

I muttered something ugly.

"Do you really think I wanted to see you? I'd like to forget you ever existed. If Steffie hadn't—"

"Who's Steffie?"

Chloe was standing in the doorway.

Karen turned to me. "You didn't tell her about Steffie?"

Chloe stepped into the room. "Who's

Steffie?" she repeated, her huge golden eyes darting from Karen to me.

There was no easy way to do this. Whatever I said and however I said it, I was screwed.

"Karen and I had a daughter, Chloe." Full-on cop mode: crisp, clean, factually correct with the emotional resonance of a tax return. "Her name was Steffie and she died two years ago."

Everyone said time would lessen the pain but so far it hadn't happened. Saying it made the whole thing real again, brought Steffie to life in front of me: a whirling, laughing, silly kid who made me feel like I had been put on the planet for a reason.

Another woman would have burst into tears or exploded with anger but not Chloe. She didn't move, blink, or seem to breathe. Her intensity was white-hot and probably laced with more than a touch of her newfound magic. Karen must have sensed something strange in the air because she shivered and shrank deeper into the couch, as if to put some distance between herself and Chloe.

"Why didn't you tell me about your daughter before this?"

Karen didn't give me a chance to answer.

"Because it's his fault she died." Her voice was taut as overstretched cable and probably as dangerous.

"Is that true?" Chloe asked me.

The cop answered her. The father couldn't find his voice.

"Steffie grabbed her bike while I was changing the oil in the garage. I didn't hear her ride down the driveway. By the time I realized she'd left, it was too late."

"I would have heard her," Karen said. "I would have known what she was doing every second."

"What about the time she grabbed that book of matches and—"

"You bastard! I wish—"

A sharp clap of thunder outside brought us all up short. Chloe's expression still didn't change but I was sure she had a lot to do with the timing.

"It's late," she said calmly. "Why don't you pick up where you left off in the morning." She turned to Karen. "Motel 6 is a little south of here. It's spartan but you'll be comfortable. I'll drive you."

Considering how much Chloe hated to drive, that spoke volumes.

Karen ignored her. "You drive me," she said to me. "We have to talk."

So do we, Chloe's look said as another rumble of thunder crashed overhead.

"Chloe's right," I said to my ex-wife. "I'll swing by the motel in the morning and we can talk over breakfast." I wanted to make a few phone calls to old friends back in Boston and see if I could get a handle on what had been going on.

Karen considered her options for a few seconds, then nodded.

She turned to Chloe. "I've been on the road all day. I need to use the bathroom."

"Fine," Chloe said. "Just ignore the litter boxes."

"No problem," she said as she followed Chloe down the hallway. "I love cats."

That should have been my first clue that it would be a long night.

6

CHLOE

The old wives were right. I never should have knitted him that sweater. My relationship was unraveling right before my eyes and heading straight for the frog pond.

Luke wanted me to sit down so he could explain why he hadn't told me about his daughter, but there was no way I was going to have that conversation while his ex-wife was in my bathroom.

First love. First marriage. First child.

Those memories all belonged to Luke

and another woman, and even the strongest magick couldn't change that fact.

I know that humans marry and divorce the way I cast on new knitting projects. They move on to new spouses and new lives with an ease I don't really understand. But when humans have a child together, like it or not, they are bound together forever.

I made another pass through the cottage while Luke stood near the front window, lost in thought. We had dodged a bullet back there at the church. Luckily the first Mrs. MacKenzie had been preoccupied with her own problems and had accepted our exploding water heater excuse without question. We couldn't expect to get away with that a second time.

I was quenching another blue flame message from Lynette when I glanced over at the grandmother clock in the hallway. An uneasy feeling settled into the pit of my stomach, right next to the huge knot of apprehension at the prospect of driving the ex to the motel.

"She's been in there over ten minutes," I said to Luke, practically my first words to him since we entered the cottage. "Does she usually take that long?"

He looked like someone awakened from a deep sleep. "I don't remember."

"You were married to her." I sounded exactly the way I felt: tense and angry. "You must have some idea."

"We didn't chart bathroom schedules."

"Go in there and check on her."

"Why don't you check on her?"

"She's your ex-wife."

"It's your house."

We sounded like quarreling children. One of us had to act the part of the adult in the equation. I walked down the hallway and tapped on the door. "Are you okay in there?"

No response.

I looked over at Luke, who was standing next to me. "Now what?"

He knocked twice, harder. "Karen? What's going on?"

No response.

He grasped the doorknob and tried to turn it.

"She locked it," he said.

"Not a problem." I placed my hands an inch away from the lock, narrowed my focus, and waited for the tiny pop.

"Try it now," I said, stepping aside.

The door swung open and there was the ex–Mrs. MacKenzie, out cold on the floor.

"Shit," he muttered, kneeling down next to her. "What the hell's going on now?"

She looked frail and vulnerable, her childlike frame swallowed up by the oceans of fluffy yellow bath mat underneath her. I refused to feel anything but indifference toward her.

"Someone give the woman a Twinkie," I muttered as he slid an arm under her shoulders and raised her to a sitting position. I was skinny but she made me look like I needed a couple weeks with Jenny Craig.

I could see where this was going and I hated it. We couldn't send the waif to Motel 6. Clearly she would have to spend the night at the cottage.

Bad enough that meant she would be sleeping in the guest room next to us, close enough to hear me snore. (Assuming I really do snore. I still think Luke exaggerated.) Now I would have to make very sure that I kept the magick under control while she was there.

The truth? I wasn't sure my powers were up to it. Somehow I was managing to keep the protective charm around Sugar Maple up and running, but for some strange reason my cottage seemed to be a free-range magick zone. Random acts of sorcery had a habit of breaking out when I least expected them, and they usually eluded my attempts to rein them in. We had the weekly cutlery run, the daily flying bath towel brigade, and the occasional let's-see-who-we-can-conjure-up-in-the-middle-of-the-night sweepstakes. Not exactly something you can easily explain away to a civilian.

Take last night when Forbes the Mountain Giant slid a massive hand under the cottage's foundation and gave us an aerial view of the valley nobody else in Sugar Maple had ever seen.

I was pretty sure Luke would be sleeping with one eye open for a long time to come.

I soaked a washcloth in cool water and handed it to him. "Hold this against her forehead," I instructed. I wasn't entirely clear what the wet cloth was supposed to accomplish, but I had seen it in enough movies and television shows to know it was the thing to do. "I'll make her some toast and eggs."

And call her a cab.

Of course, I didn't say that. It sounded

bitchy and heartless, and I didn't want the man I loved to think I was either of those things. What I really wanted to do was spend a few quality minutes with the Book of Spells and conjure up a one-way astral projection that would send Karen Mac-Kenzie back to Boston.

Which was also bitchy and heartless but a lot more efficient.

He placed the cold washcloth on the ex's forehead and she stirred. For a second I had the feeling she knew exactly where she was and what she was doing, and my stomach turned in on itself like a salted pretzel.

I turned and headed for the kitchen.

Call it sorcerer's intuition, but I'd bet my weight in quiviut she had staged this last scene like an Oscar-winning director with an audience of one in mind.

Of course, I couldn't say that to Luke either. Human males had a curious tendency to believe pretty much anything a female of their species told them at face value. Subtext, nuance, veiled sarcasm were all lost on them so you can imagine what the sight of a damsel in distress could do to them.

I cracked two eggs into a Spatterware bowl and quelled the urge to add sponsymia and partularicus to the mix. Sponsymia and partularicus were herbs prized by scorned lovers for their antierotic qualities. Half a teaspoon, and celibacy was your only option.

I'd be lying if I said I wasn't tempted to give it a try. I had promised myself that I would never use magick to keep Luke by my side, but I still hadn't worked out the rules as they applied to ex-wives.

I jumped at the sound of a knock at the window and saw a bedraggled canary tapping its beak against the glass.

"Open up!" Lynette chirped in a Betty Boop voice. "I'm freezing my ass off out here."

I opened the window. She skidded across the narrow windowsill, squawked, then landed in the sink with a splash.

"I sent three blue flames," she complained. "Why didn't you answer me?"

"I couldn't. She saw them."

Her beak dropped open. "The wife *saw* them?"

"She saw them," I said again for emphasis, "and she asked questions."

"She's not supposed to be able to see them." I could see the wheels turning in her tiny little bird head. "Maybe she's magick!" I didn't think it was possible for her voice to climb any higher.

"Luke saw them too," I said, "and we *know* he's not magick."

"Amen, sister," Lynette chirped. "Definitely no magick there."

I had the feeling she'd just insulted my man but I let it pass.

"Well," said Lynette, "I'd say we've got trouble."

"You think?" I shot back. "Isadora's on the prowl. We had an explosion in the middle of a town hall meeting. And now Luke's ex-wife is sprawled on my bathroom floor and I'm seriously afraid she might be in there for the rest of my life. So yeah, I'd say we've got trouble."

"PMS," Lynette clucked. "You should ask Lilith for one of her Saint-John's-wort potions. Works wonders."

"I don't have PMS," I said. "What I have is a shapeshifting canary giving me unsolicited medical advice when that very human woman could walk in here any second."

Lynette's beak dropped open. Her eyes closed. Her wings spread open wide. She sneezed once and in a flurry of feathers and expletives morphed into the human form I knew and loved.

"Shoot," she said. "I forgot I was still in the sink."

It occurred to me that it would be harder to explain why a middle-aged woman was sitting in my sink than it would have been to explain talking to a canary.

Lynette grabbed my hand and climbed out, dripping soapsuds on my tile floor. "They had another meeting after you left."

A wicked cold chill ran up my spine. "About Luke?"

"And his ex," Lynette said. "Renate is on the warpath. She claims you're trying to destroy Sugar Maple by bringing another human into the town."

"I didn't bring Luke to Sugar Maple. The state sent him here. Everyone knows that."

"That's not what Renate is telling them, honey."

I poured the beaten eggs into the waiting skillet and listened to the sizzle. "They can call Montpelier and check it out. I have nothing to hide."

"Renate says one full-blooded human is more than enough."

"Then she should be ecstatic that Luke is our only full-blooded human resident."

"They think the ex-wife is going to move up here too."

I wasn't prone to hysterical laughter as a rule but there was always an exception. "Renate needs some serious therapy."

"Honey, you're not listening to me. They think falling in love with a human has changed you." She pulled a tiny, bright yellow feather out of her left ear and tossed it over her shoulder for luck. "I don't think it and I know Lilith and Janice don't think it either but—" She gave one of those shrugs that were worth a thousand words. "You came into your powers, but until you have a child, we're in the same precarious position we were in before Luke showed up. They're afraid you've forgotten your responsibility to the town."

"And this is what Renate called a secret meeting to talk about? They said all that to my face tonight."

I didn't think it was possible for Lynette to look more uncomfortable than she already did but I was wrong. "She said Isadora was right and we should consider moving Sugar Maple beyond the mist."

Where anyone with human blood would be doomed.

"I'd better—" I stopped at the sound of footsteps in the hallway and flung open the window. "They're coming. We'll talk about it at the shop."

Lynette wrapped her arms tightly across her chest and closed her eyes. The footsteps came closer. She shrank down to canary size but there wasn't a feather in sight.

"Hurry!" I whispered. "They're almost here."

Lynette stretched out her wings and I held my breath as a covering of down appeared, followed by a brilliant layer of yellow, complete with flight feathers and tail.

" . . . scrambled eggs," I heard Luke say from the doorway. "Chloe's a great cook."

Lynette winked at me and flew out the open window as Luke and the ex walked into the kitchen.

Luke sniffed the air. "Something's burning," he said, glancing around.

I felt my cheeks redden with embarrassment. Some great cook. The pan of scrambled eggs I'd started while talking to

Lynette had turned to dark brown leather. I saw the look Mrs. Ex shot Luke but I decided to be magnanimous and ignore it.

I addressed the ex directly. "There's OJ and V8 in the fridge. The coffee's almost ready and the eggs will be done in a minute." Martha Stewart with magick. I should have my own DIY show.

Luke sniffed the air again like a bloodhound. "It smells like burning feathers in here."

I forced a lighthearted laugh that fooled nobody. "Feathers? I don't think so. Not unless one of the cats got into trouble."

Mrs. Ex's smile was every bit as phony. "Luke's right. There are yellow feathers in your sink."

And as it turned out, one feather was also stuck to the front burner on the stove and it happened to be on fire.

I extinguished the flames, turned on the exhaust fan, wiped up the mess, then made another pan of scrambled eggs for a woman I would have happily abandoned on the side of the road if I hadn't been cursed with a conscience.

"Bon appetit." I feigned a yawn behind

my hand. "If I don't see you in the morning, it was nice meeting you."

She nodded but she didn't say a word.
I wasn't sure if she was rude or just preoccupied and I didn't care. All I wanted
was for her to be someplace else when I
woke up.

LUKE

The last time I saw Karen, we were in the
parking lot behind the Realtor's office. It
was late August and a heavy humid haze
hung over the buildings, the trees, and us,
blurring the sharp edges. She wore a green
dress. Her red hair was scraped back in a
low ponytail. A half-smoked Salem fell to
her feet next to six more half-smoked ciga-
rettes. She reached deep into her bag for
another one and I didn't try to stop her.

The divorce was final. The house had
closed. All the bits and pieces that made
up a couple's life together had been inspected, divided, or tossed away with our
marriage. We were waiting for our respec-
tive attorneys to finish the last of the

paperwork, then call us back in to distribute the checks.

There were so many things I wanted to say to her: that I had loved her, that I would always love what we had shared in those early days, that for a little while before our world stopped spinning on its axis, we had almost been happy.

But I was all out of words. We both were. We had flung words at each other like sharpened knives and most of them had drawn blood. The only thing left was goodbye.

And now here we were, more than two years later, looking at each other across Chloe's kitchen table. The only thing we had in common was the memory of the little girl we both still mourned.

"These eggs aren't very good," she said. "The supermodel can't cook."

"Her name is Chloe."

"She burns scrambled eggs, Luke. Nobody burns scrambled eggs."

Nobody burned scrambled eggs unless they'd been distracted. The yellow feathers in the sink were a dead giveaway that Lynette Pendragon had dropped by for a visit.

I gulped down a cup of coffee while she pushed the eggs around on her plate.

"I think you need a doctor," I said. "Maybe an X-ray or something. You keep passing out. That's not normal."

"Nothing for you to worry about," she said. "Steffie really did send me here to find you. I'm not crazy and I'm not making it up."

It felt like an explosion going off inside my chest but I stayed cool. "You found me. So where the hell is she?"

"I don't know. But she'll be here. I know she will."

"Steffie's not coming. We buried her next to my mother. She's not coming back. Not now. Not ever."

"She already came back once. I know she'll do it again."

"You need help."

Her laugh was almost scary. "That's what my therapist said."

"You've been seeing a therapist?"

"A therapist, a shrink, Father Romero at Christ the Redeemer, a social worker at the hospital. They all think I'm nuts but I'm not. I swear it."

Right around now was when I'd be calling for backup.

"You told them about Steffie?"

She shot me a scornful look. "I went about the dreams."

I raised my hands in the air. I didn't want to hear about her dreams. The ones I still had about Steffie were bad enough. Ones so real that waking up was like losing her all over again. Dreams about her first word, her first step, making her laugh with the silly Rock Paper Scissors game she loved. Dreams I wished I could block forever.

"This is way above my pay grade." If they couldn't help her, what chance did I have? "I need to get back to town hall and fill out a report. Get some sleep. We'll talk in the morning."

"Same old Luke," she said. "Still running away when the going gets tough."

"There was an explosion," I said. "I have responsibilities."

"You had responsibilities to your daughter too."

She was right but that didn't mean I wanted to hear it.

"You need help, Karen," I said. "I'm going to drive you down to Boston tomorrow and see if we can find a doctor."

"Not until we do something about Steffie."

"She's dead." My neutral cop persona was starting to crack. "There's nothing we can do."

"She's reaching out to us." Her eyes were wild with grief and hope. "She sent me to find you, Luke. Doesn't that mean anything to you?"

If I had believed a word she said was true, it would have meant everything, but I didn't.

My daughter was dead and I was the reason why.

That was the only thing I believed.

It was the only thing that mattered.

I pushed back my chair and stood up. "See you in the morning, Karen."

7

CHLOE

I tried to eavesdrop on Luke and his ex-wife from the bedroom, but the astral static was so strong I couldn't hear a word they were saying. When that didn't work, I tried to send Pye into the kitchen to pick up the vibes and report back to me, but she seemed to like the redhead about as much as I did and refused to leave my side. Dinah, Lucy, and Blot weren't any help at all. The three of them were sound asleep on the window seat, oblivious to the turmoil I was going through.

Why was I pacing like someone in solitary? It was my house. I didn't have to stay locked away in the bedroom like a prisoner. I could stroll back into the kitchen, take my seat at the table with the man I loved and the woman he'd married, and find out what was going on.

If I didn't, there was the distinct possibility that I might go crazy.

I smoothed down my hair, wished for the thousandth time that small boobs would come back in style, then casually ambled toward the kitchen.

They weren't there.

They also weren't in the living room.

Or (insert loud sigh of relief) the guest room.

The familiar sound of the truck's engine turning over grabbed my attention. Okay, it didn't grab my attention exactly. What it did was grab me by the throat and practically throw me to the ground. I raced out onto the front porch and straight into the ex, who was sitting on the top step, knees under her chin, smoking a cigarette. Relief almost knocked me flat.

"He left," she said before I had a chance

to say a word. "He said he had to fill out a report at town hall or something."

"Did he say when he'd be back?"

"Hello," she said. "This is Luke we're talking about."

"What's that supposed to mean?"

"He hasn't pulled the disappearing act yet?" Her bitter tone unnerved me. "Well, give him time. He will."

She was grieving her daughter's death, and blaming Luke was one of the ways she eased her pain. I understood that, but it didn't mean I liked hearing it. Their marriage wasn't any of my business. I intended to keep it that way.

The night was moonless and foggy. The glowing reddish orange tip of her cigarette punctuated the darkness like a beacon. She was the stranger, but suddenly I was the one who felt like I didn't belong.

"The guest room's at the end of the hallway," I said. "I left some towels and an extra toothbrush on the bed."

She nodded. "Thanks."

That was the best she could do?

"Sorry about the eggs. There's a stash

of Chips Ahoy in the cabinet over the fridge if you get hungry."

"Thanks."

I had one last thing to say, and after that, I was through with polite conversation.

"I'm sorry about your daughter."

She tossed the cigarette down, and it made a soft sizzle when it hit the mud. "So am I."

"Okay then," I said. "Good night. I have an early day tomorrow but if you need any-thing—"

"No problem," she said, not bothering to look up at me. "I'm fine."

I turned to leave, and from the corner of my eye I saw a shimmering silver thought probe slithering through the mud toward the ex. To be honest, I wouldn't have minded watching her expression when the nasty little gizmo started nibbling at her ankle like a thought-hungry piranha, but there was no way I was going to let the entire town find out her story before I did.

I held my hands up and out in the stop position and racked my brain for the words to halt the probe's progress. I knew that defensive spell inside out. I had used it at the town hall. And how many times had I deflected thought probes as they tried to sneak in my bedroom window while Luke and I were—well, you get the picture. Let's just say more than my yarn shop would be an Internet sensation.

"Come on," I muttered. "You knew it a few hours ago."

The ex turned slightly in my direction. "Did you say something?"

I ignored her. I could hear the rhythm of the defensive charm but couldn't assemble the words in the right order.

" . . . walls of stone, walls of fire . . . " I waved my arms in the air.

The ex turned all the way around. "What are you doing?"

I finally had her attention exactly when I didn't want it.

The thought probe was winding its way through the mud toward her right ankle. I had maybe five seconds before it made contact. A vision of the Book of Spells danced before my eyes. The pages flipped and a beam of golden light landed on the Doomsday quick-and-dirty solution for blocking thought probes.

I threw myself on the probe a split second before it made contact with the redhead, covering the prickly, glittering missile with my body like a bomb blanket.

I don't even want to think about how I looked, sprawled at her feet. You know that dream where you're naked at your high school reunion and everyone else has had liposuction and spa treatments while you're standing there with your cellulite shimmering under the spotlight?

This was worse.

The probe was nipping at my thigh, but I didn't dare move or it would slip away and sink itself into the redhead's memory bank.

The redhead rushed over to me. "Are you okay?" She looked different, stronger somehow. She even sounded different. More engaged. More sure of herself.

I tried to talk, but like I said before, magick didn't come easy to me and it was taking all my powers of concentration to shut down the probe. I had nothing left over for conversation.

For some reason this seemed to worry her.

"Don't move," she said. "I'm a trauma

nurse. I'm going to see if you have any injuries."

It kept getting better and better. Just my luck that the incredible fainting woman turned out to be a trained medical professional.

"Don't touch me!" I warned as I struggled to wrangle the probe into submission. If she touched me, the probe would use me as a conduit to get to her.

"I won't hurt you," she said in a soothing tone of voice. "I just need to see if you broke anything."

"You're the one who keeled over in the church," I reminded her. "Maybe you should be checked for a concussion."

"I'm fine."

"So am I."

She moved closer. I pinned my knees more tightly together. Thought probes had the nasty habit of gaining power just before they went dormant, and I was feeling the heat.

"I'd feel better if you let me check you out," she said.

"I'd feel better if you'd pretend I wasn't here."

"That would be a lot easier if you'd quit twitching."

"I'm not twitching."

"Yes, you are. In my line of work, twitching isn't a good thing."

The probe unleashed its last burst of energy, sending sharp arrows of heat through my body, then went dormant. I breathed a long loud sigh of relief.

Which, as it turned out, was a big mistake because the redhead thought I was having respiratory problems. She flipped me over on my back and started doing weird things to my chest. Unfortunately I'm insanely ticklish and she hit one of those spots on my rib cage and I started laughing and then she started laughing and the next thing I knew she lost her footing and ended up in the mud next to me.

Who knew mutual embarrassment could be a bonding experience?

"I'm Chloe," I said, extending a muddy hand.

"Karen." She had a strong grip.

Too bad she was my human boyfriend's totally human ex-wife. I was starting to like her.

LUKE

Karen's arrival had knocked me on my ass, but that was nothing compared to the way everyone else in town was freaking out. I stopped by the town hall on the way to take another look at the rental car. I figured I'd lend a hand with the repairs, but there was nothing a human male could do that a sprite couldn't do a thousand times faster and better.

Midge Stallworth and her husband were there, brewing coffee and making sure the collective blood sugar didn't drop. Renate and Colm. Lilith and Archie, Frank and Manny and Rose from Assisted Living. Paul Griggs and his clan. I sensed rather than saw the spirits, a pulsing heartbeat hanging in the heavy air. With the exception of Renate and Colm, I had come to think of them all as friends. People I could turn to if I needed something. People who knew they could turn to me.

Okay, so maybe "people" wasn't the right term, but when it came to Sugar Maple, my vocabulary was still limited by my human experience.

I hadn't expected the conversation to stop cold the second I entered the vestibule or the literal icy wind blowing in my direction when I said hello.

"You gotta get rid of her." Aging vampire Frank never minced words. Usually I found that trait admirable. "The dame has bad news written all over her."

"Pay your back alimony!" The usually cheerful Midge glowered at me. "Maybe then the woman can afford some food."

"One human's enough around here." Coming from Archie, the troll who ran the electronics repair shop near the bridge, this was no surprise. "Two is going to tip the balance. Mark my words."

Renate from the Inn fixed me with one of those chilly stares the Fae specialized in. "We need to consider our options." She paused. "Without strangers in our midst."

Even I knew what that meant. They wanted me gone.

"See what you did," Midge chided the others. "You're making Luke uncomfortable. Tell him you don't consider him a stranger. He's one of us now."

"The hell he is." So Deno from Pizza

Haven was on the other side of the issue too. "No human has ever been one of us and we're not about to start now."

"Hold on a minute!" I didn't have to take this crap. "Chloe's father was human. He was one of you."

"Never!" Renate swelled to full-size human form and stared me down from across the room. "We were born of the need to escape human treachery. That will never change."

"This is no life for a man like you." Colm was turning on the one-of-the-guys charm. "You're a police detective in a town without crime. You can't be happy here in our quiet little hamlet forever."

"Of course he's happy here." Midge sprang to my defense. "He'd be happy anywhere with Chloe."

"I don't give a fig if he's happy or not," Frank chimed in. "Just knock her up, pal, and let's get on with it before Isadora grabs the whole shebang. We're not getting any younger. We want security."

Midge sidled closer to me. "You don't have a"—she lowered her voice—"problem in that area, do you?"

I knew bearing a child was part of Chloe's destiny but it wasn't something we had discussed. I had been hoping to postpone the conversation indefinitely.

"I won't be in my office tomorrow," I said, tamping down volcanic anger. "If anyone needs me, call me on my cell."

I strode toward the door, hoping I'd reach the street before I blew.

"Wait a second, Chief," Wayne, one of the itinerant house sprites, called to me as I pushed open the door. "Grayson found this in the back and figured it belonged to your ex."

He tossed a worn navy blue leather wallet to me from the top of the extension ladder where he had been working.

"Thanks, Wayne. I'll see she gets it." Karen had had that wallet for as long as I could remember. I pocketed it and took one last look around the meeting hall. "Great work. You guys could revive the housing industry single-handed."

Wayne's grin was infectious. He looked like George Clooney circa *ER*, and I had to remind myself he was a house sprite revealing himself in a form that my human brain could process.

At least that was the way Chloe had explained it to me.

If I'd learned anything these last few months, it was not to ask too many questions because sometimes the answers were more than you could handle.

The ex-husband might have kept his hands off Karen's wallet, but the cop wasn't about to let any clues to her mental state get by. Besides, I needed her car rental receipt to get the repair in motion so she could go back to Boston.

Lucky for me, she was still a pack rat. I found the rental car receipt neatly folded behind her cash. I tossed it on the seat next to me and continued searching. Her Stop & Shop frequent shopper card. An ATM card from Bank of America. Health insurance card. A receipt from Golden Wok. Nothing that gave me any idea what the hell had pushed her over the edge.

But something had. After two years of silence she'd driven up to Vermont to find me with a crazy story about Steffie and some special ringtone only the two of them knew. And where were all the photos she used to carry? She carried her life around with her on a daily basis. Our wedding day. The day we brought Steffie home from the hospital. Her first Christmas. And her second. And her third.

But now there was only one photo. Steffie and Santa taken the Christmas before she died.

"What do you want from me? I'm working on a case and I can't break away."

"It's Christmas Eve, Luke. Steffie's all excited about seeing the mall Santa. You promised you'd be there. She's counting on you."

So was the eighteen-year-old kid we found beaten half to death on campus. I switched the office phone to my other ear so I could tap info into the computer. My mind was fully engaged. I had nothing left for anyone but the young girl who was clinging to life in the ICU.

"Twenty minutes," Karen urged. "You know how much Steffie misses you when you're working all these hours."

"I've gotta go," I said, already gone. "I'll see what I can do."

I didn't make it back in time for Steffie's visit with Santa. I wasn't there when she opened her presents Christmas morning. I missed the first grade Valentine's Day pageant.

The girl in the ICU? She was a junior at BU and doing great.

That was our daughter's last Christmas.

It never got easier. I kept waiting for the day when it wouldn't hurt so damn much but so far that day hadn't come. Our marriage had been on shaky ground before Steffie's accident. After her death there was nothing left but anger and guilt.

I disappeared into my work. On the job nobody asked me how I felt. Nobody monitored my emotional temperature on an hourly basis. I did my job and I did it well, and if there were days when I felt like driving the squad car into a brick wall, that was my business and nobody else's.

Karen had it tougher. She took a sabbatical from nursing and spent her days watching old movies on AMC. She didn't have brothers or sisters to turn to. Her father died when she was in her teens; her mother lost her battle with cancer early in our marriage. She had one cousin that I knew about, a teacher in Natick who showed up every Christmas like clockwork to criticize.

It was a long shot but maybe the cousin could shed some light on what had been going on. I drove back to the office, where I kept a Bankers Box filled with old contact info that I'd brought with me from Boston.

The storefronts were all dark. The streetlamps gave off an old-fashioned yellow glow that washed the sidewalk with nostalgia. It was so quiet you could hear an owl hooting in New Hampshire. I tried not to think about all the things I couldn't see or hear.

What can I say? The place unnerved the hell out of me after dark. I let myself into the station and flipped on the low-wattage fluorescent overhead. It flickered twice, then came to life.

The police station was a renovated pet shop that still smelled like the monkey house at the zoo, but I was slowly getting used to it.

I dug through a stack of old Rolodex cards and found the cousin's number. Like everyone else on the planet, Nancy screened her calls and I didn't make it through the net. I'd be surprised if she phoned me back. I'd never been one of her favorites.

I tried calling a couple of old friends. They answered their phones but neither had seen or heard from Karen in months.

So I did what I'd done a thousand times when I worked for the Boston PD and needed help. I called Fran, the chief of police's right-hand and my good friend.

"Are you drunk dialing," she asked, "or did you forget how to tell time?"

"It's ten thirty, Frannie. Your grandchildren are still awake."

"I guess there's no morning shift up there in Sugar Maple."

"I need your help."

That was the best thing about old friends. When you needed them, they were there for you. And as it turned out, they didn't gossip about your ex-wife until you asked them to.

"You didn't know any of this?" Fran said after she'd finished. "Sorry to dump it on you but you asked."

I'd asked and now I knew. Karen had quit her job at the hospital, let her friendships go to the point where the few that remained were on life support.

"I don't know if this means anything," Fran said as we were saying goodbye, "but she called me about two weeks ago. She wanted my cousin Noreen's phone number."

"Noreen the psychic?"

"She prefers to be called a transdimensional therapist."

I let it pass. "Did Karen tell you why she wanted Noreen's number?"

"I didn't ask and she didn't volunteer."

The reason wasn't hard to figure out.

"So don't be a stranger," Fran said after we'd exhausted the Noreen/Karen connection. "If you won't come down to Boston, maybe I'll drive up to Sugar Maple to do some shopping. We can catch up." She laughed knowingly. "You can introduce me to your new girlfriend."

There's a great idea, I thought. I hadn't intended to tell my old pal about Chloe, but when she asked if I was seeing anyone, I couldn't hold back. She'd grilled me like I was the prime suspect in a murder investigation and I was lucky I'd stopped short of telling her that Chloe was a sorceress-in-training. There wasn't a protective charm in the universe strong enough to keep Sugar Maple's secrets safe from Fran.

There was nothing more I could do for

Karen. Her problems weren't my problems anymore. They hadn't been for a long time now. Whatever it was she was looking for, she'd have to find it someplace else.

I logged off the computer and was stuffing the Rolodex cards back into the file when I heard the front door open.

"Hello, hello," Midge Stallworth's cheery voice rang out. "I saw your lights on and wanted to make sure everything was okay."

"Everything's fine, Midge." I shoved the file back into the closet and smiled at her. "I had a few calls to make."

"About your ex, I'll bet. Can't make those calls with Chloe around, right?"

"Something like that."

"So what brings her to Sugar Maple to see you?"

"Just passing through," I lied.

"Oh, you can tell me," Midge said in her Betty Boop voice. "I won't tell anyone."

"Nothing to tell. She'll be back on the road tomorrow."

"She's a tiny little thing." Midge stepped farther into the room. "Not at all like Chloe. I've always loved a big tall man with a teeny woman."

Midge barely topped five feet in heels.

I nodded and took a step back. What the hell? Midge was old enough to be my grandmother—and that was just counting human years—but the vibe in the room had become sexually charged.

"I'd better get back to the cottage," I said. "Chloe will be wondering what's taking me so long."

"I brought some donuts." She aimed a full-wattage smile up at me. "Why don't you put on a pot of coffee and I'll run back to the car and get them."

"Maybe some other time, Midge."

I'd never seen anyone over two actually pout before.

"Sit down."

"What?"

She motioned toward the desk. "Sit down."

Okay, now I was getting seriously freaked out. When it's after midnight and a vampire tells you to sit down, you have reason to worry.

"Oh, don't you look at me like that," she said with one of her high-pitched laughs. "I'm not going old school on you."

"Old school?"

"*Interview with the Vampire.* Bela Lugosi." She pretended to bite down on her forearm. "My grandkids call it direct access."

"That's a relief."

She laughed again and patted my hand. "You had that scared human look around your eyes. The young ones toy with the old ways, but trust me, they'll learn soon enough. Life is easier all around without the hunt."

Which was all terrific information but I didn't have a clue what it had to do with me. Or why I needed to know it tonight.

"Midge, you know my office is open to you anytime, but tonight I need to get home and take care of some personal matters."

"Honey, I hate to say this, but it really *is* time you went back home."

"That's what I'm saying."

"Not Chloe's home. *Your* home: Boston."

"Are you joking?"

Her big brown eyes brimmed with tears. "I wish I was, honey, but it had to be said. One human was tolerable but two is something else again. Now don't get me wrong. *I* don't feel that way. I'm a firm believer in live and let live. We were welcomed here years ago by open-minded humans who believed we had rights too. There's no reason why we can't all get along together. But some of us—and I'm not naming any names but you can figure it out if you try—are seriously questioning whether or not Sugar Maple belongs in this realm at all."

"The Weavers," I said. They hadn't exactly hidden their feelings from anyone since Isadora's banishment. They were Fae so moving beyond the mist would be as natural as breathing to them.

"You didn't hear it from me."

"They're only two people. You'd need a hell of a lot more to bring about that kind of change."

"There were whispers before, but the whispers got a lot louder tonight after your wife showed up."

"What does Karen have to do with anything?"

"The general feeling—and again I'm just telling you what I heard—is that it starts with one human and then another, and before you know it, they're building summer houses and sending their kids to school here."

"Karen is going home as soon as her car's repaired."

Midge's expression lightened. "Well, that's no problem. The boys can have it ready in two shakes of a lamb's tail."

I explained to her that because the accident was already on record with the rental car agency, we needed to follow procedures by the book. "They'll probably toss her another rental and she'll be on her way."

"Honey, you'll have to make sure of it or I won't be held responsible for what happens."

"Don't worry, Midge," I said as I moved her toward the door. "Nobody's going to hold you responsible for anything."

One way or the other, the responsibility was all mine.

Just ask Karen.

8

CHLOE

Clearly this was my night for lurking. This time I was positioned outside the bathroom door when I heard the unmistakable squeak of the medicine cabinet door sliding shut. I did a quick mental inventory of the contents and breathed a sigh of relief. Nothing incriminating in there. At least nothing that I remembered. For a second I considered barging in and catching her red-handed, but I kind of understood where she was coming from. The sad truth of it was I would be up to my elbows in her battered Coach tote bag right now if I wasn't afraid I'd get caught.

All things considered, I'd rather have her poking around my medicine cabinet than unconscious on the bathroom floor looking all pale and wan and needy. I had never been the rescue-me type. When you were taller than most men of your acquaintance, damsel-in-distress wasn't a card a girl could easily play.

I left her to her investigation and walked down the hallway to the laundry room to see what I could do about getting our clothes clean.

I see hand knits every day of my life. Everything from garter-stitch dishcloths to wedding ring shawls like the one that had come close to putting me into intensive care. I knew great knitting when I saw it, and her cardi was great knitting. Even spattered with mud, the ribbon-tie sweater was a thing of beauty. Intricate trim, clever short-row shaping, a dressmaker's attention to detail.

But that unfortunate six-inch gash across the back was an affront to knitters everywhere.

I'm pretty good at repairs but this one

was beyond my skills. My human skills, at any rate.

But my magick was another story.

By the time I heard the blow dryer start up in the bathroom, the tear was gone and I was pressing the excess water into a stack of thick white towels and congratulating myself on a job well done. A great sweater should be forever . . . or as close to forever as a knitter can manage.

The ex walked in while I was gently shaping the damp sweater on my blocking board.

"You didn't have to do that," she said with a slight smile. "I was going to wash it."

"No problem," I said. "I didn't want the mud to have a chance to settle into the fibers."

"You're a knitter."

"So the mountains of yarn in the guest room gave me away."

Her smile widened just enough for me to notice. "That and the eight spinning wheels in the hallway."

"Occupational hazard. I own a knit shop in town."

She smoothed the edging on her cardi. "Luke told me." I held my breath as she ran her hand down the sleeve. "I was so proud of myself when I finished this. My daughter loved it. I used to tell her when she grew up—" She stopped and shook her head. "It has a big rip in the back. I keep promising myself I'd figure out how to mend but—" She flipped the sweater over. "You fixed it?" She looked at me like I'd cured cellulite with applications of hot fudge. "Where did you find matching yarn? It was hand-spun."

Busted. I won't tell you what I thought but it would have gotten me bleeped on *The View*.

I had to think fast. "Remember I'm a spinner too. I have boxes of samples stowed away. I can usually come up with a match for just about anything."

As far as lies went, that was a good one. I really did have boxes and bags of yarn samples tucked in every storage space both here and at the shop.

"Un-uh," she said, shaking her head. "Something weird's going on here."

My heart slowed to a crawl. I held my breath and waited for the other shoe to drop.

"I know exactly where the tear was and even I can't find your repair." She was smiling from ear to ear in a way that would have delighted me if I deserved any of the credit. "You can tell me. It's some kind of magic, right?"

I made it a habit to avoid the *M* word around humans. Instead I babbled something incoherent about grafting and needle size, and then I heard myself offering to teach her some of the basics at the shop sometime.

"Wait a minute! Are you *that* Sticks & Strings? I read about you online," she said, warming up even more. "Isn't that the place where your yarn never tangles?"

"That's us," I said, laughing. "Your yarn never tangles, your sleeves always turn out the same length, and you always get gauge."

Knitting makes strange bedfellows. It transcends race and gender and political orientation. Sit two knitters down with needles and yarn, and I guarantee they'll find common ground.

Even if it's only how to repair a ripped sweater.

KAREN

I hate the word *bonding*, but even I couldn't deny that we clicked somehow. And it had nothing to do with the fact we had both slept with Luke MacKenzie. I felt my guard drop for the first time in weeks.

We sat down at her kitchen table with mugs of tea and she tried to show me how she had repaired my sweater, but I swear to you her fingers were a blur.

"Slow down," I said. "You lost me when you threaded the tapestry needle."

"Sorry. I have a quick metabolism."

She wasn't kidding. I don't want to say there was something weird about Chloe Hobbs, but up until that moment I thought only cartoon characters moved that fast. Even though she was wielding the needle right under my nose, I still had the feeling it was the knitting equivalent of a Vegas magic trick.

Or maybe she had some weird kind of knitting superpowers, paranormal crafting skills straight out of a Harry Potter—

She stopped, needle poised above the piece of knitted fabric she was using to demonstrate her technique. "Actually I've never read Harry Potter."

You could hear my breath leave my body in one loud whoosh. "What did you say?"

"I thought you—" She stopped and shook her head. "Forget it. I thought I heard you say something about Harry Potter but you didn't so . . . " Her words trailed away.

"You're psychic!" Why had it taken me so long to figure it out? It was written all over her face. Those eyes! Nobody had eyes like that unless they saw things the rest of us couldn't. "I knew there was something different about you."

Her mouth opened but no sound came out.

"My grandmother was psychic and so was my mother. I'm not but I know when someone has the gift. You picked up on something I was thinking and then you pushed it away. My mother did that all the time."

"I'm not psychic."

"I grew up with it. You won't shock me."

"I was trying to slow down so you could read my stitches. That's all it was."

"Fine," I said with a shrug of my shoulders. "Whatever."

"I'm telling the truth."

"I didn't say you weren't."

"But you don't believe me."

"My mother didn't want to admit she had second sight either. It's okay. I get it. Some people—"

She jumped up and sent cats and yarn flying in every direction. I wanted to tell her to consider cutting back on the caffeine but I thought better of it.

"I'm sorry," I said instead, bending down to retrieve a ball of merino. "I just think you should be proud of your gifts and not hide them."

She looked like she wanted to hit me with a pair of US 15s. "I'm not psychic," she said through gritted teeth. "I can't read minds. I can barely read a menu without my contacts in. Will you just drop it?"

She's a foot taller than I am so I dropped it.

But I didn't believe her for a minute.

CHLOE

I wasn't lying when I told the ex that I'm not psychic. I'm really not. Or at least I don't think I am. My powers still aren't totally realized, but so far I haven't seen any clues that mind reading was going to be one of my specialties. Mostly I'm lucky if I can figure out what I'm going to do next, much less what anybody else will be up to.

Bad enough she was Luke's ex-wife; now she was turning out to be one of those humans who think they are somehow connected to "the other side."

Trust me. They aren't. They don't have a clue what the other side is all about, and if they did, they would probably run like hell to get away from it.

Of course, there was one problem with my thesis: I had heard her speak even though the ex claimed she hadn't said anything, which pretty much put us at an impasse. And if you think I'm bad at confrontations, you should see how awful I am at impasses.

I wiped up the tea. She saved the yarn from a wicked puddle. The cats abandoned the kitchen for the relative safety of the front room. We stared at each other for a few awkward minutes at the end of which she pretended to yawn and I pretended she wasn't pretending. The sleeping draught I dropped into her tea wouldn't take hold for another half hour.

Finally I showed her to the guest room.

Now all I had to do for the next eight hours was make sure the cutlery didn't stage a performance of "Be My Guest" at the foot of her bed.

I started a huge pot of coffee. My plan was to stay up all night, standing vigil over the dishes and other household objects that just might decide to join the chorus. I could explain away a repaired sweater but dancing spoons might be problematic.

And don't get me started on what I'd do if Isadora managed to breach her banishment and make another appearance. I had enough to worry about.

Like wondering when Luke was going to come back.

I grabbed my cell and pressed number one.

"Luke MacKenzie here. Leave a message."

"What's taking so long? Call me."

Better yet, come home. His ex-wife hadn't driven up to Sugar Maple to talk knitting. Whatever was going on, he needed to deal with it himself and send her back to Boston, where cutlery knew its place.

Another five minutes passed, then ten. Still no sign of Luke. I pressed the redial.

"Luke MacKenzie here. Leave a message."

My hands started to shake and I disconnected.

I was now officially worried.

Luke was a cop. More than that, he was the only cop in town. It didn't matter that this was the Town Without Crime. His cell was on all day, every day, even when we were making love. There was no way he would head out in the middle of the night with his phone turned off.

Come to think of it, he didn't head out much at all after dark. There was the occasional lost tourist or dustup with some of the town's teenagers, but once the sun went down, he stayed pretty close to home.

And to me.

My stomach knotted. Not that Sugar Maple posed a danger to him. Or at least it hadn't before Isadora went totally nuts tonight and trashed our town hall meeting at the same time Luke was rescuing his ex from a ditch near the outskirts of town.

The coincidental timing bothered me, but I wasn't sure why. Most of life was a series of coincidences. Some good, some not so. It was what you did after that mattered.

For all I knew, Karen's arrival might have saved his life. As the only full-blooded human in town, he would have been the most vulnerable to serious injury when the explosion tore through the old church. A pillar or a giant shard of window glass might have—

I didn't want to think about it. There were enough items on my list of worries without adding things that never happened.

I wasn't sure if the thought made me feel better or worse.

A half hour later I had finally settled down at my favorite Schacht wheel when Luke pulled into the driveway. His headlights swept the living room like a beacon, spotlighting the soft merino roving I was spinning into cobweb yarn. I felt the familiar little bump-up in my heart rate, but this time it was equal parts desire and anxiety.

Spinning was second nature to me. But love? Not so much. Just when I was finally getting the hang of it, maybe even believing this crazy connection between Luke and me might actually work out, the fates threw a curveball at me in the form of an ex-wife and the little girl they'd lost.

I pounced the second the door closed behind him.

"Why didn't you tell me about your daughter?"

"I thought you didn't want to talk while Karen was in the house."

"Why?" I asked again, my voice breaking slightly. "I need to know." I was hurt and angry and feeling more vulnerable than I'd ever felt before in my life, and I didn't like it. If I could have bartered away my all-too-human heart, I would have done so in a cat's breath.

I locked eyes with him, and I didn't even try to hide my feelings. It wasn't easy for me to open myself up that way. I'd spent most of my life putting a good face on things, pretending to be happy and content when the loneliness threatened to swallow me whole. Who would have guessed love could hurt even more?

He needed to see what keeping secrets from a woman did to her. Let him see the damage he'd caused.

He pulled back.

I pushed harder.

Maybe too hard.

His expression downshifted swiftly from surprise to self-defense to a level of pain I'd never seen before, and all the fight went out of me.

"I wanted to tell you about Steffie," he said, "but—"

I put my fingers to his lips. "I know. You don't have to explain." I wished with all my heart that he would but I wasn't going to push. Not now.

"Karen's in bad shape." He told me about his call to his old friend Fran in the department. "Fran helped me track down a nurse Karen worked with at the hospital. She didn't quit. She was fired."

"I'm sorry she's having a rough time," I said, "but I don't understand why she came up here to see you."

He slipped back into cop mode and I tensed up. "She claims she saw Steffie at the park near our old house."

I tensed up even more. "What do you think?"

"You're kidding, right? I think she needs some hospital time, that's what I think."

"Did she speak to Steffie?"

The cop façade broke for a moment and frustration slipped in. "She said something about a phone call but she has no proof." He regrouped. "I'm going to drive her back down to Boston tomorrow and see if I can get her some help."

"Can't her family take care of it?" Not that I was being territorial or anything, but wasn't that what families were supposed to do?

"She doesn't have any family." A slight hesitation. "Just me."

"You're not part of her family anymore." *You're part of mine.*

"You saw her. She's running on fumes. I can't let her drive back like that. She'll have another wreck."

"Are you sure she didn't actually have some kind of contact with Steffie?"

"She didn't see Steffie."

"You've seen the Souderbush family. Did you forget they died over one hundred years ago?" It wasn't like I hadn't briefed him on all of our villagers, especially our noncorporeal ones. I mean, there was a reason we were ranked the most popular stop on the Spirit Trail.

"My daughter isn't a ghost."

"But you have to admit that it *is* possible." I didn't think he was ready for the truth: all humans ended up in the spirit world, in one way or another. The afterlife had more options than any mortal could imagine and they weren't all wonderful.

The cop mask hardened. A smarter woman might have heeded the warning. "It's bullshit."

"What if it isn't?"

"I'm not going there."

"You're going to have to go there, Luke. Your daughter's mother is asleep in my guest room and I don't think she plans to leave anytime soon."

"I told you she's leaving tomorrow."

"Don't tell me. Tell her."

He started down the hallway toward the guest room with me close behind him. Would I never learn to keep my big mouth shut? Talk about the wrong thing to say. She wasn't going to be up for conversation until morning.

When she was conscious.

"I didn't mean tell her now. She's asleep. That's a good thing. Let her—"

"Why wait?" he shot back over his shoulder. "I'll drive her back tonight. She can sleep in the truck."

"Luke, stop! The woman's exhausted. Tomorrow morning's good enough." What was wrong with me? Wasn't this exactly what I wanted?

"She's going tonight."

"What about the rental car? How will you—"

"I'll work it out with the agency when I get back."

"This is crazy. It's almost three in the morning. When do you figure on getting some sleep?"

He wasn't listening to me. My words bounced off his back like it was a trampoline. I'd seen this behavior before: the human male quit listening when he didn't want to hear any more. He just shut down, and the more words the female threw at him, the fewer he heard.

If this was part of the human experience, they could keep it.

"Luke!" I snapped as we approached the closed door to the guest room. "I didn't want to tell you, but I gave her a potion. She'll sleep straight through until seven and there's nothing you can do about it."

"I'll wake her up."

"You're not listening to me, Luke. You won't be able to wake her up. An earthquake won't wake her up until seven tomorrow morning. Not a second before."

Nothing. No response at all. Not even a grunt.

What did I have to do to make him hear me?

For the record, I didn't mean for it to happen, but when it comes to controlling my powers, high emotion gets me in trouble every time. Before I even realized what was happening, Luke glowed bright crimson, then shrank down into a human Ken Doll, then back again to normal size in the blink of an eye.

"What the hell!?"

This was so not the way to build a relationship.

"I didn't mean to do it," I said, torn between embarrassment and highly inappropriate laughter.

He didn't take his eyes off me, and who could blame him? I wouldn't trust me either. "You mean like the time you flipped the bed when we were—"

"Exactly."

"Except this time you were pissed."

Which was an understatement but this didn't seem like the right time to quibble. "Yes."

His expression shifted. "Did you say you gave her a potion or something?"

"To help her sleep."

"You mean, like Sominex." He sounded so hopeful. I hated to burst his bubble.

"Well, not exactly like that."

"You put a spell on her?" His hopefulness was fading fast.

"I added something to her tea."

"Something you can't buy at Rite-Aid."

"Not without a very odd prescription."

Any other man would have been out the door the first time his toothbrush talked back to him but not Luke. He laughed. He didn't want to but he laughed anyway.

We stood there looking at each other for what seemed like forever, and then we fell into each other's arms. Sparks, pale ivory and yellow, arced over our heads, and I smiled against his shoulder as we held on tight. I needed his warmth the way I needed light and air and water. The stronger my sorceress side became, the more I craved his very human touch.

Tell me the fates don't have a sense of humor when it comes to love.

Love scrambles your priorities. It was easy to forget the big picture when you found yourself in the middle of a soap opera–worthy romantic melodrama. We were so caught up with the ex and her problems that everything else fell away.

He didn't tell me about his encounter with Midge, and I didn't tell him about Lynette's earlier warning. Maybe if we had, things would have gone differently, but we didn't. It all seemed so clear at the time. First we would get Karen back to Boston, and then we would deal with Sugar Maple.

We had no idea our time was running out.

9

KAREN

"Where's Luke?" I asked as I entered the kitchen a little after seven the next morning. "His truck is gone."

Chloe looked up from the laptop sitting next to her bowl of oatmeal. "He was gone when I woke up. He probably went out to see about your rental car."

That sounded like him. It was a lot easier to deal with a wrecked car than an ex-wife.

She gave me an easygoing smile. "He found your wallet back at town hall. It's on the counter."

"It must have slipped out of my bag when I ran into that wall everyone said doesn't exist."

Her expression didn't waver. Supermodels were like that. They could hold a pose forever. "Sleep well?" she asked.

"Actually I did. I guess it's the mountain air." I felt strong in a way I hadn't in months, like maybe I was moving in the right direction, no matter how crazy it seemed.

She gestured toward the big red pot on the stove. "I made plenty. Help yourself."

I wasn't much of an oatmeal fan but I figured it had to be better than her scrambled eggs. Besides, for the first time in ages, I was hungry.

I helped myself to a small bowl while she watched.

"I have raisins and dried cranberries if you like."

"Plain's fine." I sat down across from her and reached for the cream resting next to her open laptop. "Catching up on the news?"

She flashed a slightly embarrassed grin. "Knit blogs," she said. "I'm addicted."

I peered over her shoulder at Crazy Aunt Purl's latest adventures. "Brooklyn Tweed and Franklin."

She looked up at me. "And don't forget Wendy, Dawn, and Knitspot. My blogroll is so long it's embarrassing."

I smiled and went over to the stove to check out the oatmeal. I couldn't remember the last time I'd eaten anything close to a real breakfast. I wondered if my stomach would rebel from the shock of nutritious food. "So how long ago did he leave?"

"Like I said, he was already gone when I woke up."

"He's avoiding me, isn't he?"

"Of course not. He's—"

"I was married to the guy. Avoiding me is what he does best." I know this is hard to believe, but I'm really not one of those women who get off on bad-mouthing their ex to strangers, but I couldn't stop myself. I spewed venom all over the supermodel, ugly personal details of a wrecked marriage that would send a single woman running to the nearest convent. "Cops make lousy husbands and worse fathers. You're lucky he doesn't want any more kids. Married or not, you'd be a single mother."

"That's not the Luke I know." She closed the laptop and stood up. High patches of color flooded her cheeks. "I have to get ready. We're doing a Magic Loop sock workshop this morning at the store. You're welcome to join us."

But I couldn't let go. "Listen, there's a reason cops have a high divorce rate. Shutting down is what they do best."

"This isn't Boston. We don't have the same problems here. The job doesn't have the same stresses."

"But he's the same man."

"You don't know that."

"You're the one babysitting the crazy ex-wife. What does that tell you? The cop thing always comes first. You should—"

She didn't stick around long enough for me to finish the sentence.

CHLOE

I couldn't get away from her fast enough. If this was what it meant to be human, I was grateful for every drop of magick that separated me from their angry, warring race.

I had spent most of my life longing to be part of them, wishing I could step across the invisible divide that separated me from the rest of the world, but hearing Luke and

Karen speak about each other with so much bitterness and hatred, I wondered if maybe I had been the lucky one after all.

A few hours ago I had been bent into an emotional pretzel with jealousy over Karen, but now I felt nothing but sadness.

Was this how love ended? All those hopes and dreams they'd shared, the memories they had made together, were they nothing but ashes to be swept away? Was this where Luke and I were headed? If it was, I needed to know before I lost any more of my heart to dreams that would never come true.

The last time my cottage had contained so much anger, the roof had spun up into the night sky like a giant Frisbee. A mini-tornado had swept my kitchen bare in its wake as Isadora vented her rage against me. Gunnar and Dane locked in combat in midair while I clung to the counter and struggled to keep from being sucked into the twister that was destroying my house.

It seemed like another lifetime. Both Gunnar and Dane were gone now. I won't lie to you. I didn't shed a tear for Dane, but Gunnar's loss will be with me forever. In a better, kinder world we might have been more than friends, but the fates had other plans for both of us.

Plans that I was beginning to question.

You're lucky he doesn't want any more kids.

That couldn't be true. He knew that giving birth to a daughter was the other part of my destiny. Sugar Maple's future depended upon an unbroken chain of Hobbs women to keep the protective charm in place.

The time wasn't right yet, but it would be soon, and I wanted Luke to be the father of my child and I had hoped—believed—he felt the same way too. Was this the cosmic pie-in-the-face I'd been waiting for since the day we met?

I thought I'd have more time before I had to start thinking about these things. I didn't think I'd be bumping up against reality a few short months into the fantasy. I needed more time to believe that I'd be the one who broke the curse and not only kept Sugar Maple safe from harm but lived happily ever after the way they did in storybooks.

Suddenly I couldn't breathe. I felt like a

mountain climber desperate for oxygen. My fingertips were tingling and that wasn't a good sign. The last time that happened, I ended up circling Sugar Maple at five thousand feet without a plane.

I locked the door to my room and willed the Book of Spells to appear. I needed proof I was on the right path. I needed to touch the source of my powers, feel the jolt of recognition I experienced every time I moved through those pages and saw my own history reflected back at me.

What if loving Luke wasn't enough? What if I was the reason the fabric of Sugar Maple was unraveling faster than a threadbare sock heel?

What if there was nothing I could do to stop it?

"Appear!" I commanded the Book. "Appear!"

I waited but nothing happened.

"Book of Spells, appear!"

I felt myself being pulled backward through a narrow, pulsating tunnel that flattened me like toothpaste through a tube. Lights flashed all around me. Alternating blasts of fire and ice jolted me into a state of hyperawareness as I realized the Book of Spells wasn't coming to me: I was becoming part of it.

The world I knew, the life I'd lived, the days yet to be, raced past me faster than I could register their presence.

Luke watching me that first morning in the yarn shop, laughing at the way I snored.

Walking up Osborne Street with Gunnar, talking about love and friendship, wishing it could have been different between us.

Peering through the dining room window at the Inn, wishing I could be normal for one night, just a regular girl on a date with a regular guy.

Suzanne Marsden in her glorious naked dress.

Bad dates, no dates, lonely nights spent drinking too much wine and eating too many cookies, wanting to crawl inside the television and live with one of the sitcom families.

Gunnar smiling at me . . . so happy, so alive.

My surrogate mother, Sorcha, holding my hand when I cried for my parents.

And oh my parents! Young and tall and strong and beautiful and happy . . . See? It was possible. It could happen.

But it never lasted.

Not for Aerynn or Maeve, Fiona or Sinead, Siobhan or Aisling, or Bronwyn or Guinevere or me.

And there I was again with Luke, but it was too blurry to make out exactly where we were or what we were doing.

I strained against the image, trying to bring it into focus, trying to see what the future held, but I saw nothing.

Nothing.

KAREN

She drove like an old lady. White knuckles, shoulders pulled up around her ears. I could have walked to Sticks & Strings faster.

"Do you drive often?" I asked as she shuddered to a lopsided stop in front of her shop.

"Not if I can help it," she said and I could see why.

Something about her was different. I

couldn't put my finger on exactly what had changed, but I had the feeling my outburst was the reason.

The Luke she knew and loved might be completely different from the man I'd been married to. And even if he wasn't, I should have kept my mouth shut. Some things a woman in love needed to learn for herself.

Besides, it wasn't up to me to save her. Supermodel could figure out a way to save herself.

That same uneasy feeling I'd experienced when I first drove into town returned. The streets were relatively empty except for a steady stream of customers bustling in and out of a place called Fully Caffeinated. The sky was blue and cloudless. The morning sun cast a soft lemon yellow glow. But I glanced over my shoulder when she unlocked the front door just the same.

"Okay," she said, flinging open the door. "Welcome to Sticks & Strings."

She flicked on the lights and I saw heaven.

"Oh. My. God."

"Yeah," she said with a laugh. "I think so too."

The walls were floor-to-ceiling yarn in

every color of the rainbow. Pure wools, cashmere, silk, cotton soft as a whisper, alpaca, hemp, the legendary quiviut.

"You must be the happiest woman on the planet," I said as I fondled a hank of Rowan Silk Tweed in shades of morning sunrise. "I'd pay you to work here."

Soft, squishy couches. A huge fireplace. Baskets of yarn and roving everywhere. Pottery bowls piled high with stitch markers and cable needles and row counters scattered on table-tops. Ceramic pitchers filled with straight needles, felted bowls of circulars. Ott lamps positioned exactly where they were needed most. The place was a knitter's nirvana.

Well, except for the cat.

"Another one?" I asked as a giant black feline entwined itself around my ankles. "Do you breed them or something?"

"You're not a cat person."

"How can you tell?"

"That little vein pulsing in your right temple is a dead giveaway." She bent down and scooped the mammoth cat into her arms. "This is Penny. We don't know exactly how old she is, but if she were human, she could smoke, drink, and vote."

I looked at Penny, then at Chloe. "She has your eyes."

Chloe grinned. "I know. Weird, isn't it?"

It was more than weird. To be honest, it was a little creepy.

She placed Penny on top of an over-flowing basket of roving adjacent to the celery green sofa near the front window. "Feel free to fondle the merchandise. I'm going to check my messages and get things ready for the class."

I wandered around the shop, petting skeins of cashmere and quiviut, ogling the richly saturated colors in the Noro palette, trying to picture what her life was like. I mean, she was tall and blond and gorgeous. She lived in a fairy-tale cottage in a Norman Rockwell–painting town. She spent her workday playing with sticks and string. One look at her and you knew she was one of those women whose lives were blessed from cradle to grave.

CHLOE

The good thing about being at the shop was I didn't have to worry about random magick breaking out the way it did at the cottage. We definitely had magick at Sticks & Strings, but it was the kind of magick that turned a great yarn shop into a legendary one. The protective charm that blanketed the town not only kept us safe from discovery but also seemed to have a soft spot for knitters.

Not that I was complaining, you understand. I was all for anything that brought in the customers.

The bad thing was I had forgotten Janice was dropping by early to help me set up for the workshop.

"Damn it, Jan!" I said as she blossomed into the storeroom in a cloud of lavender and attitude. "Just once I wish you'd use the front door."

"What's the problem?" she asked, tugging at the hem of her red, white, and blue hoodie. "You told me to get here before eight thirty, and I made it with two minutes to spare."

I lowered my voice. "We're not alone. The ex is out front petting the yarns."

Janice brightened. "Cool. I picked up some weird vibes from her last night. I was hoping—"

"No, it isn't cool," I broke in. "It's definitely uncool." I lowered my voice even more. "She saw the blue light last night."

Janice shrugged. "So tell her you like blue lights. That shouldn't be hard to explain."

"She was sitting outside in Luke's truck while I went in to make sure everything was under control and she comes bursting into the cottage screaming, 'Fire! Fire!'"

"All because she saw a little blue light flickering in the window?"

"You're not listening, Jan: she shouldn't have seen any of it. Not the blue light in the window and definitely not the blue *flames* she saw climbing up the front of the house."

Comprehension dawned. "Ohmigod, she's one of us! She didn't look magick to me but these days you never know."

"Luke saw it too."

That stopped her cold. We both knew Luke didn't have an atom of magick in his entire body. "He saw the blue light *and* the blue flames." A totally inappropriate giggle broke loose. "He even saw flames shooting from Dinah's tail."

Janice wasn't a giggler either but she caught the wave. "What did you say to her?"

"I told her I didn't see anything."

"With a straight face? I'm impressed."

"That's the thing, Jan: I really didn't see anything."

"The humans saw the blue flames and you didn't?"

"That's pretty much what I'm saying."

"This isn't good."

"You think?"

"No, I mean this seriously isn't good. Somebody's screwing with the protective charm."

"But the charm can't be altered," I said. "The Book of Spells states quite clearly that while it can weaken over time or disappear entirely if a Hobbs woman no longer walks the earth, the basic nature of the protective charm cannot be changed by anyone. Not even one of Aerynn's descendants."

"And I say that's a load of crap." She gave me one of those looks only a good friend can give you and not end up in intensive care. "If the powers are strong enough, anything's possible." We both knew she was talking about Isadora.

"Not her style," I said. "The explosion at town hall was meant to hurt someone. This was more of a prank."

"Flaming cat butts," Janice said, grinning. "I see your point."

"Oh crap," I said, gesturing toward the front of the shop. "I left the ex out there alone with Penny."

Which started us both giggling again like two fourth graders.

"Go out there and introduce yourself," I said to Janice, "while I get the gift bags ready for class."

"Can I ask her about their sex life?"

"Off-limits."

"Can I ask her why she's here?"

"I already know why she's here."

"Don't tell me. Let me guess." She tapped her forehead with her fingertips and grinned at me. "She's here because Luke isn't paying his child support and—"

"Their daughter is dead and she's having trouble accepting the fact." I gave her a bare-bones version of the situation. I couldn't let her go on joking about child support. "But that's between us, okay?"

Janice was wisecracking, flip, and generally irreverent, but she was also the mother of four children she loved dearly. "It stops here," she said.

"He's driving her back down to Boston

as soon as he gets some paperwork straightened out. She'll be someone else's problem by this time tomorrow."

"You're that sure she's delusional?"

I hesitated. "Luke is."

"And how about you? What do you think?"

Suddenly the answer was clear and it scared me more than the idea of Isadora breaking through her banishment. "I'm afraid she isn't."

10

∽

LUKE

I drove thirty miles to the nearest McDonald's for an Egg McMuffin fix around daybreak, then cruised back to Sugar Maple in time to meet up with the tow truck driver sent out by the rental car agency. Sometimes it felt good to be just one more warmblooded human jump-starting his day with fat, protein, and caffeine the way God intended.

Jack was waiting for me when I reached Karen's car.

"She did a number on it," he said around

a half-smoked cigarette. "What happened? A deer spook her?"

"Something like that," I said. "I think it's the axle."

He squatted down and peered under the Nissan. "More'n likely. Can't take the torque." He straightened up and I could almost hear his aging joints squeak. "Got the paperwork?"

"I'll get it."

I walked along the shoulder to where my truck was idling. Jack stayed on my heels.

"So you're the new chief of police," he was saying as I retrieved the documents from the backseat. "How's that working out for you?"

"So far, so good."

"Think I know this car. A woman drove through last night wanting to stay at the Inn. Had to tell her they don't rent rooms. Looked at me like I had a screw loose."

"That's what happens when you're popular," I said. "No vacancies." I'd been around Sugar Maple long enough now to know how to burnish the image.

Jack flipped through all five pages, folded the stack, then stuffed the lot into the back pocket of his sagging jeans. "I can have a replacement brought up from Nashua by this evening."

"Don't bother," I said. "She found other transportation."

He took a long drag on his cigarette. "Hope she finds herself a square meal while she's at it."

He finally had my attention. "Wait a second. You met the driver?"

"Like I said, she pulled in last night for a fill-up. Wanted to know if Sugar Maple was close by." He took another drag. "Told her she'd be better off getting a room at Motel 6, then hitting town in the morning. Guess she didn't take my advice."

"Guess not," I agreed.

"Never met a woman who could let a phone ring like she did. Damn near drove me crazy."

"I'm not following you."

"Her cell was ringing off the hook. I told her it might be important but she wasn't paying me any attention until the ringtone changed and you never saw such a little woman kick up such a big fuss in your life."

"Kick up a fuss how?"

He shot me a look. "She isn't in any trouble, is she?"

"No trouble," I said. "I'm just filling in the blanks."

He nodded and took a third drag on his cigarette, then tossed it to the ground. "Like I said, the ringtone changed and next thing you know she's digging in her bag like she's going to China and saying things like, 'Don't hang up, Stevie! Don't hang up!'"

"Steffie."

"Steffie! Yep, that's it." He looked at me. "Lucky guess?"

"Yeah," I said as I climbed behind the wheel of my truck. "Lucky guess."

CHLOE

The morning's class, Magic Loop Socks, consisted mainly of a dozen night-shift nurses from the big medical center three towns over, and a handful of townie regulars. Given the bad blood between the Weavers and me, I was surprised that Renate's harpist daughter, Bettina, still kept coming to my classes, but I was happy to see her. It gave me hope that we'd find a way to work things out. Lilith had gone off to a librarians' breakfast in Burlington but

Janice and Lynette picked up the slack with lots of knitting chatter and jokes.

Usually I was pretty good with the patter, but today I had trouble telling knit from purl. Every time I heard a car, I leaped up to look out the window, hoping to see Luke's truck slide into the spot behind mine. How long did it take to hand over some papers to a tow truck driver anyway?

I wasn't going to breathe deeply until Karen was on the highway headed home.

"Somebody stop this woman!" Sue, one of the older nurses, cried out. "Jilly's planning to give those socks to her boyfriend."

"What's wrong with my socks?" Jilly asked, looking up from her knitting. "I know guys hate color and all that so I picked a really nice blend of black and charcoal gray."

Sue shook her headful of brassy blond curls. "Repeat after me, ladies: knit socks for a boyfriend, then watch him walk away from you."

"That's a first for me," I said, looking up from my Japanese short row heel.

"Uh-oh," Lynette said with a laugh. "How many pair have you made for Luke anyway?"

"Six," I said. "What's your point?"

At least they could laugh. At the moment I wasn't finding it funny at all.

"Knit a strand of your hair into the sock," Janice said. "That will bind him to you forever."

"A strand of hair? Oh great." Jilly rolled her big blue eyes. "That means Pete's going to run off with my cat."

"No knots," Karen said, needles flying. "Knots bring the recipient bad luck." She looked up at us and grinned. "Not to mention it's lousy knitting."

The conversation leaped from knitterly superstitions to pet peeves and it was punctuated with lots of laughter. To my surprise, the ex was a very capable teacher with a great deal of patience and a dry sense of humor that everyone seemed to appreciate.

Including me.

"I just love Karen," one of the nurses gushed as she served herself more coffee in the storeroom. "You should hire her full-time. I'd take a lace class from her in a heartbeat."

It wasn't that the ex went out of her way to ingratiate herself with the clientele; it was simply that her talent for knitting combined with the magical aspects of my shop were creating a "perfect storm" scenario that was definitely building up my bottom line. I'd never had so many workshop requests in my life, not to mention the totally obscene amount of both sock and lace-weight yarn I'd sold since we opened.

"Now that's scary," I said to Janice as she dashed past me on her way to the loo. "Bettina and Karen are acting like BFFs."

"Don't laugh," Janice said, "but I'm ready to dump you for the ex. That woman knows her way around a pair of triple zeroes."

I sighed. "She does, doesn't she?" I liked to think she was getting a helpful boost from our store's great knitting juju, but I had the feeling she was a natural.

"Too bad she's human. I kind of like her," Janice said.

"And you don't like anyone."

"Tell me about it but I like her."

"So do I," I admitted. "How weird is that." Okay, so maybe I didn't like her when she was trash-talking the man I loved, but the rest of the time she was pretty good company.

"Not that it's any of my business, but I'm not getting any crazy vibes from her. Lots of sadness but nothing crazy." She paused for a second. "Except when it comes to Luke. She's not too crazy about him."

"I know. She told me."

"At least you don't have to worry about them running away together."

"There's that."

I went back up front and dived into the fray. Turning a heel was my favorite part of sock knitting. You didn't need magickal powers to feel like a wizard when a piece of flat, one-dimensional knitted fabric suddenly turned 3-D with nothing more than a few artfully placed increases and decreases. And when you managed it all on one crazily twisted circular needle and a skein of yarn, it was worth applause.

Not that anyone ever actually applauded when I showed them how to turn a heel or pick up the gusset stitches, but I wouldn't have been at all surprised if one day they did. Sock knitting is that great.

The nurses were enthusiastic students. A few of them were already Magic Loop fans, and the others took to the technique easily. Bettina was struggling painfully with the concept, and I suggested she go back to her familiar double points and not look back. Karen offered to demonstrate the two-circ method (why didn't I think of that?), and suddenly Renate's daughter was zipping right along like a pro.

Score another one for the ex.

Not that I minded. (Well, not much anyway.) If we were going to be trapped together in the shop waiting for Luke to show up, at least we were having a good time.

Until we weren't.

It happened so quickly I didn't have a chance to deflect the question away from Karen. One second we were chatting away about stretchy cast-offs and the next we were talking about kids.

"How about you?" one of the nurses asked Karen. "How many do you have?"

People say "I feel your pain" all the time, but mostly it's a self-serving, meaningless statement meant to convey compassion you really don't feel. But when that question landed in Karen's lap, I swear to you I really did feel waves of pain radiating outward from her. The kind of pain I hope I never feel firsthand.

Her cheeks flushed but her expression didn't waver. "A daughter," she said, then reached into her tote bag and pulled out her wallet. "I only have one photo with me."

She sounded sad and apologetic and so achingly vulnerable I wanted to somehow shield her from whatever might be coming her way.

The nurses pulled out photos of their kids, which was all the encouragement Lynette needed. She whipped out her digital album, an action that sent Janice digging in the depths of her knitting bag for her youngest's latest school photo.

"What about you?" the youngest of the knitting nurses asked. "Any kids?"

"None for Chloe yet," Lynette piped up, "but we're all hoping it won't be long now."

"We're thinking it might be anytime," Bettina said, continuing Lynette's train of thought. "Now that she's found Luke and all." An awkward silence ensued, followed by Bettina's muttered, "Oh crap. I'm sorry."

"About what?" I asked lightly. Good shopkeepers kept a bright face no matter what idiotic thing their customers just said. "No problem here."

"Chloe's dating my ex-husband," Karen said in a cheerful tone of voice. "I told her he's not exactly a family man, but she'll find that out for herself soon enough."

How does an awkward silence to the tenth power sound?

We all threw ourselves into admiring the photos being passed around and pretending Karen had been speaking in a language we didn't understand. I made the requisite oohs and aaahs over kids I'd never seen before and would probably never see again, nodded approvingly at Lynette's brood and Janice's, admired Bettina's tribe, then felt the world slip out from under me when I saw Luke's daughter for the first time.

I would have known her in a crowd. The big dark green eyes. The tumble of copper penny hair. The silly gap-toothed grin. She was everything you would want in a little girl: bright and funny and so full of life it spilled from the photograph and through my fingers.

My eyes burned with tears. I wanted to lower my head and cry until I couldn't cry anymore. I wanted to cry for Luke and Karen, for Steffie, for the little girl of my own that I might never have.

I met Karen's eyes across the table. What was there to say? Not even magick could make this right.

11

LUKE

Five minutes with a tow truck driver named Joe and everything had changed.

There was still a strong probability that Karen had some kind of mental health problem, but for the first time, doubt entered the picture. What if Karen was telling the literal truth and not just the truth as she believed it? The idea scared the shit out of me. I didn't want to think of my baby girl out there in some other dimension, alone and reaching out for us.

Karen and I had been together when

Steffie died. Not happy. Not one of those couples you wish you could be. But the three of us were a family, and right or wrong, we probably would have stuck it out together if Steffie hadn't—

No point going there. Steffie was dead and we were still trying to pick up the pieces of our lives in whatever way we could.

I couldn't go back to town. Not yet. Chloe expected me to drive Karen back down to Boston this morning. Karen expected me to sit down and talk. The truth? All I wanted to do was get as far from Sugar Maple as possible.

How could I make a rational argument against communication with the dead when I lived in a town that was the number one overnight resting spot on the Spirit Trail? There was a reason why the Sugar Maple Inn never had any vacancies. They really were booked up every night, every week, every month, year round, but not with happy Homo sapiens toting Amex cards and Canon PowerShots. The rooms at the Sugar Maple Inn were occupied by World War II flyboys who died over the English Channel, by Samurai swordsmen and French seamstresses from the time of Louis XIV and Egyptian scribes and Colonial farmers from Braintree and any other soul who needed a place to rest during his travels.

I interacted with ghosts every day in Sugar Maple. A werewolf was one of my closest friends. I shot hoops with his kids. Vampires, shapeshifters, and trolls walked through my office on a daily basis. The woman I loved was half sorceress.

Hell, I didn't even blink anymore when I found Fae babies asleep inside my glove box.

What I'm saying is that I knew better than most humans ever could that the world was bigger and richer and more varied than any of us living in our familiar dimension could ever imagine.

I got it.

But when it came to my daughter, the little girl we had buried, the unexplained was more than I could deal with. I'd been running from her death from the moment the EMT pulled me away from her and said it was too late. Karen's wild story about otherworldly phone calls and ghostly playground visits had been strangely easy for me to block. I could accept the fact that Chloe could turn me into a Ken Doll, then back again to human size with nothing more than a passing thought, but I still refused to believe my daughter's spirit needed me.

I was a cop. I needed proof.

Proof that wasn't likely to find me on the highway, a few miles from the New Hampshire state line.

"Come on," I muttered. "Gimme a sign, a smoking gun, something I can hang on to. Call me, Steffie . . . I'm here waiting . . . Call me—"

The shock of the ringtone almost blew me off the road. A cross between Brahms' Lullaby and the old Barney theme song, it filled the cabin with an unfamiliar melody that raised the hairs on the back of my neck.

I grabbed for the phone and flipped it open.

"MacKenzie."

The song didn't stop.

I clicked the ON button.

"MacKenzie here."

Not only did the song not stop, it got louder.

I started to sweat.

"Say something, goddamn it."

But the song kept on playing, an endless loop that made me want to drive into a brick wall if that was the only way to get it to shut the hell up.

And then without warning, Steffie's voice spilled from the phone with the music and I flung the cell down like it was on fire. What the hell was happening?

I skidded to a stop on the shoulder. Steffie's voice, sweet and babyish, blended with the ringtone's music. I couldn't make out the words to the song but her voice—Jesus, her voice was unmistakable.

I felt like she was dying all over again, like she was slipping away from me, limp in my arms like a discarded doll, and this pain made the pain I felt the first time seem like a warm hug.

And something inside me finally broke and I howled her name, louder and louder, the sound tearing up from my gut, ripping my throat, as I tried to send my guilt up into the somewhere so she would know I loved her and would trade places with her in a heartbeat but the fucking song wouldn't stop and my little girl kept singing singing

singing and I knew there wasn't one goddamn thing I could do that would ever
make this better.

At least not in this world.

Maybe it was time I found out what
Sugar Maple had to offer.

CHLOE

By the time noon rolled around, the ex,
Penny the cat, and I were the only ones
left in the shop.

Penny slept soundly in the self-
replenishing basket of roving I'd inherited
from my mother while Karen worked on a
gorgeous cabled knee sock. There was
still no sign of Luke, and we were both
moving from anxious to worried.

"I ordered out for sandwiches," I told
her. "Hope you like tuna."

"Whatever," she said, looking at me over
her sock. "Thanks."

I knew what she was thinking: *See? I
was right. I told you he would disappear.*
But she didn't say it and neither did I. We
really hadn't said too much to each other

since her unexpected outburst at the work-table.

I sneaked into the bathroom once and dialed Luke's cell, but it rang through without even flipping to voice mail. Something that didn't exactly make me feel all warm and fuzzy inside.

As it turned out, the fun was just beginning.

Luke didn't show up but everyone else in town did. Now, I know Sticks & Strings is a world-class yarn shop, but even I didn't believe the entire female population of Sugar Maple suddenly had an overwhelming need for sock yarn. The chance to check out Luke's ex-wife up close and personal proved impossible to resist.

"Is it always this busy in here?" Karen asked after Clara Bains from the children's day care center bustled out clutching her new two-dollar plastic crochet hook.

"No," I said. "I think they're coming to see you."

"Typical small town," she said with a quick smile. "They probably want to check out the bitch who embarrassed you this morning."

I wasn't sure how to respond so, for a change, I said nothing.

"Sorry about that," she went on. "My social skills have eroded the last few months."

I nodded my acceptance of her apology but I wasn't really feeling the love. She had meant every word she said at the worktable. Even worse, she might have been telling the truth.

Shelly, the pretty werecat who worked at the Assisted Living facility, pushed open the front door. "Hi, everyone!" she trilled, pointedly not looking at Karen. "Time for a new project."

Shelly wanted yarn about as much as I wanted moths, but I waited patiently while she checked out every skein of Manos del Uruguay in the store and pretended she wasn't really checking out the ex.

When it came time to pay, she made a big production of checking her watch. "Oops! Coffee break's over. Gotta run." She dashed toward the door. "Hold that pretty pink for me, would you?"

Verna Griggs was next in the parade. It was a known fact that Verna would rather sit naked on an iceberg than fiddle with sticks and string.

"You too, Verna?" I asked, rolling my eyes. "Please don't pretend you're here to buy yarn."

Verna gave me a wink. "Why would I pretend I'm here to buy yarn when we both know I wanted a look at Luke's ex?"

"Tell that to the rest of the villagers," I said. "I almost sold more yarn today than I actually sold last year."

"How're you handling"—she paused with atypical delicacy—"this new development?"

"I know you're too polite to ask, but Luke plans to drive her back to Boston later today. Feel free to pass the news along."

The lines of worry on her forehead eased dramatically. "That should help."

I didn't have to ask what she was talking about. Everyone in town had made it crystal clear that the addition of one more human into our mix would send us spinning straight into Isadora's grasp.

It was hard to believe a ninety-pound woman could throw a town into a frenzy but she had.

Phil from the sub shop dropped off a bag of tuna salad sandwiches and some diet soda while we were talking to Verna and, fates love him, he didn't even glance in Karen's direction. I was saying goodbye to both of them at the door when I glanced up the street and saw Beansie from the farmer's market marching a brigade of quilters toward Sticks & Strings.

Enough already. I had to draw the line somewhere.

I darted back into the store, locked the door, then posted the CLOSED sign. No more trotting busybodies through the shop like we were an exhibit in the Museum of Lost Humans. They could pretend to buy yarn someplace else for a while.

"I should have done it hours ago," I said over my shoulder as I double-checked the lock. "Now we can eat in—"

I didn't mean to scream, but when you turn around and see your boyfriend's ex-wife floating toward you in a giant transparent bubble, screaming seems like a pretty reasonable option.

"Don't panic!" I ordered her even though I was doing a pretty good job of panicking myself. "You're fine! Just calm down and I'll figure out how to get you out of there."

I guess you wouldn't be surprised to

know that the first thing I did was check for purple glitter. The second thing I did was start breathing again when I didn't find any.

I was glad I couldn't read lips. The hand gestures, however, were self-explanatory.

She kicked at the pliable membrane of the bubble like a crazed soccer player. The more she kicked, the more the bubble bounced around the room, careening off walls, tumbling over the back of the sofa, shooting up to the ceiling, then down to the floor like Mr. Toad's Wild Ride.

"Stop fighting it," I yelled, not sure if she could hear me in there. "You're making things worse."

Which, all things considered, was hard to imagine.

I tried to grab the giant bubble but it was like clutching at quicksilver. The thing had a mind of its own.

And quite possibly a gyroscope, because no matter how crazy its trajectory, Karen remained upright through it all.

Seriously pissed, but upright.

Had I caused this to happen? I tried to reconstruct my thoughts seconds before she got gobbled up by the bubble, but I'd been more fixated on my nosy neighbors than on Luke's ex-wife. If I suddenly had bubble powers, I would have encased the Sugar Maple Garden Club, not Karen MacKenzie.

But if I wasn't responsible, who was? There were no signs of Isadora anywhere, no smears of purple glitter. No glitter of any color that I could see, which pretty much ruled out Fae intervention, but there was always the possibility. Vampires? It was still too sunny out for most of them. The bubble was too ephemeral for the earthier trolls among us. Mountain giants lean more toward smash-and-grab. We had a large shapeshifter population, but they usually liked to be right in the middle of things, not watching from—

"Holy crap!"

I jumped at the sound of Janice's voice behind me. "How did you get in? I locked the doors."

She offered me a bite of her slice of pizza but I shook my head. "Not the back one," she said. "You always forget to lock the back one. I was cutting through on my way back to the shop." She gestured toward Karen, who was glaring daggers at both of us. "I have to admit that's one way to keep things under control."

"Which would be terrific if I had anything to do with this."

"You didn't pop her into that bubble?"

"Nope," I said as Karen drifted past us. "And I don't know how to pop her out." I tore my eyes away from the sight of Luke's ex-wife dancing on the ceiling. "You've seen this before, right? Please tell me you've seen it."

"Only on *Seinfeld* and it didn't end well." Janice took a bite of pizza. "Did you try poking it?"

"It's like poking a jellyfish."

Karen glared out at me, and I made an I-wish-I-could-help kind of gesture, which only seemed to make her angrier.

"Dude is seriously pissed off," Janice observed. "Guess the magickal cat's out of the bag now."

"Oh God," I moaned. "I hadn't thought of that."

"You'd better start thinking of it. She's going to have questions when you get her out of that thing."

"Assuming I can. Remember I'm not the one who turned her into Bubble Girl."

"I'm thinking Midge," Janice said. "She's been dying to know what goes on with you and your hunky cop."

I shook my head. "It's daylight," I reminded her. "Midge doesn't get rolling until after dark."

"Maybe she preprogrammed her prank."

"And miss the payoff? Definitely not Midge Stallworth." Midge loved nothing more than a good practical joke that wasn't aimed in her direction.

Vampire humor is to Sugar Maple what bathroom humor is to the human world. Classless, embarrassing, and sometimes very funny as long as it wasn't at your expense.

"Luke isn't back yet," I said as we kept our eyes locked on Karen. "I called his cell but it rang through."

"You know what it's like up here in the mountains. The signals get lost when you turn a corner."

"He left before dawn, Jan. He should have been back hours ago. What if—"

"You worry too much," Janice said. "If Luke was in trouble, every busybody in this town would be lined up to be first to tell you.

Around here bad news travels faster than it happens."

"You're making my head hurt."

"Sit down," Janice advised. "Pour yourself some red. Maybe the Book of Spells has a bubble antidote."

"And if it doesn't?"

Janice shrugged. "Then you pour yourself another glass of red and wait."

12

LUKE

Chloe's Buick was parked at the door of Sticks & Strings, its right front passenger wheel up on the curb. It was only four in the afternoon and the CLOSED sign was in place.

I tapped on the glass. Seconds later Chloe flipped the dead bolt, then opened the door a crack.

"This isn't a good time," she said.

"Listen, I'm sorry I left you alone with Karen. I shouldn't have stormed out this morning."

"Luke, I'm not kidding. Go home. We'll talk later."

She made to close the door but I stuck my foot in the opening. Sometimes size twelves came in handy.

"I know you're pissed. I should have called. Things got away from me."

She glanced over her shoulder, then back at me. "I'm over it."

"So let me in."

"Luke—" She groaned. "Oh damn."

"What's going on?"

"Nothing." She pushed on the door. "Will you just go home and let me finish up?"

"Is Karen with you?"

"She's with me."

"I need to talk to her."

"Not a good idea."

"So she's pissed too."

"It's not all about you, Luke."

"I'm the one who should be pissed," I reminded her. "You turned me into a Ken Doll."

"I told you it was an accident." She didn't look even a little apologetic. "Could we talk about this later?"

I wasn't big on strong-arm tactics, but sometimes a man's gotta do what a man's gotta do.

I expected her to turn me into a garden slug but she didn't. I took it as a good sign and stepped into the shop.

"Chloe, we—holy shit!"

My ex-wife was floating three feet above the ground in the bottom of a giant soap bubble.

"Oh Jesus," I said, unable to tear my eyes away from the sight. "Tell me she isn't dead."

"She's not dead."

The holy-shit aspect was gaining momentum. "Is she in a coma?"

She hesitated a second. "She's sleeping." A pause. "At least, I think she's sleeping."

"But you can wake her up."

She hesitated again. "I don't know."

I watched as the bubble floated past us, gently tapped against the far wall, then began floating back toward the other side of the room. "You've got to be kidding."

"Do I look like I'm kidding?" She was starting to sound pissed again. "In case you've forgotten, this hasn't exactly been a great day for me. Watching your ex-wife float around my shop in a soap bubble wasn't way up on my to-do list."

"What the hell has been going on around here?"

"Other than the fact that every fake knitter in town walked through the store so they could take a good look at my competition?"

It was going downhill faster than I could stop it.

And I didn't try to stop it.

"And how about the fact that when I figure out how to break her out of the bubble, I'm going to have to explain how she ended up inside a bubble in the first place without mentioning the words *magic*, *spell*, or *deep shit*."

How many holy-shit moments could you handle in one day? "So that's why you stuffed her in a bubble."

"What kind of woman do you think I am?"

"A woman with magical powers she can't always control." And a temper I wasn't going to bring up right now.

"I didn't put her in that bubble."

"She didn't jump in herself, did she?"

All around the shop, lightbulbs shattered in a hailstorm of glass. Like I said, she has a temper.

"Okay," I said, backing up a step or three. "If you didn't do it, who did?"

"You're the detective," she snapped. "You tell me." Her cheeks reddened noticeably. "Sorry. It's been a bad day."

I knew I was walking out onto thin ice but what the hell. I'd been there before. "Are you sure you didn't do it?"

"Absolutely."

I waited.

"Well, almost positive."

I waited some more.

"If I did, it was involuntary."

"Like turning me into Barbie's boy toy."

"You really need to let that go, Luke. It's getting old."

"It happened yesterday."

"You know what I'm talking about."

"I know weird things happen when you get pissed off."

"I'm not pissed off."

I mimed extreme relief. "Good to know. That last trip to miniature land knocked me on my ass."

I expected a laugh or at least a bare-minimum smile but I got nothing. Our eyes met and the truth hit me hard. She wasn't laughing. She wasn't pissed off. She was hurting and hurting bad.

"She said you don't want another child. Is that true?" Pure Chloe. Straight to the heart of the matter.

"Yes." No point playing word games. This was too important. "I'm not saying things won't change but right now it's true."

"I guess your ex-wife knows you better than I do."

"We're still new to each other." I reached for her hand. The sparks were there same as always but she didn't respond. "We'll get there."

"She said you were a lousy husband."

"She's right about that too."

"She said you buried yourself in work whenever things got tough at home."

"I guess it seemed that way to her."

She met my eyes. "Is that why you stayed away today? Things were getting tough here and you took off."

"That's not what happened."

"Where were you, Luke? Why didn't you call? I mean, did you have to turn off your voice mail?"

This was as good a time as any. If we

were meant to get through this, I'd find out now.

"I need your help." The words felt strange and unfamiliar to me. Cops were supposed to make things better for other people, not go around asking for help.

Next to me, she grew very still. "What kind of help?"

"I want to contact Steffie."

She was silent for a few moments. "Last night you were dead set against it. What happened?"

On cue, my cell phone erupted into the same sweet lullaby I heard earlier. Steffie's voice, soft and babyish, wrapped itself around us like a hug.

"That's what happened," I said. "My daughter called."

CHLOE

Time stopped. Or at least it seemed to. There was nothing but the sound of his little girl's voice and the heart-wrenching melody that kept her afloat.

I saw her laughing face in the photo Karen kept tucked away in her wallet and suddenly I knew that she loved a pink plush bunny named Mr. B., strawberry ice cream, and knock-knock jokes. She was funny and fearless, and more than anything, she wanted to see her parents one more time.

And I wanted her to go away and take her mother with her. I wanted to spin us back to the beginning when it was all bright and shiny and new. Our love. My powers. My beloved Sugar Maple. This thing called a future that had never seemed real to me before.

The town was slipping away from me. My powers were still unpredictable. Our love was so much more complicated than I ever could have imagined possible. And the future? It was anybody's guess.

If I could have snapped my fingers and erased the sound of her voice from Luke's memory banks, I would have. He was in pain. The kind of pain that changed a man forever.

But I didn't have the power, and more important, I didn't have the right. That pain was all he had left of his daughter.

It was all in my hands. I could say no to Luke. I knew I didn't have the skill set to reach out to his daughter, but there was someone who did.

"We can hold a séance and try to bring Karen and Steffie together. Janice put herself through Yale holding séances all through Connecticut and New York. I think she'd do this for us."

"Janice went to Yale?"

Nothing in Sugar Maple was the way it seemed. Didn't he know that yet? "Summa cum laude, business degree."

"I'm not turning my daughter's death into a sideshow."

"Do you really think Janice would summon your daughter into a sideshow?" More important, did he really think I would? "You asked for my help, Luke. That's what I'm offering."

"Séances are bullshit."

"Don't get hung up on a word. A séance is a means to bridge two worlds, nothing more. That's what you want, isn't it?"

"Karen needs help, not witchcraft."

"This is Janice we're talking about. The woman who cuts your hair and makes that lemon cake you like. Since when are you bothered by her bloodline?"

"I'm not."

"What kind of help did you think I was going to offer? A Ouija board and a DVD of *Ghost*?"

That seemed to hit a chord and he nodded. "I'm being an asshole. You're right. I'm in."

"We have to work fast," I said to him as his phone fell silent, "and we have to keep this a secret." I told him about the stream of villagers who'd passed through the shop to see Karen up close and personal. "If they even suspect I'm doing anything to prolong her stay, all hell will break loose. She has to be on the way back to Boston by midnight no matter what."

Luke went across the street to get Janice.

And then I did what I probably should have done hours earlier. I grabbed a pair of US15 bamboo straights, whispered a prayer to my ancestors for guidance, then popped the ex's bubble.

KAREN

One moment I was dreaming about soft Hawaiian beach balls and the next I was bouncing across a hard wooden floor on my unpadded butt. I looked up at the supermodel from the doorway, where I finally skidded to a stop. "What the hell—?"

The supermodel was wielding a wicked long pair of knitting needles and a look of extreme relief. "You fell off the sofa."

It took a second for her words to penetrate. "I was asleep?"

"You don't remember?"

I shook my head.

"Napping," she said. "You said you wanted to take a nap. I think you're playing catch-up."

"And I think I'm turning into a narcoleptic." I glanced around the quiet shop. "Where's Luke?"

"Across the street talking to Janice." That look of extreme relief vanished. "I think she can help you."

"With what? I'm not looking for highlights."

"But you are looking for your daughter."

Everything else fell away. "If you're screwing with me—"

"I'm not screwing with you."

The weird, prickling sensation I'd felt a split second before I walked into their church/town hall came back full force, and all I could manage was a nod of my head.

"If we do this, you're going to have to follow my lead when we're with Janice, no matter what."

"If it means reaching Steffie, I can do anything."

Maybe she wasn't psychic but she knew where they held their club meetings. You could stop fifty people on the street and I'd bet not a single one would be able to rustle up a séance like it was a take-out pizza. And that would explain the weird vibes I'd been picking up ever since I arrived in the village. Don't get me wrong. I'm not like my ex-husband. I don't have anything against people with the gift, but I can't help getting an itchy feeling every time I meet one.

And she made me itch like I'd fallen into a mosquito breeding ground.

No wonder she had overreacted back at the cottage when I confronted her about her abilities. If she wanted to pretend it was her friend Janice with the psychic gift, that was okay with me. The Luke MacKenzie I'd been married to had a major problem dealing with my mother's and grandmother's ESP. Maybe she had been keeping it a secret from him, like her real hair color. (I might believe in psychics but I don't believe in natural blondes.)

Still, I had to admit I was impressed that she was willing to put herself on the line for someone who had been a complete stranger less than one day ago.

Maybe I was her psychic charity project. I didn't care. Steffie was out there somewhere and she needed me, needed her father, and if Chloe could help bring us together, I would spend the rest of my life figuring out a way to thank her.

13

∂

CHLOE

Cut & Curl closed at 7 P.M., and by seven fifteen Janice was slipping in through the back door.

"I hope you ordered Chinese from Golden Wok," she said as she breezed into the shop. "I can't do this on an empty stomach."

"Luke's picking it up," I said. "He should be back any minute."

"Where is she?"

"Up front working on that gansey I started last week."

"What happened to the bubble?"

I grinned at my friend. "I popped it with a straight."

"Good thinking." She grabbed a can of diet soda from the store fridge. "What kind of mood is she in?"

"She has a million questions."

Janice rolled her eyes. "They always do. Let's get started."

Janice nimbly deflected Karen's queries and started asking questions of her own. Karen worked on the gansey while she answered Janice's almost-embarrassing barrage of inquiries. I wasn't sure how many of those questions actually pertained to the séance and how many were barely disguised attempts to ferret out information for me. If Karen was annoyed, it didn't show. She answered with painful honesty, sparing neither herself nor Luke in the process.

Janice grilled her for details about Steffie's attempts to break through the barrier that separated the spirit world from this realm of existence, taking notes on a crumpled index card that she didn't really need. She used it to make the humans comfortable.

"She wanted her father," Karen said, eyes on her knitting. "That's the only reason I'm here."

"Unfinished business," Janice said with a nod of her head. "Too bad we're not doing this next week when there's a full moon. The portal will be more porous."

"There's a portal?" Despite what Karen thought, I'd never been anywhere near a séance in my life.

Janice shot me a look. "Of course there's a portal. There's always a portal."

"Even I know that," Karen said.

"Where is it?"

"The cemetery is the closest."

"I don't like cemeteries," Karen said.

Nobody liked cemeteries. "Can't we do it someplace else?" I asked.

Janice barely disguised her annoyance. "You go where the spirits gather."

"Won't they gather wherever you tell them to gather?" Karen asked. "I thought the medium tells them what to do."

"They gather where they gather. It's up to us to make it easy for them."

"They gather where they gather?" I started to laugh. "You sound like you've been hitting the Zen tapes again."

"The cemetery is on sacred ground," Janice explained to Karen, pointedly cutting me out of the loop. "It shares land with an Indian burial site that preceded the white man by hundreds of years. Your daughter's spirit will recognize she's safe there."

It was clear the thought of midnight in a cemetery didn't make Karen feel either safe or comfortable.

"Don't look at me," I said to her, pushing down my own uneasy feelings on the subject. "This is Janice's ball game. I've never been to a séance in my life."

Karen remained unconvinced. "They didn't hang around a cemetery in *Ghost.* They sat around a table."

Could it get any worse? I could feel Janice struggling to control her temper. If there was one thing my friend hated, it was movie mediums who got it all wrong.

"Fine," she said. "Maybe you're right. We'll do it here."

"But we don't have a portal," I said.

"A second ago you didn't even know we needed one."

"But you did," I shot back. "How can you proceed without a portal?"

"We can use a proxy." She got up and walked over to the counter. "Help me take down the tapestry."

"The tapestry?" I went totally blank.

"D'oh," Janice said, imitating one of her kids. "The tapestry that's been hanging behind the register since the shop opened."

The needlework representation of Sinzibukwud Falls had been part of my life for so long that I barely noticed it anymore. Before I opened Sticks & Strings, it had held a place of honor in Sorcha's cottage, and before that it had been my mother's and her mother's before her right back to Aerynn.

These days it served as a makeshift bulletin board. Notes, sketches, receipts, pending bills, magazine clippings, all manner of things were pinned to the surface until you could barely see any of the lovely, even stitches peeking through. And yes, I felt a little guilty.

"I wish I knew who made this," Janice said as we carried it over to the table. "You can feel the energy popping off the fabric."

Karen walked around the table and studied the tapestry. "You have waterfalls around here?"

"Just that one."

She shivered. "There's just some-thing . . . uncomfortable about it."

Janice rolled her eyes. I said nothing. Nobody had ever expressed unease about the Falls before. Good to know I wasn't the only one who found the place less than welcoming.

"Okay," Janice said, "now we need a round table."

"I have a card table in the storeroom."

Janice provided the white candles, frankincense, cinnamon, and sandalwood.

And the music.

"Enya?" Karen wrinkled her nose as the music from Janice's iPod filtered through the tiny speakers.

"The spirits love her," Janice said. "Go figure." She glanced across the table at me. "Did he go to Sichuan province for the food?"

Something told me it wasn't the Chinese food that was holding things up. I excused myself and ducked out the back door, where I found Luke leaning against the Dumpster.

"You can't stay out here forever," I said to him. "We need to get started."

"I'm out."

"No, you're not. You asked me to put it

together and I did. Now you have to follow through."

A faint smile flickered, then died. "You're tough."

"You don't know the half of it."

He grabbed the bag of takeout from the ground, then followed me into the shop.

"About time," Janice said as we joined them at the table. "Did you get spring rolls? I'd kill for a spring roll."

"Can't you eat after?" I aimed a pointed look in her direction.

She couldn't. We toyed with our food and waited while she wolfed down a spring roll, a handful of crispy noodles, and a bottle of water.

Finally she nodded for me to dim the lights.

"The lights went down," Karen said, glancing around. "Are we having a power outage?"

Note to self: next time do it the old-fashioned way. "Remote control switch," I lied.

Lucky for me, the woman had other things on her mind.

"We are all here of our own free will," Janice said. "Is that true?"

Luke hesitated but he concurred.

"We'll be joining hands. I'll offer a short invocation. We'll close our eyes and open our hearts and allow the benevolent spirits entrance."

"Spirits?" Luke interrupted, sounding grim.

"I don't want to see my great-uncle George," Karen said. "I want my daughter."

"People, this isn't rocket science. I can't guarantee who or what will slip through the portal. I can't promise you that any-thing will. But if you could wait until tomor-row when Saturn transits the full moon—"

"We can't wait," Luke snapped.

She glared at him. "Then you have to accept the limitations. If you can't accept them, let's call it a night."

"Sorry," Karen murmured. "We're freak-ing out. Ignore him."

Luke muttered something that sounded a lot like "bullshit."

"I'd tell you to leave if your daughter hadn't asked for you specifically," Janice said to him. "Spirits sense lousy attitudes."

It wasn't a lousy attitude; it was fear. I wanted to tell Janice to ease up on him, but there was no way I could do it without embarrassing him so I let it go.

"Let's try again," Janice said, aiming a pointed look in Luke's direction. "Clear your minds of negative thoughts. Join hands and close your eyes."

I didn't close my eyes at first. I was too busy making sure Luke closed *his* eyes. And I have to admit I wanted to see if Janice had any nonmagick tricks up her sleeve, like jiggling the table or switching on a sound machine.

I guess I was hoping for some fireworks, maybe some flashing lights or spooky noises. Everything looked disappointingly ordinary.

Janice lifted her chin slightly and took in a long deep breath and closed her eyes. I did the same.

"Spirits, thank you for giving us your time this night. We gather together in love and harmony and invite you to join with us and share your wisdom."

We sat quietly for what seemed like a week and a half. I caught the scent of cinnamon wafting from the shallow dish on the side table, Janice's lavender essence, and the aroma of Kung Pao chicken from the bag of deliciousness I intended to dive into the second this was over.

Which was probably not the right attitude. I pulled together my random thoughts and centered myself again. This was for Karen and Luke. This was their chance to contact their daughter. I wasn't going to be the one who screwed it up by daydreaming over a bag of takeout.

"Spirits, we welcome you with open hearts," Janice said. "We bid you enter this blessed circle of protection."

Are you out there, Steffie? Your mommy and daddy miss you so much.

I felt silly and self-conscious and everything in between but there was no denying the sorrow that suddenly seemed to rise up and surround us all. An emptiness that pulled the oxygen from my lungs and made me light-headed.

"Steffie?" Karen broke her silence. "We're here, honey. Come talk to us."

"Nobody's coming," Luke said. "This is all bullshit."

"You're not helping," Janice snapped. "If you can't keep a positive attitude, at least keep your mouth shut."

"Janice!" My eyes popped open. "Telling Luke to shut up doesn't promote tranquillity."

"He lacks respect," Janice said. Respect was huge in her world and I understood why. The witches of Salem had been treated with anything but respect. But she knew the situation going in. She really needed to give him a little breathing room. "The spirits don't appreciate that."

"Please!" Karen sounded desperate. "I know Steffie is out there. Can't we try again?"

"Fuck this." Luke pushed back his chair. "And you put yourself through college with this stuff?"

Janice, her face scarlet with anger, turned to me. "This is one of the reasons why we don't need another human in town."

"*Another* human?" Karen was all over it. "What does she mean, *another* human?"

"Figure of speech," I said, my heart slamming into my rib cage. How many bullets could I dodge in one day? "Janice is the queen of hyperbole."

"I can't believe I said that!" Janice looked downright horrified. "Damn it, that's not what I wanted to say at all."

Suddenly I had the feeling this wasn't going to end well. "That's okay, Jan. Let it go."

"You know I'm vigilant about protecting Sugar Maple. I'd never let the cat out of the—"

"Let the cats stay where they are," I said as tiny beads of sweat trickled down the back of my neck. "The cats are just fine."

"I can't." She looked like she was going to burst into tears. "I want to shut up . . . I'm going to shut up . . . but the magick won't let me. We all know what's going on and I can't seem to—"

I ordered myself not to freak out. "Everything will be fine, Jan, if you shut up right now," I whispered so only she could hear.

Janice, however, was talking at full volume. "The ex spent the afternoon in a transparent bubble. I think she knows she's not in Kansas anymore." Tears flowed down her cheeks. "I didn't want to say that. I swear I didn't!"

Karen leaped to her feet. I grabbed her cup of tea a micrometer before it skidded off the table. "I thought that was a dream."

"Of course it was," I said. "There's nothing to worry about. It was just a little blip."

Janice clapped her hands over her mouth. "Oh gods, I'm sorry! You have to believe me, Chloe. I'd never do anything to compromise the town. It's like someone's shut down my internal censor."

I swung around to glare at my friend. "What is wrong with you, Jan? Aren't things bad enough?"

"Hey, don't blame me! You're the sorcerer. You should recognize an interruptive chaos spell when you see one."

Please tell me she didn't really say that.

Karen stared at the two of us. "Did she just call you a sorcerer?"

Okay, so she really did.

"That's my Ravelry nickname." I congratulated myself for being quick on my feet. Ravelry was a popular online gathering place for knitters where screen names tended toward the creative. "Queen of the Universe was already taken."

Karen shook her head. "I don't think that's what she meant."

"Feel free to jump in anytime," I said to Luke.

He looked like he had been to hell and back, but he slid behind his cop face and pretended none of this was happening. "We gave it a shot and it didn't work. We have our answer. Let's call it a night." He turned toward his ex. "There's no magic here, Karen. You know it and I know it. I'll drive you down to Boston."

Karen looked from Luke to Janice to me. Our eyes held for what seemed like an eternity, and I felt a shifting deep inside. Part of me wanted her to acknowledge what was right in front of her, that she was surrounded by magick of every kind imaginable and she would never be closer to contacting her daughter than she was right here, right now. I wanted her to fight for her daughter, to take a stand against the impossible.

But the other part of me, the part who loved Luke and Sugar Maple, just wanted her to go away, and that part won.

"Luke's right," I said. "If Janice can't make a connection with your daughter, no one can. You've done everything you could to reach Steffie. You might as well go home to Boston."

She nodded. What was there to say?

"I'll straighten up in the morning," I said. "Let's go."

Janice didn't bother to say good night. I think she was afraid of what she might say next. Interruptive chaos spells have ruined more marriages than snoring. Luke grabbed the bag of takeout. Karen gathered up her stuff, including her ever-present cell phone. I made sure Penny the cat had sufficient food and water.

Luke and Karen stepped out onto the lamplit street. I closed the door behind us, set the lock, then drew in a breath of the damp spring night. You could almost smell the disappointment in the air.

"I'm coming with you," I said as Luke and Karen walked toward his truck. "I'm not in the mood to drive."

Actually I wasn't in the mood to do much of anything, including knit. I guess without realizing it I had expected something to come of the séance, that contact (however fragile) would be made with Steffie MacKenzie.

And maybe it would have if Luke hadn't been such a horse's ass.

Which I told him as soon as we were in the truck.

"What was wrong with you?" I demanded of Luke as soon as Karen climbed into the rear seat. "You didn't give Jan a fighting chance to reach Steffie."

"A white candle and oregano?" He shot me a look as the engine sprang to life. "Like that's going to call down the spirits."

"That wasn't oregano. It was frankincense, cinnamon, and sandalwood."

"It smelled like room freshener," Karen piped up. "One of those stick-on things you buy at the supermarket."

"No wonder the spirits stayed away," I muttered. "I wish I had."

"Janice was humoring you," Luke said. "I'm surprised she made enough money to get through freshman year. She's a lousy medium."

"And how many mediums have you known in your life?" I threw back at him. "You're not exactly a New Age-y kind of guy."

Luke opened his mouth to say something, then stopped. "Did you feel that?"

I frowned. "You mean that little bounce?"

"It's more than a bounce," Karen said. "It felt like we were flying for a second."

Which would have been crazy talk except for the fact that the ground suddenly dropped away and we were sailing up over the treetops, over the lighthouse monument, over town hall and the Inn and the Playhouse, and were headed straight toward Snow Lake.

14

CHLOE

I used to have fantasies that I was Sandy in *Grease*, and one day my own personal Danny Zuko would find me and we'd fly up up and away from Rydell High in a vintage Ford convertible.

Let's just say the fantasy was a whole lot better than the fact. For one thing, Danny Zuko's ex didn't pass out cold in the backseat the second we went airborne.

Luke was struggling with the steering wheel, which struck me as oddly endearing, this very human, very male need to control the clearly uncontrollable.

For some reason I wasn't scared. I suppose that sounds ridiculous, but I somehow knew the point of this exercise wasn't to slam the three of us into the ground at two hundred miles an hour. It was just the beginning.

We skimmed the woods that surrounded Snow Lake, dipped slightly, then glided in for a landing on a dock that suddenly appeared on the west side of the lake.

"Holy shit," Luke muttered, still death-gripping the wheel even though we were on solid ground. "Holy shit."

I scrambled out of the truck with Luke right behind me. A wild, squirrelly wind kicked up, bending the trees to the ground, then snapping them straight a second later with a sound like machine-gun fire. A violent crack of thunder shook the dock beneath my feet and the sky above split open, showering me in a storm of purple glitter that stung my skin like acid rain.

The glitter only confirmed what I already knew. Isadora was back for Round 2.

And this time Luke saw the glitter too.

He winced as the crystalline shards bounced off his face.

"Oh my God!" Karen's voice took us both by surprise. Why couldn't she stay unconscious for once? "Was it a tornado?"

This wasn't exactly the time to explain the history of Sugar Maple and the rage of the Fae.

"Don't move," I ordered Luke and Karen. "No matter what happens, don't say anything."

I wanted to add, *And don't be afraid*, but who was I kidding? You'd have to be flat-out crazy not to be scared out of your mind with the sky ripping apart over your head.

"What's going on?" Karen's voice was shrill and loud. "What *is* this stuff?" She frantically brushed glitter off her shoulders with quick stabbing motions.

"Stand behind me," Luke ordered his ex.

"This has something to do with the séance, doesn't it?" She looked from Luke to me. "Maybe it's Steffie." She was sliding from shrill to manic. "Maybe she's trying to let us know she's—"

The thunder/lightning combination exploded over us like a hydrogen bomb. The earsplitting, bone-crushing sound was accompanied by a blinding blue-white bolt of light and energy that raised the temperature around us by a few degrees.

Karen clapped her hands over her ears and dropped to her knees. Luke remained motionless. He'd been through this before. He knew what was coming as well as any human could.

Not that I knew much more than he did. Isadora was fighting her way through the banishment, exploiting any weakness she could find. Why else would she have brought us to Snow Lake, the scene of Luke's friend's death back in December? The scene of Sugar Maple's only murder. Proof positive that even the best of protective spells can fail.

The sky was now a blackened shade of purple. The towering pine trees ringing the lake were bowed in submission, branches snapping and breaking as a hollow wind howled around them.

And then suddenly the world went quiet. Karen rose from her knees and glanced quickly around the perimeter of the lake. "Maybe it was a tornado," she said, her voice high and tight. "They say tornadoes sound like freight trains and—"

"I see I have your attention."

Isadora's voice swelled like an overture in the hands of a world-class philharmonic. It filled the silence and pushed away any thoughts we might have had of making a run for it.

Huge fountains of water erupted like minivolcanoes at the center of the lake, all rich purples laced with molten pink. While we were taking in the floor show, Isadora suddenly rose up from the water on a cloud of oily purple mist that suddenly coated my exposed skin.

"Ohhh!" Karen exhaled on a sigh. Isadora's Fae beauty could be overwhelming and it was working its magic right now. The ex looked over at me. "Don't even try to explain *her* away."

"I wasn't planning to." I figured the flying car had pretty much let the last of the cats out of the bag.

Isadora had never looked more breathtaking. Flawless creamy skin. Huge turquoise eyes with dark lashes that cast shadows on her cheeks. Shimmering hair the color of a raven's wing, hanging straight to the floor. She wore a dark purple velvet cloak embroidered with every color of the rainbow and studded with jewels. An amulet of platinum and amethyst hung between her full breasts.

Every man's dream. Every woman's nightmare.

"We meet again," Isadora said, her words floating across the surface of the lake toward us. "How interesting to see you've surrounded yourself with your own kind."

"Enough, Isadora," I said, willing myself to sound more confident than I actually felt. "You've been banished. You have no power here."

On the other side of the lake, one of the centuries-old maple trees ripped free from the muddy earth and shot across the water heading straight for us.

"Down!" I screamed and the three of us hit the wooden dock a moment before the massive tree split Luke's truck in two, then slammed into the lake with a mighty splash.

Karen was trembling so hard I could feel the slats vibrate beneath me. Luke was partially covering me, another of those deeply human gestures that touched the human part of my heart in a way nothing else ever had.

"Don't move," I whispered to the two of them. "No matter what happens, don't react to anything she says or does. I can fight her but not if I have to worry about the two of you."

"What's going on?" Karen demanded. "Luke's a cop. He should be—"

Luke clamped his hand down across her mouth. "Shut up," he growled. "We do what Chloe says."

"Release me." The sound of Isadora's voice made the hairs on the back of my neck stand up and salute. "You've seen a sample of what I can do from within my banishment. Your magick is too new and raw to contain me permanently. Ultimately I will be victorious. Release me now and I will show compassion."

I couldn't help it. I started to laugh. "Compassion? You mean like trying to kill Luke at the knit shop in December? You mean like the compassion you showed my parents when they were dying or the way you watched Suzanne struggling to keep from drowning in the icy lake? Tell me all about compassion, Isadora, because I really need to know."

I guess I went too far because suddenly I was being flung across the length of the dock by an unseen force greater than anything I had ever encountered. Rough splinters of wood tore at my jeans and slashed at my sweater. I skidded past the wreckage of Luke's truck, then sailed off the edge of the dock and who knows what would have happened next if I hadn't managed to somehow bend my body like a boomerang and sail right back to where I'd started.

Both Luke and Karen were staring at me like I had danced on the rings of Saturn.

But there was no time for taking bows. Isadora's anger was taking physical form and the three of us watched, frozen in place, as her small, slender body began to grow until she all but blotted out the sky from our sight. The wild winds whipped her velvet robes around her legs. Her ankle-length mane of ebony hair swirled around her magnificent face. Her huge turquoise eyes burned with the need for revenge.

She zeroed in on Karen, and I stopped

breathing. Next to me, Luke tensed like tempered steel.

Stay calm . . . Don't let her get to you . . . It's all an illusion . . . She's still under banishment . . . She can't hurt us . . . Just stay calm and we'll get through this . . .

Isadora didn't move but suddenly a blizzard of glitter spilled over us so thick and fast I had to shield my eyes with my hands.

Karen was shaking so hard she needed to lean against Luke in order to remain standing. Who could blame her? I would have traded places with her in a heartbeat, but as much as I hated to admit it, Isadora was running the show.

"She killed my son." Isadora's words were expelled on an oily breath of smoky flowers. "Did you know that, Mrs. MacKenzie? Our Chloe killed my son Dane. She picked up a sword and she sliced him in half . . . my beloved son."

Don't listen to her, Karen . . . Don't let her see your reaction . . . Stay still . . . Don't give her anything to work with.

"I don't believe you," Karen whispered and my heart dropped to my knees. Her emotions were fuel for Isadora's raging fire.

"Tell her, Chloe." Isadora's voice was supple, seductive, a heartbeat away from irresistible. "Tell her what you and your human did that night."

I stayed silent even though I wanted to scream, *You had twin sons, Isadora! You lost Gunnar that night too and he was worth a thousand Danes.*

The lake slid into total darkness. Moon, stars, streetlamps, ambient light from houses three blocks away. All of it gone. To be human, even part human, is to have the need to banish the darkness. We'll do almost anything to bring back the light.

Some of that primal need for light lived inside me too. The part that came from my human father knew the terror they were feeling. It was bred into our bones.

The eerie stillness was shattered by Luke's cell phone, followed almost immediately by Karen's. The ringtones were the same, the slightly syncopated lullaby that I'd heard earlier.

"Steffie!" Karen cried out into her cell. "Talk to me, baby!"

"It's Daddy, Steffie," Luke shouted into his phone. "Say something!"

But their phones kept on playing that

choppy lullaby I suddenly knew by heart, joined by the sweetly reedy voice of a child rising up over it.

"Mommy! Daddy! Help me! Please help me!"

Karen's anguish split the night in two. Her howls of despair pierced my heart.

"This isn't real," I said to her and to Luke. "This is an illusion. She's tapping into your histories and reflecting powerful images that will get the deepest response. Don't buy into it. That's not your daughter talking."

"Chloe's right," Luke said. "Isadora will do anything to get what she wants. That's not our little girl. Keep telling yourself. No matter how real things seem, that's not our little girl."

A glimmer of light appeared at the western edge of the lake. It hovered about one hundred feet above the treetops, spinning lazily, growing brighter with each revolution until it reached the dock and Isadora's face was revealed at its center.

An Isadora I'd never seen before. The turquoise eyes were streaked with blood. Her teeth had lengthened into yellowed fangs. The flawless porcelain skin was pockmarked and sallow, sagging around her neck like a baggy sock around a skinny ankle. The oily mist that had surrounded her earlier spilled from her mouth in noxious clouds that made the bile rise in my throat.

All things considered, I'd rather face down the giant anaconda she had conjured during our last battle than this hideous alternative version of Isadora. At least a snake had standards.

"You understand," this giant Isadora crooned into Karen's ear. "You're a mother. You know how it feels to lose your child. Chloe took my Dane away from me. She killed him, Karen. She took my baby's life."

Karen was strong. Her entire body shook with fear but she stood fast and said nothing.

Isadora exhaled another cloud of putrid oily smoke. Karen swayed but she didn't fall. My respect for Luke's ex-wife climbed another notch.

"Maybe I should show you what happened," Isadora said in a mock-friendly tone. "Sometimes humans need to see things with their own eyes before they can let themselves believe the truth."

"It's not the truth," I said quietly. "It's not the truth. She's using our memories for her own purpose."

Next to me, Luke was coiled and ready to strike. The analogy wasn't lost on me. I reached for his hand and squeezed it, but I'm not sure it registered. He had disappeared behind the cop mask.

The sky began to curl back from the center, illuminated around the edges with shimmering streaks of silver and purple. Quick splashes of color burst onto the empty rectangular patch, random blasts of white and red and gray that added up to nothing at all.

I felt smug. She had nothing. Okay, so maybe she could fight against the banishment and cause explosions and make the winds go squirrelly and send us flying in Luke's Chevy, but those were all parlor tricks. Anyone with the most basic set of powers could do all that and more.

I mean, a big fat sky filled with nothing but Jackson Pollock spatter? Come on. Give me something I can use. Something that would make a good story one rainy night over a box of wine and some Chips Ahoy.

"Show's over, Isadora," I said in my best been-there-seen-that voice. "We've had enough of your pathetic little magic tricks."

"Not a good idea," Luke muttered. "You don't want to piss her off."

For the record, I should have listened. But I was too full of myself, too high on my own burgeoning powers, too pleased with Isadora's obvious limitations to pay attention to a man who had spent his adult life defusing dangerous situations.

"That's it," I said, turning toward Luke and Karen. "She's depleted her energies. She'll—"

Luke grabbed my arm. "Don't turn around," he said. "Don't look."

But I did.

In time to see my parents' car go into a death spin on a patch of black ice and slam into a tree all those years ago.

In time to see my beloved surrogate mother, Sorcha, crying for me in the next dimension.

In time to see Gunnar killed by his mother's black magick anaconda.

In time to see Isadora's death bolt ricochet off the crystal shield I held up high and sail straight toward Dane, slicing him in two.

In time to see Karen and Luke on their wedding day . . . gazing with wonder at their newborn baby girl . . . staring down, mute with grief, at her tiny open casket—

Luke made a sound like he'd been gut punched, but it was Karen's cry of despair that will never leave me.

"Steffie!" Her voice bounced off the mountains and slammed back into us with the force of a thousand battering rams. "Oh, baby, I'm so sorry!"

"Karen," I cried, "listen to me. This isn't real. She's in a different dimension. These are nothing but home movies. That's not your daughter. You have to believe me."

She didn't hear a word I said. All she could hear was her daughter's voice.

The screen was gone. The images absorbed back into the night. The dock beneath us began to sway, then vibrate. A bolt of lightning sizzled from the sky to the lake, sending steamy mist spiraling upward to where Isadora, glowing pale against the darkness, seemed to reach from horizon to horizon. The shackles of her banishment glittered like captured moonlight.

Banish again! Banish for all time!

I raised my hands high and called upon all the knowledge I had gained so far. "Banish forever! Return never!"

I'd studied everything I could find about banishment spells and applied it to keeping Isadora contained, but there was still one piece missing, and that piece was the key to sending her away forever.

Karen was looking at me like I'd taken leave of my senses, which struck me as pretty funny considering we'd arrived by flying Jeep and she had witnessed astral movie projection without blinking.

Isadora was fading fast.

"Banish! Banish into eternity!"

With a roar that sent us sprawling backward onto the dock, a giant Isadora swooped down on us in all her restored beauty, her giant turquoise eyes blazing with emotion, burning hotter than the sun. She swept in close enough for us to feel her oily breath against our skin. Her eyes closed for a moment and I prayed this was the last gasp of power at her command for tonight, but then they slowly opened wider, then wider still, and the image of a small child in a transparent box appeared deep within her pupils. The child was curled up on the floor of the box, head resting on her arms, red curls tumbling over her shoulders. She wore the same simple white dress they had buried her in.

"Wake up, Steffie," Isadora crooned. "You have company!"

15

CHLOE

This time it wasn't an illusion. I'm not sure how I knew, but the second the little girl stood up and looked out at us through that glowing prison, I knew this was Luke's daughter.

Not a hologram. Not a reflection. Not a construct of memories gleaned from her parents.

This was Steffie MacKenzie.

The look on her face when she saw her parents was a mixture of joy and terror that not even Isadora at the height of her powers would have been able to replicate. She opened her mouth to scream but the sound was swallowed within her prison. She pounded the elastic walls with tiny fists, her face turning red as her hair. Tears, shimmering like freshwater pearls in the glowing light, ran down her face and splashed to the floor.

Luke seemed to be in some kind of emotional lockdown. I thought I knew him, knew the landscape of his face, but at that moment he was a total stranger to me. He stared at the image that was his daughter and betrayed nothing at all. He had gone someplace where I couldn't reach him, and I wondered if he would ever return.

It took a few seconds for the new reality to register on Karen, but when it did, I didn't have to tell her that this was truly her daughter. She knew it in her bones.

"Steffie." The name was a whisper, almost a prayer. Then, "Steffie! Baby, Mommy and Daddy are here! Where are you? Tell us where you are and we'll come for you!"

The child locked eyes with her mother and pounded harder on the walls of her prison within a prison.

"What's happening?" Karen grabbed my arm. "Where is she?"

"I don't know," I said honestly. "I only know what I see, same as you." Somehow Isadora had been able to absorb Steffie's spirit into her own banishment. I had no explanation and, even worse, no idea what to do about it.

"It's a miracle," Isadora cooed. "The grieving parents have a chance to apologize for their mistakes."

Luke took a step forward.

"Hit a nerve, did I, Detective? Maybe if you'd been paying more attention that day, your daughter would be standing next to you instead of rotting in a—"

With a howl of rage, he flung himself in Isadora's general direction, but she closed her turquoise eyes and Steffie disappeared. He bounced off an invisible barrier that was part of the banishment and fell back onto the dock.

Karen's cry of anguish hung in the air like a bad dream. She screamed things at Luke, things I wish I hadn't heard, things I wish I could forget. Horrible, intimate, ugly words meant to destroy. The depth of her pain made me dizzy. The worst part of all was the way Luke let it rain down on him without flinching. As if he agreed with her.

My world was changing around me, and I knew there was nothing I could do to stop it. If Isadora was looking to hurt me in ways that went beyond giant snakes and flaming death bolts, her aim had been dead-on.

Karen's focus shifted from Luke to Isadora, and I watched, mesmerized, as the ex seemed to gather strength. "I don't know who you are and I don't care," she said straight to Isadora. "But I do know you have no right to hold my daughter's"—she struggled for the right word—"spirit prisoner. Let Steffie go." She drew in an audible breath. "Take me instead."

"Karen!" I couldn't hold back. "You don't want to do that."

Luke was on his feet and moving toward us when Isadora swooped in again and opened those terrifyingly magnificent eyes of hers to reveal Steffie one more time.

The child's eyes slid over me without any sign of recognition, then rested on her mother. Karen started to sob as she pleaded with Isadora to release Steffie. The look in the little girl's eyes was older than time, a blend of deep compassion, sorrow, and the kind of knowing that takes centuries to achieve.

Behind me, Luke's breathing was ragged and harsh, like he was struggling to hold himself together and almost failing. Steffie turned slightly and her dark green eyes, so like her father's, rested on him. His breath caught on the cusp of a sob, and I thought my heart would break apart.

He took a step forward, hand outstretched, and Steffie flattened herself against her translucent prison, crystal tears running fast over fists soft and small as a rolled-up sock. There was something almost ritualistic about the way she moved her fists, the splash of tears, the eerie repetition of movements.

"Tell us where you are, Stef!" Luke bellowed. "Help us find you!"

She was saying something, yelling something, but her words were trapped inside the container with her. The tears flowed faster and those tiny fists couldn't keep up with the flow. The tears spilled over them like rapids over rocks.

Isadora closed her eyes and telescoped backward to a spot over the treetops where she glowed like a shimmering purple cloud. There was nothing else in the world but Isadora. I heard nothing but her voice, saw nothing but the harsh glow of her essence in the night sky.

"Twenty-four hours." I heard her words from someplace deep inside me, as if the sound was working its way out through my bones. "The clock starts now."

She knew my thoughts before I gave them voice.

"Humans leave tracks through this world and the others. A guilty conscience is better than one of their tracking devices. His child wasn't difficult to find." Her laugh made me shiver. "Even easier to control." She paused while her words sank in. "We can end this now, Chloe. Undo this patchwork of spells you've put on me. Release me from my banishment and the child's spirit is free. Refuse me and an eternity of despair is all she'll know."

The sky ripped apart. The cage around Steffie shattered and I screamed as she started falling falling falling through staggering darkness, her small, defenseless body smashing against the jagged rocks at random. She had nothing to hold on to, no solid ground beneath her feet, only the darkness and the pain. We saw her body break against the rocks, saw her face smashed beyond recognition, heard her terrified cries, felt her terror, her loneliness, her despair as she called out for her parents in an endless plea for help.

A part of me wanted to say to hell with Sugar Maple and undo the banishment spell right then and there. Was the town worth the horror Steffie would face at Isadora's hands?

"You're losing them," Isadora crooned. "You've been losing them since your human came to town. Let them go. It's what they want. It's what you want. Make a new life with your lover the way your mother should have years ago."

She was twisting the story. My mother loved Sugar Maple, and Sugar Maple loved her. She would never have considered walking away from her responsibilities as a descendant of Aerynn, not in a million years. Wasn't I living proof of that?

"But you don't have a child of your own, Chloe, and maybe you never will. Why delay the inevitable when it could all be taken care of now with so little fuss? Release me from this imprisonment and we'll let the fates determine the outcome for all of us. You'll be golden in your lover's eyes and I'll offer the good villagers a chance to make a new start beyond the mist where they can exist free and independent."

I couldn't gamble Sugar Maple's safety on the hope that Isadora would keep her word and release Steffie. The Fae weren't known for tolerance. Navigating life beyond the mist, in a world governed by the Fae, might prove far more dangerous than navigating through the human realm ever had.

"You don't trust me," she said. "I'm hurt, Chloe. After all we've been through together. I'll admit I badly underestimated your abilities last time but I won't make that mistake again. But are you willing to sacrifice this innocent human child's eternal peace to keep happy a town that doesn't belong to you any longer?"

I needed time to think. Time to figure out what to do next.

The huge tower clock that stood near the municipal parking lot burst from the lake like Shamu at Sea World. Flames shot from the face, crackling and hissing like an out-of-control forest fire.

"Twenty-four hours." Her words tore through my brain like gunshot. "You will always be a half-blooded human. Release me now and the child's soul will be allowed to complete its journey and I will allow you and your human to live your lives henceforth without fear. But mark me well: my powers are strong even in banishment. If you choose to reject my offer, the time will come when I unravel this spell, and from that moment on, you and your precious human will not know a moment's peace."

A loud, blustery wind started moving toward us from the west. The trees twisted and swayed as if following some weird forest choreography. The sky went cloudless, moonless, starless black, and we instinctively reached for one another's hands.

"Oh God," Karen groaned as the dock began moving out from under our feet.

"Hang on!" Luke cried out as we flipped backward like a trio of Russian gymnasts, tumbling end over end over end through the velvety darkness until we found ourselves standing in front of Sticks & Strings, right next to Luke's truck.

A truck that was in perfect condition.

The sky overhead was filled with stars.

A sliver of moon continued its transit across the sky. The streetlamps glowed gently, same as always.

We stared at the truck, the sky, and then at one another.

"That didn't really happen, did it?" Karen asked.

But she knew the answer as well as we did.

And like us, she also knew that time was running out.

16

CHLOE

When we finally got back to my cottage, I did what people do when life knocks you on your ass: I broke out the Ben & Jerry's, the Chips Ahoy, and a box of wine, then sat down at the kitchen table to figure out what to do next.

"You're kidding, right?" Luke asked as he surveyed the calorie-fest. "You can eat after that?"

"Watch me," I said, popping the lid on the Ben & Jerry's. "Fat and sugar help me think."

"You're going to eat all of that?" Karen asked from the doorway.

"I'm going to give it my best shot," I said, reaching for a spoon. "If either of you wants any, you'd better stake your claim now."

"Consider my claim staked." She grabbed a spoon from the counter and sat down opposite me.

"The Cherry Garcia is all mine."

"No problem," she said. "I'm a Dulce de Leche girl myself."

"Things might get ugly with the cookies."

"I'm willing to take my chances," she said with a tired smile.

Luke watched us with a look of amazement. "Any chance you have some single malt hidden away?"

I looked up at him. "What kind do you like again?"

"Glenfiddich."

I closed my eyes, focused deeply, then felt the answering ripple between my shoulder blades. "Check the cabinet over the fridge. You might find some."

Which of course he did. Sometimes magick came in handy.

He grabbed a juice glass from the dish drainer near the sink and poured three fingers' worth.

"Cent'anni," I said, lifting my box of wine in his direction.

"Bottoms up," he said and downed every last drop.

We ate (and drank) in silence. We ignored the cats, who periodically jumped up on the table, surveyed the proceedings, then jumped down again. Suppressing a feline insurrection was so far down on the to-do list that they could have smacked us around, then polished off the wine with a whiskey chaser, and we probably wouldn't have noticed.

"Your phone's ringing again," I said to Luke. I was almost relieved to hear the bland everyday ringtone I'd grown accustomed to. "What's up with that?"

"Isadora's light show. They saw it two towns over and think it was a UFO. The reporters are coming out of the woodwork. One of them even called NASA." He grabbed his bottle of single malt and excused himself to return some calls and explain away the incident.

"Is your brain on overload?" I asked Karen as I refilled my mug of wine.

"I passed overload when the car went airborne," she said. "I think I'm moving from seriously delusional to totally fried right about now."

I laughed and scooped up another heaping spoonful of cholesterol-heavy lusciousness. Luke and I had given her a condensed version of *The Idiot's Guide to Sugar Maple*, complete with audiovisual aids, courtesy of the Book of Spells.

"Do I get to say, 'I told you so'?" she asked as she popped a piece of chocolate chip cookie into her mouth. "I knew you were psychic all along."

"You're still wrong. Do you think I would have let us walk into that trap if I'd seen it coming? I don't have any psychic abilities at all. I'm what you'd call a sorceress-in-training."

We all had our labels. Psychic. Sorcerer. Part-time witch. Full-time shapeshifter. None of it seemed to matter anymore.

"How long do you think Luke will be in there?" she asked, gesturing toward the back of the cottage.

I shrugged. "I don't have a clue."

"That's exactly what he used to do when we were married." She jabbed her spoon into her ice cream. "He'd hole up at the office and wait until everything cleared."

"This is hardly the same thing, Karen. He's the chief of police. He has to return the calls."

"Nothing dangerous about that."

I narrowed my eyes in her direction. I'd always wanted to narrow my eyes at someone, and this seemed as good a time as any to do it. "What's that supposed to mean?"

"You saw him back there at the dock. Why didn't he do something? He's a cop. He knows how to handle dangerous situations. He could have taken her down."

I laughed out loud. "Do you really think a one-hundred-eighty-pound human male could take down an immortal? Isadora and Dane almost killed Luke back in December. Trust me, he did the right thing." The *only* thing he could have done under the circumstances.

"I still think he should have tried."

"So we could bury him tomorrow?" I slugged down some more red. "Let's not have this conversation."

"I don't understand the problem. Give that Isadora creature what she wants and she'll release Steffie's spirit. It sounds pretty simple to me."

"It isn't."

"It should be."

Of course it should be. In a more perfect world, hers or anyone else's, a child's innocent spirit wouldn't be trapped in some hazy netherworld of loneliness. That wouldn't happen. But none of our worlds was perfect. Not even close.

My head was pounding so hard I thought it was going to explode. "I know Isadora. You don't. She used her own *son* to murder my parents. What makes you think she'd keep her word on this?"

"What makes me think you'll keep your word?" she tossed back at me. "You lied to me. You pretended to be normal. How do I know you haven't put a spell on Luke and trapped him here the same way that creature trapped Steffie?"

I shoveled more cookies and ice cream into my mouth. "Tell me how you really feel."

"You scare the hell out of me," she said. "I mean, my God, you killed her son. I saw it playing out on that screen."

"It was an accident. The sword bounced off my shield and split him in two." But I wasn't telling the entire truth. I wanted Dane dead, and if that accident hadn't happened, I would have found a way to kill him.

"Almost everything you and Luke told me since I got here has been a lie. There's nothing normal about this town. None of you is even remotely normal."

"Depends on how you define *normal*," I reminded her. "To us, you're the abnormal one."

She put down her spoon and locked eyes with me. The urge to turn myself into a tree frog was almost irresistible but I held steady. "Maybe you're screwing with me. Maybe you're not. Maybe that whole freak show out there tonight was the result of some magic mushrooms you slipped into my Kung Pao. But if there's even the slightest chance that my daughter is out there, that her spirit is in some kind of danger, then I'm going to fight as hard as I can, do whatever I have to do, and there's nothing you can do to stop me."

I believed her. She was maybe five feet tall. I doubted if she weighed one hundred pounds. But there was something intensely powerful about her, something so fierce and primal that it defied the physical realities.

When it came to her daughter, the first Mrs. MacKenzie was a warrior.

Steffie was gone but Karen was still her mother. Even now, even when all of her human reality must be telling her it was futile, she was willing to fight for her daughter to keep her safe from harm.

My mother loved me but she never fought for me. When faced with the choice to join my human father in death or stay in this earthly realm and raise her little girl to adulthood, my mother chose to leave me in the collective hands of the villagers of Sugar Maple and ultimately in the loving embrace of Sorcha the healer.

After many earthly years in this realm, Sorcha had been ready to pierce the veil into the next dimension. But a needy six-year-old girl with no powers to her name and a sullied half-human heritage came into her life and she stayed until she was sure I could fly on my own.

Karen didn't care if I liked her, loathed her, or wanted to put her in a psychiatric institution. All she cared about was Steffie.

Maybe on some level she was crazy,

but it was a crazy I understood. Grief could do terrible things to a human's heart and soul, make you see things that weren't there and overlook the things that were. And maybe sometimes it led you to exactly the place where you were meant to be at the moment in time when you were meant to be there.

I wish I knew if this was one of those times.

"I saved the town," I said quietly. "I don't mean the buildings and the woods and the lake. I'm talking about the families who've been living here for over three hundred years. That's what Luke and I were doing the night Isadora's sons were killed. I regenerated the protective charm and managed to drive Isadora into banishment. When my parents died, this town became my family. They'll be here long after—" I stopped myself. "Let's just say if Isadora succeeds, she'll pull the town through the mist just like she promised. She has to be stopped permanently."

"Is that the worst that could happen?"

"The worst that could happen to the town is that not everyone will make it through to the other side. It's a violent process and there will be casualties." I met her eyes. "Luke would be one of them."

"So go live somewhere else. You all have magic powers. Wouldn't it be easier to live somewhere you didn't have to hide what you are?"

"I can't." Assuming such a place even existed.

"But Luke can."

The truth really does hurt, especially when it's aimed straight at the center of your heart. I looked down at the table, unable to think of anything clever or insightful to say.

"I don't see the problem," Karen persisted. "You can use your magic to keep him safe. I've seen what you can do. Pop him into one of those bubbles you wrapped around me. Think of something!"

"Shut up."

"What did you say?"

"I said shut up. Maybe if you quit talking for a minute, I'd be able to think of something."

"Come on," she urged. Her voice held a manic edge. "I mean, you're practically a knitting superhero."

"This isn't a joke."

"That's my child that creature's holding. I know it's not a joke."

My cheeks flooded with color. It took every ounce of self-control at my command to keep from grabbing her by the shoulders and shaking some sense into her. Protecting Sugar Maple and Luke and even freeing Steffie were only part of a wider picture I was just now beginning to understand.

The loss of her son Dane had pushed Isadora over the edge into obsession, turning her dislike of humans into an all-encompassing hatred of the race. If she managed to take Sugar Maple beyond the mist, who would be able to stop her from taking another town and then another?

But Karen couldn't see any of it. The loss of her daughter blinded her to everything else.

The parallel between the two grieving women, however, wasn't lost on me, and a part of my heart ached for them both.

The truth was I could study the Book of Spells like a Talmudic scholar but there wasn't time to learn even a tenth of what I needed to learn in order to construct all the protections we would need to fight off a full-powered onslaught from Isadora.

The Book revealed itself on its own schedule, according to the sorcerer's skill level, and my level was still rank beginner.

I should have done more, worked harder, dedicated myself to mastering my craft. That was why I'd been born, wasn't it? To protect Sugar Maple and her citizens. And to make sure another Hobbs woman walked the earth after I was gone. So far I was failing on both counts.

Only the most basic banishment spells were available to me, which was why I had to construct a web of spells in order to contain her.

Suddenly I felt very old and very tired. I had been outmaneuvered by the Fae leader, and the only weapons I had in my arsenal were two heartbroken humans and the Book of Spells. I realized once again how much I had depended on Gunnar, not only for friendship but for guidance in dealing with his mother's eruptions.

There was only one way we could save Steffie, and that was by completely vanquishing Isadora once and for all. Surrender wouldn't work. Neither would compromise. Luke understood that, but I knew Karen never would.

I wasn't sure I wanted her to.

"Karen, I can't tell you not to fight for your daughter. The only thing I can do is tell you we're on the same side."

"Then why aren't you doing anything?"

I had nothing left to offer her but the truth. "Because I don't know where to start."

"You're pathetic." She sounded almost sorry for me. "You both are. Steffie was trying to tell us something, and I'm not going to rest until I figure out what it is."

She met my eyes. I wasn't crazy about what I saw reflected back at me: the last descendant of Aerynn.

The one who lost it all.

17

CHLOE

I watched from the living room window as Karen walked halfway down the driveway and lit a cigarette. She said she needed to think. All things considered, I probably should have tried harder to keep her inside, where I could protect her, but I wasn't sure I cared any longer. I hadn't been able to keep Luke's truck from sailing across town like a detailed Cessna. Why did I think things would be any different now?

With a little luck, maybe she would keep

walking down the driveway and never come back and we could forget any of this ever happened.

I had never felt like a bigger loser than I felt at that moment.

"Where's Karen?" Luke's warm breath brushed against the side of my neck.

"She went out. Said she needed to think."

"And you let her go?" He wrapped his arms around me, and silver-gold sparks flickered all around us.

"I'm not sure I could have stopped her without dropping another bubble over her." And I wasn't sure how I did that the first time.

"Do you think she's safe?"

"As safe as she would be in here with us. Doors and walls don't mean much to the Fae. I could always—"

"Shut up."

I turned slightly and looked up at him. "What?"

"Shut up," he said, then closed his mouth over mine.

His mouth was hot. His lips. His tongue. I couldn't get enough of his heat. I couldn't get close enough to the source.

It wasn't magick but it seemed like it. He slid his hand under my sweater. I unzipped his jeans. He teased my nipple with the pad of his thumb. I found him with my hand.

There wasn't time to get naked. There wasn't time to tease or stroke or prolong.

We stumbled across the room, still kissing. He pressed me up against the wall, then slid my jeans and panties down my body. His tongue burned a line down between my breasts, over my belly, lower and lower still until he found me and I cried out in the quiet room.

"Wrap your legs around my waist." His words were muffled against the side of my neck. "I want to come inside you."

His hands grasped my hips and I gasped as he lowered me onto his rigid shaft. I gripped him hard with my thighs. He was ferocious in his need and I met him thrust for thrust. The sparks between us turned to flame.

Nothing lasted forever. Not people. Not things. Not even love.

This time tomorrow it might be too late.

KAREN

I forgot just how far north Sugar Maple was. Spring nights weren't always gentle up here. The light sweater I had borrowed from Chloe wasn't cutting it so I turned back toward the cottage to grab another one.

My mind was a blank. It scared me that, with all there was at stake and a clock ticking away the minutes, I could be so totally devoid of ideas, but I guess there is just so much the human brain can take before it shuts down in self-preservation.

Human brain. Strange to think having one put me in the minority around here.

Shivering, I jogged up the driveway and was almost at the porch steps when I caught sight of movement in the front window. Luke and Chloe, shadowy in the darkened room, were wrapped in each other's arms, ivory and gold sparks shooting in every direction like fireworks gone crazy.

It's not that I didn't know they were lovers. All you had to do was look at them to know that. But knowing it and seeing it were very different things.

Life went on.

No matter what happened, no matter how battered and bruised you were, sooner or later life swept you up again and threw you back into the river. Luke had moved on while I was still standing onshore, unable to make peace with Steffie's death. There had always been something unfinished to it, as if I'd caught only part of the story and needed to know how it ended.

Or even if it ended.

Clearly I couldn't go back into the cottage without embarrassing all three of us so I checked Luke's truck for a jacket or blanket, then opened the door of Chloe's Buick, where I stumbled on the mother lode. I grabbed a phenomenal Aran cardie with vintage buttons and front pockets. It fell practically to my knees, which considering the fact I was freezing, wasn't a bad thing at all.

The creep-out factor was sky-high as I walked toward town. I jumped at every sound in the bushes and looked over my shoulder so many times I would have been better off walking backward.

Maybe Chloe didn't know what to do next, but scarfing ice cream at the kitchen table while Luke made phone calls wasn't going to get us anywhere. Steffie was out here somewhere. I'd seen her with my own eyes. I'd watched as she pounded helplessly at some supernatural cage.

My baby . . . caged.

I stopped walking as the image flashed before my eyes.

She had looked angry and terrified and lonely, and if I could have breached the divide between worlds, I would have torn that creature Isadora apart with my bare hands and enjoyed every moment of the carnage.

How could Luke stand there and do nothing? I knew he had moved on. The supermodel was proof of that. He had gathered up his memories of our marriage and of Steffie and compartmentalized them the way he used to separate his job from his family. But that was his baby girl up there. He'd been there when she was born. He had cut the cord, heard her first cries. How could he maintain that icy distance?

If you can hear me, Steffie, talk to me . . . I'm going to find you . . . Don't worry, baby . . .

Nothing. No visions appearing in the sky. No secret ringtone.

"Steffie!" I screamed into the unyielding silence. "Where are you, Steffie?"

Still nothing.

I broke into a run. "Steffie, talk to me! Help me find you!"

She was out there. I knew she was. Even Luke believed me now. Somebody had to find her before it was too late.

I stumbled over a branch and fell head-long in the road. Shards of gravel and dirt cut into my palms. My brain registered a sharp pain in my right knee, then dismissed it as irrelevant. I got back on my feet and resumed a limping run toward town.

I had nothing to do with Sugar Maple or Chloe's problems with magic types. I didn't care about their ridiculous feuds. All I cared about was my daughter.

I had to get back to the lake. I wanted to stand in the same spot where I'd been standing two hours ago when I saw Steffie trapped in that hideous cage. Maybe without Chloe and Luke and all their baggage, I would be able to talk to that Isadora, mother to mother. She had lost her sons. She knew how it felt to grieve for a child. I would open my heart to her. I'd hold nothing back.

Anything Isadora wanted. *Anything.* She could have it. There was nothing I wouldn't do for my child.

But wouldn't she know that already? She had magical powers. She was some kind of wizard. She should know I was on whichever side was best for my baby girl.

"That's not how it works."

I jumped at the sound of a high-pitched woman's voice.

"Over here," the voice said.

I turned to my right. "Where are you?"

"You're looking at me."

And suddenly I was. She was about my height, twice my weight, and impossibly rosy-cheeked. "You realize you're going about this all wrong."

"Have we met?" I asked. "You look familiar."

"You remember! I'm so pleased. I was with you at the town hall last night when you passed out." Her eyes were the deep brown of strong coffee. So dark I couldn't differentiate pupil from iris.

"I didn't pass out," I said. "Luke said I passed out but I know I walked into a wall."

"You're half right," she said. "It wasn't a

wall. It was Isadora's force field. No point pretending. You know everything now."

She had a crazy-wide smile. Lots of big white teeth. Really big white teeth. Especially those incisors.

"Oh God." I jumped back a step, unable to tear my eyes away from those teeth.

"You humans," she said with a merry laugh. "How many times have I told Luke we don't feed that way anymore? This is the twenty-first century. Why shackle ourselves to messy, archaic methods when modern science is at our disposal?"

I assumed it was a rhetorical question. At least I hoped it was because I was too shocked to speak. I mean, what do you say to a short, fat vampire with a bad perm and press-on nails?

"We know all about what happened tonight," she said, linking her plump arm through mine. Those eyes! I couldn't look away. "Someone should have taught Isadora some manners. I always said half of our troubles could have been avoided if she understood the difference between honey and vinegar."

I finally found my voice. "Um, who are you exactly?"

Again that helium-enhanced laugh. "Oh, honey, didn't I introduce myself? I'm Midge Stallworth and I'm the answer to your prayers."

18

LUKE

We barely had time to put our clothes back on before the first blue flame message flared to life.

Nothing like a hologram of your lover's best friend in her bathrobe and bunny slippers to quench the afterglow.

"Fair warning," Janice's image said. "Half the village is on the way over. They want to show their support."

I looked over at Chloe, who was finger-combing her hair. "Can they see us when we—?"

She shivered visibly. "I try not to think about that."

I replayed the last ten minutes and almost singed my brain. "I figured there was some kind of spell to keep them out."

"And there used to be a spell that kept you from seeing blue flame messages," she reminded me. "Things are changing around here."

"Some things won't," I said. "We're in this together."

She wasn't the kind of woman who cried easily. Seeing her eyes well up with tears hit me hard. "You wouldn't be in this at all if you hadn't decided to stay here with me."

"No magic spells," I reminded her. "It was my choice to stay."

"You didn't know what you were getting yourself into. You didn't know your daughter's spirit would be involved."

"You didn't know either."

"The thought probes," she said, shaking her head. "I must have missed one."

"Thought probes? What the hell is a thought probe?"

She looked extremely uncomfortable as she explained the small missile-shaped objects that copied both memory and emotion and added the components to mystical data banks the Pentagon would envy.

"You're telling me my memories are being stored someplace?"

"I'm not sure," she said uneasily. "Maybe not. I wove a pretty good spell around you to—"

"You put a spell on me?"

"Think of it like a flu shot. Just a little extra protection."

"What else aren't you telling me?"

"You know as much as I do now."

I wasn't sure I believed her. Not because she was a liar but because even Chloe didn't know the depth of her knowledge.

Or her powers, for that matter.

"I know what you're thinking."

I met her eyes. "I thought you weren't psychic."

She forced a smile. "You're thinking you never should have left Boston."

"That's not what I'm thinking."

"But you've thought it before."

I wouldn't lie to her. "A time or two."

"I'll understand if you want to leave when this is over."

I tried to find the right words but there

weren't any. I loved her. I wanted to see where that love would lead us. But there was little doubt I was done with Sugar Maple.

CHLOE

It was the middle of the night and my living room was filled with friends who had all converged on my cottage to tell Luke and me they were standing with us no matter what Isadora threw our way. Janice and her entire family. Lynette and her daughters, sadly without Cyrus and the boys, who were leaning in Isadora's direction. Paul Griggs and his sons. Lilith from the library and, to my surprise, her husband, Archie, as well. The entire crew from Fully Caffeinated.

I tried to be grateful for those who were there and not worry about the ones who were missing.

Or the fact that Luke and I hadn't exchanged a word in more than two hours.

"What's wrong?" Janice demanded as we retreated to the kitchen to brew another pot of tea. "Did you two have a fight?"

"I'm not sure," I said. "One second we were fine and the next we weren't."

"Oh, honey." Janice looked genuinely distressed. "You know I think he's all wrong for you but I was hoping it would work out."

"Maybe it will." Lynette joined us in the kitchen. She was still half-feathered but was quickly assuming her usual form. "Most humans would have run for the hills after what Isadora did tonight."

"*I* wanted to run for the hills," I said with a small laugh, "and I'm only half-human."

"See?" Lynette sounded triumphant. "That's exactly what I'm saying. He's staying because of you."

"Or his daughter." Janice was the official glass-half-empty part of our equation. "He's not going to leave his child in Isadora's clutches. That's not how he's made."

I tried to stifle my sigh but failed. "He says he's not even sure that was really Steffie's spirit."

"What does he need?" Janice shot back. "DNA proof? The ex knew."

"Maybe he doesn't want to know," Lynette offered as the last of her brilliant yellow canary plumage disappeared. "Men don't like not being in control. If he doesn't know for sure it's his daughter, he can't blame himself for failing her."

"He hasn't failed," I snapped at one of my dearest friends. "This isn't over."

"Not yet," Janice said, "but the clock's ticking."

Isadora had charmed the clock that hung over the Playhouse so that it glowed deep purple, casting an ominous reminder of her power over the entire town.

"My great-great-grandmother told me about this when I was a little girl," Lynette said. "She said one day a Fae leader would find a way to punch holes in the Hobbs shield and take control."

Janice rolled her eyes. "I thought you stopped smoking those strange herbs of yours."

"I don't smoke anything," Lynette said, clearly offended, "and you know it, Janice Meany. Granny was there when the separation happened. She told us all about it. It was only a matter of time."

"Separation?" I asked.

"The war between Aerynn and Isadora's ancestor Da'elle."

"It wasn't really a war," Lynette said. "I mean, they didn't have soldiers or anything."

"The hell they didn't," Janice said. "Half the villagers supported Aerynn's view of Sugar Maple's future in the world they already knew. The other half would have given their lives in support of Da'elle's plan to pull the town through the mist, where they would be safe from human predation." She flashed me a look. "Guess who won."

"I can't believe Sorcha never told me about this."

"I can't believe you didn't learn it in grade school along with the rest of us," Lynette said with a shake of her head. "It's basic Sugar Maple history."

"You know how everyone always coddled Chloe when she was growing up," Janice said without malice. "They probably figured she already had enough on her plate, what with being born without magick. Aerynn's a tough act to follow."

"All this time I thought it was something between my mother and Isadora and here it's been going on between our families from the very beginning." Who knew?

"The Fae have long memories," Lynette said. "They'll wait for centuries if necessary to achieve their goal."

"But we've lived in harmony with the

Fae for over three hundred years now. It was only when my mother and Isadora clashed—"

"When your father entered the picture, things began to change and Isadora saw an opportunity to strike."

I fell silent as the puzzle pieces snapped into place. "And now there's Luke." Another human living intimately with a descendant of Aerynn.

Lynette looked down at her hands. "I didn't want to be the one to say it."

"I'll say it," Janice piped up. "You know what they did to witches at Salem. The fear of humans is ingrained in the New England Fae. It will never go away."

I nodded. Everyone in Sugar Maple knew. We had been founded as a sanctuary for women and men who'd escaped persecution at the hands of a town gone mad. The Fae had been tortured almost to extinction by humans. The enmity ran deep and wide.

"How did Aerynn defeat Da'elle?" I asked. "Were her powers that much greater?"

"No," Lynette said. "Her resolve was and that made all the difference."

"No offense," Janice said, "but sometimes I think you're afraid of your magick."

"That's a ridiculous thing to say. I welcomed my magick. I waited all my life for my powers to come in."

When I needed it most, I had summoned up the strength to do what I had to do to vanquish my enemies, even though it meant losing my dearest friend in the process. I had used my father's mortal resolve and my mother's magick to make it happen. Those didn't sound like the actions of a woman who was afraid of anything.

"That's all swell," Janice said, clearly unimpressed, "but until you decide who you really are, you'll never come into your full gifts."

"No disrespect meant, sweetie, but if you'd been more comfortable with your powers, the ex never would have happened."

"Don't go blaming the ex on me," I shot back. "I didn't summon her to Sugar Maple. I didn't even know her name until she showed up at the meeting."

"So why is she still here?"

"Come on, Jan. It was the middle of the night. You saw her. The woman was a mess. What did you want me to do, toss her out or ask her to sleep on the porch?" Not that both ideas hadn't occurred to me.

"Janice has a point," Lynette said. "You have magick. More magick than you've allowed yourself to realize. You could have settled this whole thing in the first thirty seconds if you weren't so worried about what your human would think."

I tried to stay on point. "She came to see Luke, not me. It's their business, not mine."

My two friends exchanged a look that wasn't lost on me.

"Okay, so it's my business now." Isadora had seen to that. "But you know what's at stake. Do you really want me to turn away from a child in trouble?"

"A human child who has already pierced the veil."

"Died," Janice corrected her. "Humans die."

"Whatever," Lynette said. "She's gone. She's not of this realm any longer."

"You don't understand. You're not—" I stopped short.

"Human?" Janice asked with an arch of her brow.

"I didn't say that."

"You were going to."

"But I didn't."

"Honey, I know what this is about and I feel for you. I really do. You see yourself in that little girl. We get it. But step away from the human side of your heart and rethink this. Your Luke isn't forever, but Sugar Maple is."

19

LUKE

Chloe and her friends were holed up in the kitchen while I tried to fit in with the crowd milling through the rest of the cottage.

"We're not blaming you," Archie the troll told me over a single malt the size of his arm. "Not your fault all hell broke loose when you came to town."

"Thanks, Arch." I downed the second of what I assumed would be many shots before daybreak. "If you're looking to lay

blame, you might want to aim it at Montpelier. They gave me the assignment."

"I know, I know. Bureaucracy sucks and
all that. Any human would've set off shock
waves, but nothing like this. Chloe fell in
love with you. That's what changed everything."

And here I thought triggering her powers was a good thing.

"Glad you're on her side," I said, clap-
ping him on his rounded back. "We need
the support." If not the lukewarm endorse-
ment of our romance.

Support was good but what I really
needed were some answers. I had inter-
rogated everyone in the room about Isadora, but she remained as big a mystery
to me now as she'd been from the beginning. They respected her. They feared her.
They didn't have a clue where she lived or
how she lived. Did she have a consort?
Children besides Dane and Gunnar? How
old was she? Who was her family? Where
did she get the power to break through her
banishment and capture my daughter's
soul? Was there a source she went back
to again and again, or was her power in-
ternally generated?

Easy questions like that.

I pulled Paul aside and we stepped out onto the porch. Maybe I was crazy but I knew this guy had my back the same way I had his. I could be straight with him.

"Is this it?" I asked him. "Is this all the support Chloe has in town?"

He shifted uncomfortably and looked out into the darkness of the middle distance. "All that's willing to be seen."

"Verna," I said. His wife. "She's on the other side?"

He met my eyes. "Sorry, MacKenzie. With the recession and everything, she's thinking it might be time for a change."

"You've got yourself a problem, dude."

He forced a smile. "Yeah," he said. "Sooner or later we'll have to come down on the same side."

I didn't have to tell him that sooner was about to bite him on the ass. Isadora had made that clear earlier tonight.

"Where's your ex-wife?" Paul glanced toward the cottage. "Sleeping off the excitement?"

"She went out for a walk."

"After the show Isadora put on tonight? The chick's hard-core."

"Definitely. It takes a lot to scare Karen." In many ways Steffie was just like her.

"I'm sorry about your kid."

I nodded. "Steffie was—" I couldn't finish the sentence.

Paul knew how to ride the silence while I pulled myself together. His sons were everything to him. He got it.

"She's grieving hard," I said when speech returned. "She's not here for me or to cause trouble for Sugar Maple. All she wants is Steffie."

I felt a rush of wind moving past my cheek, followed by a familiar laugh.

"Am I a lucky girl or what?" Midge Stallworth appeared in front of us dressed like Betty Crocker if Betty had a Bedazzler and wasn't afraid to use it. "The two handsomest fellas in town out here to greet me."

I recoiled, then quickly covered up with a cough and a tug at the sleeve of my sweater. For the second time in as many days I had to remind myself how much I liked the vampire matron with the espresso bean dark brown eyes.

Paul gave her a peck on one of her rosy cheeks. I wasn't ready to commit to physical contact.

Just call me cautious.

"So where's the family?" Paul asked on my behalf. "We know they're not sleeping."

Laughter all around. Like I said before: vampire humor.

"Billy took the kids up to a convention in Quebec City on Sunday. I've been a bachelor girl all week." She mimed a pout, which wasn't a good look if you were over sixteen. "You both should stop in for supper tomorrow night. I'm so used to cooking for a crowd that I don't know how to cut back."

Could someone be too normal? The conversation flowed easily. The laughs were unforced. Midge was her usual overly made-up, overdressed self with a wristful of watches and bracelets, fingers bedecked with rings, and more piercings in her plump ears than I could count. So why the itchy feeling moving its way up my spine?

I glanced over at Paul, who had retreated into the shadows. His body language was loose and natural. If he was picking up any weird vibes, it didn't show. Then again the guy was a werewolf. Weird was his normal.

But Midge Stallworth unnerved the hell

out of me, and it wasn't just the bloodsucking thing. I mean, I get along fine with Manny and Frank and Rose from Assisted Living and they were all vampire. I hit a few buckets at the Sugar Maple Driving Range with Midge's husband, Billy, last week and didn't feel I had to guard my carotid artery.

"Lipstick on my teeth?"

I felt an embarrassed flush burn its way up my throat. Want some advice? Never get caught staring at a vampire's smile. "Sorry, Midge. I was thinking about something else."

She patted my hand with motherly affection. "No apologies, honey. I never complain when a man stares at me." She winked. "All natural, in case you were wondering."

Dirty Grandma was back again.

Time to change the subject.

After the obligatory small talk about gas mileage, the price at the pump, and the great fiscal meltdown out there in the real world, Midge went inside to offer her support to Chloe.

Paul stepped out of the shadows. "You don't trust her."

"Jury's out but I'm leaning that way."

"Midge plays both sides in a conflict. Always has. I've never had a problem with her, but she makes the hair on the back of my neck stand up every time I see her."

Which was saying something when those neck hairs belonged to a guy who spent half his life tearing through the woods on all fours.

"I'd better push off." He fished his car keys from the front pocket of his jeans. "Verna's on the warpath as it is about this situation."

"Listen, I really appreciate your support." I stumbled over my words. Why the hell was gratitude so damn hard? "Both of us do. It means a lot."

"No sweat," he said, equally uncomfortable. He took a few steps down the driveway, then turned around. "They don't want to hurt you. They like you and they love Chloe, but they're scared that the human world is making inroads and Isadora offers a way out. Your ex tipped the balance and it scared them."

"I told you Karen's not here to stay."

"Tell it to them," he said. "They see Chloe surrounding herself with humans.

They think she's pulling away from her obligations. All they want is for things to go back to the way they used to be."

"You sound like you're starting to rethink your own position, Paul."

"Not me," he said, "but Isadora and the Fae are part of our history. She's one of us and so were her sons. Sugar Maple is different without them."

"In a good way, if you ask me. Nobody needs that much crazy. She's a psychopath."

"She's the chieftain of her clan. She fights for what belongs to her."

"Dude, she tried to *kill* me."

The guy was my friend and he didn't blink. "She lives by the rules of the Fae." He shot me a look. "And it's not all Tinkerbell and Disney."

Not unless Tinkerbell was a commando.

CHLOE

"I'm going out to look for Karen," Luke said from the kitchen doorway. "She should've been back by now. Don't wait up."

"Don't wait up?" Janice muttered as soon

as he left the room. Then she muttered a few things I don't want to repeat.

"This isn't good," Lynette, the optimist, said with a rueful shake of her head. "He didn't kiss you goodbye. You should always kiss the ones you love goodbye because you never know if you'll see them again."

"You really know how to ruin a party," Janice said. "Why don't we work on our obituaries while we're at it?"

I tried to laugh but couldn't quite manage it. Some party this was. I had spent most of my time reassuring people who claimed to know and love me that I wouldn't let them down. And to make it worse, Luke had seemed distant, preoccupied, borderline rude in a way I'd never seen him before. Was this more of Isadora's handiwork or just a side of him I could have lived without?

The side Karen had lived with during their marriage.

"We had a fight before you showed up."

"Before or after the hot sex?" Janice asked.

I shot her a look. "After."

"After?" She glanced over at Lynette. "I

thought humans believed in postcoital cuddling."

"It wasn't really a fight," I said, the words spilling out like they had lives of their own. "I don't know exactly what it was, but I don't think he's going to be here in Sugar Maple much longer."

Janice's sigh was long and loud. "I don't want to say 'I told you so' but—"

"Then don't."

"But I—"

"Just don't," I said. "I get it. I've heard it before. I know the drill. I just don't want to hear it again. Isadora's breaking out of her banishment. Luke's daughter is trapped in some other dimension. And I was stupid enough to let the ex wander off on her own at midnight. If you say one more word, I might turn you into Wayne Newton."

Janice opened her mouth but Lynette, with cobra speed, clamped a hand over it. "We don't want to hear it, Jan."

Suddenly I felt so exhausted I could barely keep my eyes open. Time was ticking away, and I was no closer to a solution to the mess we were in than I was when Isadora threw down the gauntlet. "I need to crash for a half hour," I said to my friends.

"If you could clear the house, I'll let you have the pick of my stash."

Five minutes later I was alone with my cats and my Chips Ahoy. The box of red was history. I tried not to think about the fact that Karen was still out there wandering around Sugar Maple. Without my protection she was helpless as a baby rabbit.

I didn't like to think that might be why I let her go, but I felt the sting of truth at the possibility.

Because I knew the answer to this whole mess. I'd known it from the beginning. All I had to do was let her go. Let her child go. They weren't part of Sugar Maple. They had no bearing on my future or the future of anyone else in this town. Nothing I did would bring Steffie back to the realm of existence she had shared with her parents. No magick was that strong. Not Aerynn's or Isadora's and definitely not mine.

Luke and Karen had already lost their daughter. There would be no more hugs, no more bedtime stories and snuggles, no watching her grow up and go to college and get married and have a baby of her own. Even if I managed to vanquish Isadora once and for all and free Steffie's spirit, none of those very human experiences would come to pass. Steffie's time in this realm had come and gone.

Was I willing to risk the future of Sugar Maple and the people I loved on the slim chance that I could find a way to undo Steffie's imprisonment *and* banish Isadora once and for all?

The risks were enormous. If I screwed up, there was every reason to believe Isadora would make good her threat and pull the town and everyone in it beyond the mist.

But what if I did nothing? What would happen if I just sat back and let the tower clock toll midnight?

The thought was ugly but compelling.

Isadora would still be trapped within her banishment, which would give me time to grow my skills.

Sugar Maple would still be part of this earthly realm, same as it had been for three hundred years.

And Luke would still be here with me. We would have a chance to get it right, a chance to push closer to forever.

All I had to do was let Steffie go.

20

KAREN

"Lie down and get some rest." Bettina Weaver lit a vanilla candle, then dimmed the lights. "Someone will get your things for you."

"Tell Luke where I am," I said, sinking deep into the feather bed.

"Of course," Bettina said. "We wouldn't want him to worry, would we?"

Actually I didn't care if he was worried or not. I just didn't want him storming over here and ruining everything the way he had at the séance.

They were going to contact Steffie. Midge and Bettina and Verna and the others were going to do what Chloe and her friends couldn't: make it possible for me to talk to Steffie. They said Isadora was nothing but an annoyance, that Steffie's spirit wasn't in any danger at all. It was all an illusion conjured up to make Chloe look bad.

"Don't you pay any attention to all that nonsense between Chloe and Isadora. The trouble goes back to the very beginning, but it has nothing to do with you and your daughter. Isadora was trying to stir things up, that's all."

They were so apologetic. They loved their town and didn't want me to think badly of them. And I didn't. They were kind and helpful and they believed that Steffie was trying to contact me. I had to keep reminding myself that Midge was vampire, Bettina was a faerie, and Verna the wife of a werewolf.

Not that it mattered. All I had to do was relax and they would do the rest. As far as I could see, I had nothing to lose. I already knew that Chloe and Luke couldn't help me and that when it came to Isadora, I was in way over my head. If they had a plan they believed would work, why not go with it? They had nothing to gain from helping me reach my daughter. They were doing it because they were good—well, *people* wasn't the right word, but you know what I mean.

So I did and a heartbeat later Bettina opened the door to a gorgeous guest suite at her parents' Inn.

"You might want to keep a low profile," she said with a slightly guilty smile. "My parents aren't big fans of Chloe."

I let it pass. My feelings for the knitting sorcerer were mixed, but for the most part I liked her. Even if she had stuffed me in a transparent bubble and left me there to age like cheese.

"I thought there were no vacancies," I said as I marveled at the hand-painted wall coverings, the incredible quilts, the enormous four-poster of glowing mahogany. "I would have dumped Chloe's cottage in a second for this."

Which probably wasn't the most politic thing I had ever said, but if you saw my room at the Inn, you would understand.

"Saturn is in close transit tonight," she said by way of explanation. "The spirits will stay close to home until it passes."

I didn't understand half of what they'd said to me about spirit trails and rest stops and journeying souls. All I knew was that they were going to put me in contact with my daughter. Nothing else mattered.

Not even the ragged, haggard-looking Revolutionary War–era soldier sitting on the edge of the windowsill, looking at me with sad eyes.

"Abigail?" he asked, a note of hope in his rum-soaked voice. "Have you come for me, Abby?"

Except for the fact I could see the window behind him, he looked as alive as I did.

"I'm not Abby," I said, struggling to sound like I spoke to ghosts every day of the week. "I'm Karen."

"Where's Abby?" he asked. "I'm here for Abby."

"Abby's in the parlor, Ethan. She's waiting for you there."

I shrieked at the sight of a glamorous woman in full 1940s movie star attire sitting on the foot of my bed.

It was getting seriously weird around here.

She smiled at me and pressed her index finger to her lips.

"Out with you, Ethan," she said in a friendly tone of voice. "You have no business being in a lady's room."

Ethan was gone in an instant.

"Cute as a bug in a rug." Her bright blond hair swooped over her right eye and fell to her shoulders in a shimmering skein of gorgeousness. "He and Abby have been playing hide-and-seek for over two hundred years."

"Wow." That was the best I could do, given the circumstances.

"So how did you get here?" she asked, curling her silk stocking–clad legs under her and getting comfortable like we were two good friends at a slumber party.

"Midge and Bettina brought me."

"No, no." Her laugh was pure movie goddess. "I mean, how did you die?"

"Die?" I leaped up from the bed. "I'm not dead." I pinched myself to be sure. "I'm absolutely alive."

"Honey, it's okay. It takes some of us longer than others to make the transition. You'll be fine. I promise you."

"No," I persisted. "Seriously. I'm not dead but my—my little girl is. That's why I'm here."

Her brilliant smile dimmed a little. "Holy

cow," she said. "I guess there's a first time for everything." She patted my leg but all I felt was the faintest movement of the air. "I saw an adorable little redhead around here yesterday."

"Steffie! Dark green eyes, lots of freckles, about six years old?"

"That's the one."

"Where is she? Can you take me to her? Did she say anything? You have to—"

"Hold your horses!" She rose from the bed and straightened the seams of her stockings with her fingertips. "I don't make the rules around here. Nobody does. We're just travelers looking for a way to complete our journeys."

"What does that *mean*?" I snapped in exasperation. "Everyone keeps saying things like that but it doesn't make any sense."

Too bad I was talking to thin air. The forties movie star had gone the way of the Revolutionary War soldier.

Was it possible Steffie was close by? I had always thought my maternal instincts would lead me to her no matter where she was, but I wasn't picking up anything at all. Still, the movie star claimed she'd seen a red-haired girl who met Steffie's description, and from what I'd seen, spirits really did feel comfortable here at the Inn.

Just lie down and rest. We'll take care of everything.

I didn't exactly hear the voice, but the words blossomed inside my head.

"Bettina?" I asked the empty room. "Is that you?"

Just lie down and rest. We'll take care of everything.

The voice was soothing. Authoritative in a hang-loose kind of way.

Put your head down. That's right. Now close your eyes and think about your daughter.

I almost laughed. Like I didn't think of Steffie every moment of every day.

But I did what the voice told me to do. I'm not sure I could have done anything else.

Forget everything that's happened here . . . Forget Sugar Maple and Chloe . . . Think about Steffie . . . when she was still there with you . . . Nothing else matters . . .

༄

Nothing else did.

21

CHLOE

I couldn't do it.

Every time I closed my eyes and tried to catch a nap before daylight came flooding in through my windows, I saw myself at Steffie's age, remembered how it felt to lose my parents, felt that deep loneliness inside my heart, and I flat out couldn't do it.

I wanted to let her go, but my human blood wouldn't let me. She was real. Spirits were real. I had lived among them all my life. The Harris family. The Souderbushes. All the souls who passed through

our town, searching and yearning for connection with the family and friends they
had left behind.

Why had it taken me so long to realize
this wasn't about Luke or Karen? I saw myself in Steffie. I knew how it felt to be a very
small child alone in a very big adult world.
I knew how it felt to miss your parents so
much it hurt to breathe. I knew how it felt to
want one more story, one more silly bedtime song, one more memory to tuck away
against forever.

There was order to the spirit world. A
tightly woven fabric of laws that governed
what happened and when and why. A fully
evolved spirit who had completed his or
her journey was far beyond the reach of
religion or magick or even love.

Isadora wouldn't have been able to hi-
jack Steffie's spirit if Steffie hadn't still been
in transit. Spirits were dimensional travelers on a mission to right a wrong, deliver a
message, achieve some kind of closure
before they reached their destination. If
Steffie had completed her journey and
claimed her own afterlife, even Isadora's
considerable powers wouldn't have been
able to touch her.

There was something Steffie needed to do in this world, some message she needed to deliver to her parents, and somehow Isadora had discovered that fact. Maybe I hadn't done as good a job of protecting Luke from thought probes as I'd thought. It had all been there waiting for Isadora to grab: his marriage to Karen, Steffie's death, their bitter divorce. And from there it was a simple dimensional leap to connecting with Steffie's spirit and setting this whole thing in motion.

If Steffie was ever going to find peace, I would need to use all the magick I had at my command to make sure she completed her journey.

Unfortunately I didn't have a clue where to start. I couldn't blue-flame Janice and Lynette. I already knew where they stood on the topic of helping humans find their afterlife bliss. Lilith the librarian was unfailingly compassionate, but she wouldn't understand putting a dead human child's needs before the needs of Sugar Maple.

I paced the cottage, trying to gather my thoughts into a cohesive whole. I tried sitting down at my Schacht and spinning some Bluefaced Leicester as a way to regain my focus, but my rhythm was off and I couldn't seem to manage a simple drafting motion. I picked up one of the dozen works in progress scattered around the place, but even plain old stockinette was beyond my ability.

I wasn't a chess player. I didn't know the first thing about the parry-and-thrust of fencing. Even love had me stumbling around like I had two left feet. Figuring out a plan to steal back a child's soul without setting Isadora free as well was like trying to reconstruct the blueprints for the space shuttle when you could barely push past the five times table.

The thought had barely formed when the room began to spin. Not in an I-think-I'm-going-to-faint kind of way but really spin like a carnival ride at the county fair. I sat down on the floor, hard, as the spinning turned into tumbling that sent me rolling across the room into the opposite wall. Before I had a chance to pull myself to my feet, I was yanked backward once again through that bizarre light-and-magic show that had made me feel like toothpaste being squeezed through a tube.

Who would think something like that could become old news?

Come on, I thought. *You can do better than this.* I'd barely scratched the surface of what the Book of Spells was capable of doing and it was already treating me to reruns? I mean, I knew exactly what was coming next: another audiovisual replay of *Great Moments in Chloe's History* meant to remind me that Sugar Maple was my first and only destiny.

"I don't have time for this!" I shouted into the twinkling lights. "Send me back now!" Didn't the Book know there was a clock ticking out there?

I was the sorcerer-in-charge. I ruled the Book of Spells; the Book didn't rule me. If I said stop, it stopped.

"Stop!" I yelled. "Stop!"

Instead of stopping, I was pulled faster through a tunnel of disco lights leftover from the seventies, a tunnel that was growing longer instead of shorter with every millisecond until I was dumped on the floor of a very dark, very weird room. Earsplitting elevator music made thinking an exercise in futility.

"Not funny," I shouted to the Book. "Take me home now!"

Nothing. Not even a ripple of acknowledgment.

I forced myself to block out the bad music and creepy décor. When it came to the Book of Spells, everything happened for a reason. Was this the answer to one of my questions? Was it a warning? I guessed this was the human part of my equation talking, but I wouldn't have minded a few plain old declarative sentences right about now.

"Okay, Book," I said, moving deeper into the room. "You brought me here. Now, what is it you want me to know?"

Nothing happened but I had the sense I wasn't alone.

"Is it about Steffie? Can you show me Steffie? Can you let me speak to her?"

Still nothing but I was getting warmer.

Literally.

I was too young for hot flashes but sweat started pouring down the back of my neck.

The music grew louder. The walls of the room began to ripple like a sixties-era psychedelic dream, pushing inward until I found myself standing at the midpoint and able to touch opposing walls with my fingertips.

I'm not exactly claustrophobic, but when the room really did start closing in on me, fight-or-flight syndrome definitely kicked in.

No doors. No windows. No way out.

My heart was beating so fast I couldn't breathe. I was a half second away from total meltdown when the music stopped, the walls disappeared, and the ceiling lifted away. There was no sky, no horizon, no sun or moon to help me orient myself. The ground beneath my feet was cushioned, and it felt like I was standing on a bed of whipped cream. Ambient light emanated from the surroundings. Each particle of air glowed from within. Tightly swirling clouds, like minitornadoes or dust devils, rotated all around me as concentrated pulses of light shot off in different directions from under my feet. As soon as a thought formed in my head, no matter how fragmented or foolish, one of the clouds rushed toward me and transformed that thought into my own private virtual reality.

Was this the next level of understanding? I felt strangely energized, lit up from within like the glowing particles that traced the contours of my body in a free-form CT scan.

My human concept of time and space was irrelevant here. I knew instinctively that it would take hundreds of earth years to master the possibilities offered by this new level. The thought of how many other levels might exist was staggering.

As soon as that thought formed itself, a small round cloud raced toward me. It stopped inches away from my face, shuddered, then turned a pearlescent white as thousands of platforms appeared before me, rising into the distance.

"Focus," I said out loud and turned my thoughts to Karen. The second her image formed in my brain, the platforms collapsed and drifted off into the distance. The round white cloud in front of me evaporated and a silvery gray cloud took its place.

"Show me Karen," I commanded. I wasn't comfortable with commands but they were big in magick circles.

Karen was lying flat on her back in the center of what I assumed was a bed. Her face was the only detail I could clearly make out. Her eyes were closed. For a second I was afraid she was dead, and a sick feeling of dread grabbed my chest and squeezed hard.

"Stay with us," I murmured. "Don't pull away."

I moved deeper into the room, sinking, then rising into the buoyant floor with each step. A midrange tone seemed to fill the air around me. I had the sense there were others in the room besides Karen and me, but they remained invisible to me.

The thought probes, however, weren't. Tiny crystalline devices radiated from Karen's head like a glittering crown. I frowned and moved closer. These were nothing like the torpedo-shaped thought probes I was used to. I reached out and touched her shoulder. At first contact a sizzle of current burned through me and my mind swelled with images of Sugar Maple. People. Places. Magick. All from Karen's perspective.

Even the sight of Steffie trapped inside that transparent cage.

It was all being siphoned away by the probes and replaced with newly constructed memories of a knitting workshop in northern Vermont that had never happened.

The magick at work was powerful because not even the Book of Spells was able to pierce the camouflage that cloaked her location. I tried every trick I could summon up to slide inside the shield surrounding Karen. Astral projection. Mind-twinning. Locus charting. They all failed.

There was only one thing left to try: old-fashioned police work.

I needed Luke.

22

LUKE

The village blazed with screaming purple light from the clock tower. And if that wasn't enough, the purple light was coupled with a steady fall of purple glitter that made a snapping, crackling sound when it hit the ground. Not to mention the oily stink of sour ashes from a long-dead fire.

The tourists were going to get an eyeful when they rolled into town later that morning.

Daybreak was less than a half hour away. I drove out to Snow Lake figuring

Karen might have gone there to see if she could contact Steffie. I pulled into the small lot and walked the perimeter, but there was no sign of her. The water was still. The park was empty. All traces of Isadora's fury were gone. I tried Karen's cell but it flipped into voice mail. I drove up and down our small grid of streets but the only thing I saw was one of the Weaver boys loading newspapers into the basket of his bike in front of the Inn.

He didn't acknowledge my wave.

There was only one way out of town, straight up Osborne to the Toothaker Bridge, then follow the two-lane road to the highway.

The road intersected with some old logging trails at various points, but if you weren't looking for them, you'd never find them. I popped on my high beams and scanned left and right as I drove. She could have tripped over a branch or stopped for a rest. Anything was possible.

Winter was brutal on the roads in northern Vermont. Endless days of subzero weather, snow, and ice took their toll. The road was littered with gigantic mud-filled potholes I had to navigate around or lose a wheel.

I swung right to avoid a nasty one when the truck began to vibrate at a decibel level high enough to take out your hearing. I'd bounced over a fallen branch a mile or so back. Maybe it had punched a hole in an exhaust pipe.

Or maybe it was the sound a sorceress made before she crashed through the roof of your truck.

"Holy shit!" I slammed on the brakes and skidded to a muddy stop in the middle of the road.

"Holy shit!" I said again for good measure.

Chloe was half on the seat, half off, clinging to the roll bar. "Ohmigod . . . ohmigod . . . ohmigod . . ."

"Breathe," I told her as I unsnapped my lap belt. "Does anything hurt?"

She met my eyes and a strangled laugh escaped. "You mean besides my dignity?"

"You crashed through the roof of my Jeep," I said. "Something's gotta—" We both looked up at the same time. The roof was intact. "What the hell—?"

"Don't ask me," she said. "I was inside the Book of Spells and then I wasn't."

"You were *in* the Book?"

"It's not the first time." She gripped my hand in hers. "I saw Karen. They're trying to erase her memory."

There was a limit to how much a human brain could absorb without exploding. "Karen's in the Book?"

"I don't know where Karen is. All I know is they're draining all of her memories of Sugar Maple."

"Who are they?"

"I don't know."

"You have to have some idea."

"Colm and Renate. Verna Griggs. Cyrus Pendragon and his sons. And that's just for starters." She spread her hands wide. "It could be just about anyone. Karen doesn't seem to be in any distress. For all I know, our friends might think they're doing us a favor."

"How do you know they're only screwing with her short-term memory?"

Her cheeks reddened. "I don't know that either."

"Looks like we're flying blind."

"Pretty much." She leaned against the

door and closed her eyes. "I wouldn't blame you if you let me out on the side of the road and drove as far away as you can."

"I've thought about it."

Her eyes opened. "Any decisions?"

This was a hell of a time for a discussion of our future together. "Boston could probably use another yarn shop."

Her eyes filled with tears.

"Just throwing it out there," I said. "Something to think about."

"Luke, I—" She stopped. "Did you hear that?"

"You mean that whooshing sound?"

Which was when the giant ball of fire smashed through the back window of the truck and engulfed us in flames.

CHLOE

"Get out!" Luke ordered as the car skidded to a stop again. "Run and don't look back."

"I'm not leaving you here."

"I'm behind you. Now run!" he roared.

I flung open the door and took off at top speed, breathing a sigh of relief when I heard his footsteps close behind me.

He caught up to me, grabbed me by the wrist, then threw me down into a ditch, where he covered me with his body a split second before the gas tank exploded.

We lay there together for what seemed like a lifetime. His heart pounded hard against my back. Even blanketed by his warmth, I couldn't stop shaking. How many times could we escape disaster? Sooner or later our luck was going to run out.

We lay there for a few moments while the truck blazed.

"Isadora?" he asked, his breath hot against my neck.

"Probably." I shivered despite his warmth. Her presence was almost palpable.

The sun was rising over the woods to the east, bathing us in the pale lemon glow of morning.

"We'd better get moving," I said. "We don't have much time left."

A bright yellow school bus rumbled by, then disappeared around the bend.

"The driver didn't even slow down," Luke remarked as he helped me to my feet. "What's up with that?"

"He probably couldn't see it," I said, try-ing not to laugh at the absurdity of the situation. "Guess at least some of the protective charm is still working."

You had to love a man who recognized irony when he saw it.

"We're near the waterfall," I said, pointing west. Our eyes met and a wave of sadness washed over me as I thought about our lovemaking a lifetime ago. "I know a shortcut back to town."

In the movies the stalwart hero and feisty heroine would throw caution to the wind and make love right there on the side of the road while the hero's truck burned all the way down to its rims.

I wish I could tell you that was what we did but I'd be lying. We were both tired, muddy, and (speaking for myself) scared so we linked hands instead and I led him deep into the woods surrounding the waterfall.

Neither one of us mentioned the missing sparks between us when we touched.

The woods were dark and cool. Only the faintest rays of morning sun filtered through the canopy of pine trees.

"How the hell do you know where we are?" Luke asked as we picked our way through brambles. "I don't see a path."

"It's not on the ground," I said. "The path is carved into the trees." I pointed toward the sugar maple up ahead. "See the line of maples? They point north toward town."

"You learned this in Girl Scouts?" A flicker of a smile crossed his face.

"Sorcha taught me. She knew all of the old Sinzibukwud ways."

I described Sorcha's herb garden, the healing potions she made from them, her uncanny talent for zeroing in on exactly what was wrong with you, then making it right with the touch of her hand.

"I wish you could have met her," I said as we left the deepest part of the woods behind. "You'd understand why Sugar Maple means so much to me."

"Somehow I don't think she'd be too happy you hooked up with a human."

"She—" I stopped and shook my head. What was the point?

"I know how they feel around here. You don't have to look so guilty."

"Actually she thought I might not be good for you."

Last month that would have made both of us laugh. Now it carried the ring of truth in every word.

23

LUKE

The good thing about fighting the forces of evil was you didn't have time to sit down and talk about your relationship.

The bad thing was you were too busy trying to stay alive.

We exited the woods behind the cemetery, cut across the grounds, then moved at a run toward the center of town.

Under different circumstances we would have split up so we could cover more territory, but after barely escaping death by fireball, I figured there was safety in numbers.

Especially if the other person had magickal powers.

First stop was Fully Caffeinated. They had a steady morning crowd of regulars, and it didn't hurt that the staff was solidly on our side.

"Do we tell them right out that we're looking for Karen?"

"Might as well," I said. "Half of them probably know where she is."

"Crap," Chloe said as we turned onto Osborne. "I'd hoped daylight would wash away the purple." The street looked like an Easter egg.

"Gonna blow Sugar Maple's cover when the tourists roll in any minute."

"I have to do something about it. Order me an espresso with three sugars. I'll be right back."

One second she was there, the next second she was on top of the clock tower overlooking the municipal parking lot. What the hell?

I'm a man, which means XY chromosome and everything that comes with it. We're built to defend and protect, not stand on the sidewalk while the woman we love does her Spiderman impression fifty feet off the ground and there isn't a damn thing we can do to help her.

When I saw her climb out onto the minute hand, I ducked into the coffee shop.

The place was standing room only. Half the staff of Sugar Maple Day School were comparing notes at a rear table. Paul waved from his seat at the counter. The booths had been claimed by house sprite work crews, Archie the troll and his pals, Verna and the Weavers. Janice, Lynette, and Lilith were slumped over coffee and bagels at a table near the door.

"Hey, Jackie." I smiled at the cute teenage selkie behind the counter. "One regular, one espresso triple sugar."

She didn't smile back. She didn't meet my eyes. She gave me a quick nod, then turned away to fill the order.

"Don't even try to get her to talk," Janice said when I joined them at their table. "The Weavers got to her mother and now she's all exorcist about going beyond the mist."

"What happened to you?" Lynette demanded. "You look like you were rolling in the mud."

"Close," I said, then told them the abridged version of the flaming truck story.

"A ball of fire?" Janice practically sneered. "How Wizard of Oz. You'd think Isadora could come up with something more original than that."

"Trust me," I said. "It was pretty damn effective."

Lilith glanced around. "Where's Chloe?"

"Hanging from the minute hand on the tower clock."

They didn't blink. It was one of the things I liked best about the villagers of Sugar Maple.

"The purple haze," Lynette said, nodding her head. "I was hoping she'd get on it."

I took a slug of coffee, then waited while it scalded its way down my throat. "Karen's gone missing."

Now *that* got a reaction.

I filled them in on what little we knew.

"Maybe she decided to go back to Boston," Lilith offered. "Someone might have given her a ride to the bus station in Grover's Notch."

"You heard what Luke said." Janice sounded exasperated. "She's lying on a bed somewhere with a crown of thought probes poking out of her head."

"Maybe it's not so bad," Lynette said.

"The selective memory-erasing probes are still in development. Nobody knows whether or not they work."

Great. Karen was being used as a guinea pig. It just kept getting better and better.

I took another gulp of high octane and glanced out the window. The purple wash that had stained everything in sight was gone, and the street had been restored to its usual state of rustic perfection.

I was glad to see Chloe breeze through the door and join us at the table. Magic or not, scaling the side of a building was serious stuff.

"Good job," Janice said, giving her a high-five across the table. "Enough with the purple already."

"Seriously," Lynette said. "She might as well announce herself with a bullhorn."

"Isadora likes purple," Lilith said. "Nothing wrong with that."

"Since when?" Janice demanded. "You hate her as much as the rest of us do."

"I don't hate anyone," the librarian corrected her. "I hate what Isadora is doing but I don't hate her."

"Well, excuse me." Janice rolled her eyes.

"I guess my sensibilities aren't as finely honed as yours."

"I don't hate her either," Chloe said. "I mean, at least I didn't until she tried to kill Luke and me."

"But she hated you," I said, growing seriously confused.

"She doesn't hate the town," Lynette said.

"She loves the town," Lilith agreed.

"It's Chloe she hates." Janice bit off a piece of bagel. "That whole family feud thing."

Chloe looked at me and shrugged. "I just found out about that myself." She brought me up to speed. "I knew she didn't want me hooking up with her sons, but I thought that was because she didn't want human blood muddying up her pristine Fae gene pool."

"They've had over three hundred years to make a move," I said. "Why now?"

"It's not like Isadora's clan didn't try before." Lilith was the town's historian as well as chief librarian. She knew where all the bodies were buried. Metaphorically speaking, that is. "In fact, Isadora made a run at pulling us beyond the mist not that long ago." She grew quiet for a moment. "I wish I could pinpoint it exactly but I think it was around when Chloe was born."

"That's thirty years ago," I said. "Can't be much of a priority."

"In human years maybe not," Lilith said, "but it's the blink of an eye to the Fae. They're very patient."

Chloe polished off her espresso, then stood up. She moved into the center of the crowded coffee shop. "Can I have your attention?"

The place fell silent.

"Luke's ex-wife stepped outside last night for a cigarette and she didn't come back. I know she's being held somewhere in town. I know she's safe. I'm *sure* she's safe. But we want her back. If you know anything at all, if you can help us in any way, we won't ask questions and we won't cast blame. She's not one of us. She doesn't want to be one of us. She wants to go home to Boston. Let's make it happen."

The silence grew deeper.

"Okay, then," she said, meeting my eyes. "I gave it a shot. You know where to find me."

We did the same thing in the hardware

store, the grocery, the farmer's market, the high school auditorium, the assisted living facility. We skipped Cut & Curl, the library, the Playhouse, and the pizzeria only because they weren't open yet.

It was the same every place we stopped. Chloe delivered her speech and was met with total silence. Friends and opponents alike stared solemnly at her and offered nothing.

"What about the Inn?" I asked as we headed to the knit shop to regroup. "Maybe someone on staff knows something."

"The Inn is the belly of the beast," she said. "Do you really think Colm or Renate would let me talk to their staff?"

"Don't worry," I said. "Let me handle this."

Maybe they could say no to the de facto mayor of the town, but they couldn't say no to the chief of police.

CHLOE

"No." Renate didn't even bother to expand to human size or form. "Absolutely not."

Luke went deep into scary-serious cop mode. "I can go all official on you, Renate, or we can come to an agreement on our own."

She looked down at us from the curtain rod suspended over her front window. "Your ex-wife is not here at the Inn. Your ex-wife will never be here at the Inn. I can't make myself any clearer than that, Chief MacKenzie."

"So you don't mind if I ask your staff a few questions."

"I mind very much."

"If you have nothing to hide, I don't see the problem."

"The problem is you aren't welcome here. Neither are your ex-wife or girlfriend."

"Oh, come on, Renate." I had finally heard enough to push me over the edge. "What's the big deal? I know you have a problem with humans, but isn't it in our mutual interest to find Karen so we can take her back to Boston?"

I might as well have been speaking Hindi. She fixed her beady little eyes on Luke.

"I like you," she said. "You're one of our favorite restaurant customers."

"You run a great place," Luke said. "I see why you have a four-star rating."

"I like you," she said again, "but not enough to make up for the fact you're human. If you want to talk to my staff, you'll need to do it through official channels or not at all."

Okay then.

"That went well," I said as the door slammed shut behind us. "I can't believe I used to like that woman." We started walking back toward town. "If she's not hiding something, I'll eat my entire stock of sock yarn."

"She's not hiding anything."

"Of course she's hiding something."

"I don't think so," Luke said. "I think she's telling the truth."

"What makes you think that?"

"Cop's intuition," he said. "Body language. Tone of voice. The whole package."

"You could see all of that with her the size of a budgie?"

"What can I tell you? I'm good at my job."

We stopped in at the bank, the pizza shop, Cut & Curl, and the sub shop.

Nobody knew anything.

Or if they did, they weren't telling.

We walked back to the yarn shop, where

eleven boxes of yarn waited by the front door.

"UPS must love you," Luke said as we dragged the boxes inside.

"You should see what it's like around here when the new fall yarns hit."

Which would have been the perfect spot for him to say something about how he couldn't wait to see either our great autumn yarns or foliage, but he didn't.

I pulled one of yesterday's tuna sandwiches out of the fridge and grabbed two bottles of water.

"What do you know about Isadora's last power grab?" he asked as I cleared a spot for us at the worktable.

"Just what Lilith said this morning. That was the first time I heard about it."

"Sorcha never said anything?"

"Not a word."

"There's something—" He stopped and shook his head. "Every time I get close to it, it fades away."

"What?" I asked. "A suspicion? A guess? An idea?"

"I don't know. Whatever it is, I can't grab hold of it fast enough."

I took a breath, then jumped into the deep end of the pool.

"Steffie's here for a reason, Luke. She wants to be here. Isadora's only capitalizing on something that was already in motion."

The mask started to slip into place.

"Don't go all cop on me. Listen to what I have to say."

His jaw was set in that familiar line but he nodded. "I'm listening."

"You were raised Catholic. You know about the spirit . . . the soul."

"They didn't teach us anything about Fae battles."

"Some people pass into the next dimension in peace and harmony, and once they leave this plane of existence, nothing can reach them. There isn't a medium on the planet who could find them and lure them back for a visit. If Steffie's spirit had completed her journey, Isadora wouldn't have been able to capture her."

"If that was Steffie we saw."

"After all that's happened, you still don't believe Steffie's—"

"I don't know what the hell I believe anymore."

What was wrong with him?

"You believe in giant anacondas, vampires, werewolves, mountain giants who can give you an aerial tour of the town, and a girlfriend who can turn you into a Ken Doll, but you can't bring yourself to believe your daughter's spirit needs you?" I took another deep, steadying breath. "Steffie wants to tell you something, and Isadora or no Isadora, she won't rest until she does."

He pushed aside his sandwich, stood up, then left the shop without another word.

And for the first time since this whole thing started, I began to wonder what would happen if I won the battle but still lost the war.

24

KAREN

"Welcome back," the friendly male voice said. "We've been waiting for you."

I opened my eyes, then closed them again. It looked the same either way.

"I can't see you," I said.

"You can't see anything. You're not supposed to." He had a warm, reassuring voice. I could tell he was on my side. I didn't have to be afraid.

"Am I dreaming?"

"You're fully conscious."

"Then I must be blind."

"Only to this dimension."

"I don't understand."

"You will," he said.

And then a small voice whispered, "Mommy?"

"Oh God . . . Steffie! Are you here, baby? Are you with me?"

She was close, so close. I reached out to touch her, but there was nothing except the smell of warm, clean, fresh air.

"Where are you, baby? Mommy's here. Take my hand!"

I felt a soft, warm rush of breath against my skin . . . so soft. My heart yearned for just one hug, one moment with her.

"Daddy?"

"He's not here with me, baby. What do you need? Tell me and I'll get it for you."

"She can't stay this time," the man with the kind voice said. "She has to go."

"No!" I reached out into the darkness. "Stay with me, Stef! Don't go!"

I woke up suddenly and completely. I felt refreshed, rejuvenated, and disappointed to see I was still at the Inn, still in the beautiful four-poster bed with the fancy quilts and blankets. The blinds were closed. A vanilla candle flickered softly on the nightstand.

And my daughter was nowhere around.

"Hello?" My voice sounded tentative, not at all like me. "Is anyone here?"

"You're awake." It was the same cordial male voice I'd heard in my dream. "I thought you'd sleep all day. Trying to cross dimensions usually wipes humans out."

"Who are you?" I sat up and glanced around. "*Where* are you?"

"Right here."

He was sitting on the foot of my bed and yet he wasn't. The bed didn't register his weight. I could see through him to the painting on the wall, but what I saw took my breath away. He was easily the most beautiful creature I had ever seen in my life. No movie star, no work of art, even came close. He glowed with a golden light that radiated off him in soft waves of energy that warmed my face.

"Are you a ghost? I couldn't see through the other ghosts."

"I'm not a ghost." He laughed but there

was no mockery in it. "I'm just not of your dimension."

"I know your voice. You were with my daughter in my dream." It was my turn to laugh softly. "Except it wasn't a dream, was it?"

"No," he said, "it wasn't."

"Where is Steffie? Why isn't she here with you?"

"Do you want the long answer or the short one?"

"Long," I said.

His smile dimmed and so did he. "For that, you'd have to ask my mother."

LUKE

The tiny library was swarming with kids. I was almost trampled by a quartet of second graders hell bent on creating as much destruction as they could in as little time as possible.

"It's Love Your Library Week," Lilith said with a shake of her head.

"Followed by Send a Librarian to Hawaii Week?" I said and she laughed.

"Speaking friend to friend, this probably

isn't a great time, Luke. If you need to concentrate, you should come back later."

"Clock's ticking," I reminded her. "I'm the oldest of five. I can handle noise."

"Tell me what you need and I'll try to find you a fairly quiet corner."

I told her what I was looking for. She nodded and grew quiet for a few moments. "We're not digitized," she said, "so you probably won't find anything on Google. Not to mention that most of what happens here stays here."

Like Vegas with a twist of magic.

"Do you have old Sugar Maple newspapers on microfiche?"

"We have the actual newspapers in the archive and daily logbooks kept by earlier town historians. You might find something there."

"You said you were around the last time Isadora made a move. What do you remember?"

"Not much." She glanced across the room at a pair of middle school girls who were giggling over a vampire book. "Chloe's mother was ready to deliver anytime. Her father worked at the hardware store with Paul but things weren't going well. Isadora was spending more time in this dimension because her boys and the Weaver kids were friends. She seemed to get angrier with every day that passed. She hated Chloe's father because he was human and she despised the fact that the next leader of the town would be a half-blooded human."

"And that's when Isadora made her move?"

"I guess she figured this was her best chance. Before Guinevere gave birth and the next generation of Hobbs was in place."

It sounded reasonable enough, but my gut said there was more.

"I have to lead story hour," Lilith said, "but let me think about this. Maybe there's something I'm missing."

She handed me the key to the archive, and I let myself into the long narrow room. Floor-to-ceiling bookshelves lined the walls, and each shelf was stocked two and three deep with newspapers, booklets, pamphlets, journals, photo albums, all in eerily mint condition and all clearly labeled by date. A computer with high-speed Internet access rested on a side table near a bank of filing cabinets.

I zeroed in on the six-month period surrounding Chloe's birth and stacked up the material on the mahogany worktable. I found a roll of parchmentlike substance stowed behind some of the annual journals, and I unfurled it across the table. It looked like it might be from the side of an old canoe, decorated with drawings burned into the surface. An eagle. A brilliant star. Indians in full dress. Trees. A waterfall. At least I think it was a waterfall. A fierce catlike creature was positioned over it, and lines like the rays of the sun radiated out from the centerpoint.

Interesting but it got me nowhere.

"Focus," I told myself. There wasn't time for anything else.

I was halfway through a long account of damage caused by spring flooding when my cell vibrated.

"Dawn Eckhard, *Vermont Country Daily*. What's the official explanation for the light show over Sugar Maple last night? I checked with NASA public relations and they said it was either Saturn orbiting closer to the earth or space junk flaming when it hit the atmosphere. I'd like your take on it."

"Nothing much else to tell, Ms. Eckhard."

"Damn," she said. "I was hoping for a UFO. We haven't had a good UFO sighting in years."

"Sorry to disappoint you."

She had an easygoing laugh. "Hey, I would have settled for another Saturn story if it got me a few extra column inches."

Another Saturn story? On another day I would have asked what she meant by that, but she had already launched into giving me her phone number and e-mail address and the moment passed.

I went back to searching the archive. Chloe's birth was heralded in the local paper. The town historian gave her arrival a full page, single-spaced, in the ledger. Her human father didn't merit a mention.

I fielded another phone call about Isadora's light show, wishing I could come up with a better explanation than space junk, but it was the best I could do.

Maybe that Saturn angle was our best excuse.

You've got to love Google. I typed in *Saturn* and the date, and the screen filled with hundreds of page options. I picked the first and scanned the contents. Ap-

parently two things were happening today. Every thirty years or so, Saturn
reached the point in its orbit when it was
closest to earth and easily visible to the
naked eye. At the same time the planet
was in direct opposition to the sun, making it glow noticeably brighter in the night
sky. UFO sightings usually rose accordingly.

Like any celestial event, it brought out
the sky watchers, the crazies, and the
hopeful.

I owed Dawn Eckhard a big thank-you.
Now I could blame Saturn for everything,
and science would back me up. The galaxy
was filled with all sorts of events, random
and regular. You could find an explanation
for just about anything if you wanted to.

But as I looked at the chart, the numbers started to form a pattern. Saturn swung
this close to earth approximately every
thirty years. Chloe was almost thirty years
old. The last time Isadora tried to pull Sugar
Maple through the mist was within seven
days of Chloe's birth.

I cross-referenced stats on Saturn's orbit with a date one week before she was

born. Not a match. I tried six days. No luck. Five was the lucky number.

I went back another thirty years. I cross-referenced Saturn with the same time period in Sugar Maple's history and found a small mention of earthquake activity near the center of town, followed by a spectacular thunderstorm.

I searched back sixty years, ninety, one hundred fifty, one hundred eighty, as far back as two hundred seventy years ago, and every single time I found references to unusual disturbances in and around Sugar Maple that tied in with the transit of Saturn, and they all spanned a narrow twenty-four- to thirty-six-hour period.

With the help of the archival records and the computer, I was able to roll it all the way back to the early eighteenth century when the Abenaki Indians were making room for the new settlers from Salem. You couldn't argue with the math.

Isadora had been working toward this since before Chloe was born. This wasn't an impulsive, emotional decision on her part. It was the well-thought-out, deliberate action of a powerful entity with single-minded intent.

To take back what belonged to her, no matter the cost to herself or Sugar Maple.

Or to my daughter.

We had been working on the classic witching hour deadline of midnight, but according to the charts, Saturn would reach the closest point in its transit at 10:42 P.M.

If Isadora was going to make a move, that was when it would happen.

Which meant we had less than seven hours to find Karen, save Sugar Maple, and free Steffie's soul.

25

CHLOE

At some point when I wasn't looking, knitting became trendy.

Don't get me wrong. I'm not complaining. *Trendy* meant lots of new knitters joining the fold, which meant a healthier bottom line for me.

I think it was the *New York Times* that called knitting the new Zen not long after 9/11 happened. I'm not sure I'd go that far (trust me, there is nothing Zen-like about a knitter who just realized she has to frog three months of work on an Orkney Pi shawl), but when I need to think deeply about something, I reach for a plain old cuff-down sock and start knitting.

Which was what I did the second Luke went out the door.

Too bad the thinking part didn't kick in as fast as the knitting part.

My mother taught me to knit when I was four or five years old. I had wanted to learn how to spin the way she did, but I was too little to sit at the wheel so she taught me to knit and purl instead. She figured there would be plenty of time later to teach me her other art.

"Your grandmother taught me," she said, "and her mother taught her, all the way back to Aerynn, and one day you'll teach your own daughter."

I wondered if Karen had taught Steffie how to knit. I imagined them sitting together in the MacKenzie kitchen on a snowy winter afternoon, happily working on a scarf for Luke while a pot of soup bubbled on the stove.

Yeah, I know. Most of my domestic fantasies were lifted straight off the Hallmark Channel and Nick at Nite. But it made me happy to think at least one little girl lived the life I'd longed for.

Except she hadn't. Steffie had barely lived at all. Six years in this dimension were barely a running start at a life. Six years with your parents weren't close to enough.

Maybe I was approaching this from the wrong angle. Isadora knew exactly what she was doing when she imposed her arbitrary deadline. Humans reacted strongly to countdown clocks. Even half-blooded humans like me. Our adrenaline pumped hard and fast and made us act on instinct instead of intellect. It made us make mistakes.

"Slow down," I said to the empty shop. "Think it through."

I had known Isadora all my life. Her son Gunnar had been my best friend. Our lives had threaded in and out over the years, and I still didn't know one single thing about how they lived or where they lived. Even Janice, who had gone beyond the mist many times to visit clients, didn't have a clue. That was how good the Fae were at covering their tracks. For millennia it had been a matter of survival.

All I knew for sure was that their powers emanated from some source beyond the mist and dissipated the longer they were away from that source. Isadora's eye-catching display last night had taken its toll on her powers, weakening her visibly toward the end. She was beyond the mist right now, gathering up whatever it was that gave her those powers.

Which meant I didn't necessarily have to be stronger than Isadora to win; I had to be smarter. I had to figure out a way to wear her down and drain her energies. If I could outlast her, I could outsmart her and steal back Steffie's spirit so the child could complete her journey.

Assuming that I knew the first thing about stealing back spirits.

Pretty much everything I knew about spirits had been gleaned from repeated viewings of *Ghost* and *Grey's Anatomy*. Janice had tried on more than one occasion to bring me up to speed, but I had my hands full with vampires, werewolves, selkies, witches, trolls, sprites, brownies, and the rest of my neighbors. I found myself wishing I'd paid more attention.

One thing I knew for sure about Isadora

was that she didn't delegate authority. She was your original hands-on bad guy, more than happy to do the dirty work herself. To be honest, I believed she liked it. Plucking a child's soul from the afterlife would be more fun than a week in the Bahamas in mid-February.

Holding the child's soul hostage? Priceless to someone like Isadora.

It was clear Isadora's powers had increased exponentially in the last few months. Even within the restrictions of banishment, she was able to reach into other dimensions and snag Steffie's spirit and hold it captive.

Each time she exploited another weak spot in the banishment, she came one step closer to breaking free without my help, and when that happened, we would be done for. That clock was ticking even more loudly than the one I had scaled a few hours ago.

I had no doubt that if Isadora were released from her own imprisonment, she would be able to pull Sugar Maple beyond the mist right now. She had the skills and the power necessary, and equally important, she had a score to settle and she didn't mind using a child's soul as the bargaining chip.

Which meant that wherever Isadora was right now, Steffie was close by.

But where?

I kept circling back to Snow Lake. Isadora showed a marked affinity for the place. Witness last night's command performance. Her sons, Gunnar and Dane, had also spent much of their time in our dimension out at Snow Lake. And come to think of it, the Weavers were always flitting about, either ice skating in the winter or boating in the summer.

It seemed as likely a spot as any.

Across the room, Penny the cat yawned, stretched, then hopped out of her basket and padded her way toward me, meowing loudly.

"You just ate," I chided her gently. "I thought we agreed to cut back on the Fancy Feast."

"When you cut back on Oreos and Ben & Jerry's," the cat shot back.

The last time Penny talked to me was just before the battle with Isadora and Gunnar back in December, and she hadn't mentioned my eating habits. Of course,

Penelope hadn't really been talking; she was just providing a gateway for Sorcha to visit this realm one last time.

My heart started to pound, and I placed the cat down on top of the worktable, where she sprawled across the waterfall tapestry I'd forgotten to pin back up on the wall.

"Okay," I said, heart pounding. "Who's in there?"

"Now you're hurting my feelings," the cat said, pausing her vigorous grooming. "I've only been gone a few months and you've forgotten all about me."

I felt like my heart stopped beating. *Please, please, Aerynn and all the other Hobbs women before me, let it be Gunnar.* "Gunnar? Is that really you?"

Penny looked up at me and her eyes shifted from their familiar golden hue to brilliant blue, and I threw back my head and laughed out loud.

Penny was a gateway companion, an old soul who had provided Sorcha, my surrogate mother, entry into this dimension just a few months ago. I waited for the cat to shapeshift into my beloved friend, but we just stared at each other.

"I've been trying to get your attention for

weeks, and you haven't picked up on it," he said. "What's up with that?"

I don't know about you, but I had trouble taking a talking cat seriously. "Shift over," I told him. "I can't stop thinking about litter boxes."

"This is the best I can do, kid. Let's enjoy it while it lasts."

It turned out he had been responsible for the odd occurrences around town recently. Flaming cat butts. The visible blue flame messages. Janice's verbal diarrhea the night of the séance. The bubble Karen suddenly found herself in. All Gunnar's handiwork.

"Please don't tell me you hurled that ball of flame at Luke and me."

"Give me some credit. I was trying to get your attention, not kill you."

"Oh God, Gunnar, I wish I could see you. Everything's changed. I don't know who my friends are anymore. Your mother has Luke's daughter's spirit trapped. His ex-wife has disappeared and I think someone's trying to erase her memory. The—"

"Don't worry," he said. "I know all about it. Karen's with me."

I felt my legs go out from under me, and I grabbed for the edge of the worktable.

"Put your head between your knees."

"Why don't you put your tail between your legs," I muttered as the room began to spin.

"She's not dead," he said, "if that's what you're worried about."

I sank to the floor in a pool of relief. "I wish you'd told me that first."

"You always did have an overactive imagination." I could almost see him smile. "Must be all those old movies you love."

I didn't want to cry but it was all too much. I was so filled with emotion it had no place to go but out through my tear ducts.

"Damn it," the cat who was Gunnar said. "You know I hate it when you do that."

"S-sorry," I sniffled. "It's just life has been so crazy. Down is up. Up is sideways. And I've been missing you so much."

"I thought you had the cop to take up the slack."

I cried even harder. "I don't think we're going to last."

"Then he's an asshole."

I started to laugh. "Gunnar . . ."

"A major asshole. If he doesn't have the balls to live with magick, then screw him. You can do better."

"I can't do better."

"The hell you can't.

"You saved his life. I thought you liked him."

"Hell, yeah, I like him, but not if he doesn't go the distance with you. I didn't cash in my chips so he could go back to Boston."

See what I mean? Gunnar always had my back. It was like he'd never left.

Except he had. He was dead. Or as close to dead as a Fae ever got, and he wasn't coming back to this dimension no matter how much I wished he could. Isadora could curse me to hell and beyond but I wasn't the one who had created the instruments of destruction that took her sons from her. Isadora had called those weapons into being to use against me, and she would pay the price for that act of vengeance into eternity, separated from her sons' spirits in every dimension. There may not always be justice in the world of humans but it was good to know the Universe would not be denied.

But how I wished Gunnar could have been spared.

Penny stretched out full length on top of the tapestry and looked up at me. Gold flecks were starting to appear in the blazing blue eyes.

"You're shedding all over my heirloom tapestry." I waited for his retort but there wasn't one. "Gunnar? Are you still here?"

Penny's eyes were swiftly returning to their normal color.

"Gunnar! Don't go!"

The gold in Penny's eyes receded and Gunnar's familiar blue returned.

It was like a bad cell phone connection. Any second the line could go dead.

"You said Karen was with you."

"Same room, different dimension."

I nodded as if I knew what that actually meant. "And she's okay?"

"For the moment. Good thing Midge doesn't know her butt from a hole in the ground. They're trying to erase Karen's memory of Sugar Maple, and so far all they've done is make Bettina's right eye twitch and give Verna hives."

I tried to wrap my brain around the fact that my friends had been plotting against me. I must have made a few pithy and unprintable comments because suddenly poor Penny was laughing so hard by proxy that she hacked up a Noro-sized hair ball.

"Calm down, Terminator," Gunnar said. "It's not what you think."

"Oh, so now you can read minds. That Fae afterlife must be some special place."

"They're trying to keep the peace."

It was my turn to laugh up a hair ball. "By kidnapping Luke's ex-wife and stealing her memories? Somebody call the UN. Sounds like ambassador material to me."

"They like things the way they are. They want to support you but the whole human thing is freaking them out. All they want is to keep the status quo, and the only way they can think of to do it is to send Karen back to Boston and maybe then they can pick up where they left off."

"I don't see the connection."

"She came to town and my mother went nuts. She leaves and my mother settles back down. And as a bonus, maybe Luke goes after her. It's win-win."

"Have they met your mother? Who in her right mind would ever believe Isadora would back away from a fight?"

"Solve the human problem and every-thing else will fall into place."

"Except it wouldn't," I said. "She's not giving up until she breaks through the ban-ishment."

"They haven't thought it through," he said with a shrug of cat shoulders.

"They should have," I snapped. "And what happens to Steffie if their idiotic plan succeeds? Are we supposed to just let her go?"

Another one of those long silences that made me crazy even when I wasn't talking to a cat.

"It's different for us," he said finally. "You die. We move on."

"Don't play the semantics game, Gun-nar. We've been friends too long."

"And don't kill the messenger," he shot back. "You wanted to know what was go-ing on and I told you."

"I'm not letting Steffie go."

"I didn't think you would."

"And they have to stop screwing with Karen's memory."

"Agreed."

"That's it?" I asked. "You tell me all of these terrible things are going on but you don't tell me how to stop them. You don't tell me where Karen is being held or where your mother lives or where she gets her power. The only thing I know for sure is that there is no way in hell I'm going to let your mother win."

"Good," he said. "Now let me show you how to fight her."

26

KAREN

They weren't trying to help me reach Steffie.

They were trying to brainwash me.

Literally wash away all my memories of
the last few days in Sugar Maple.

Which, considering the fact that I'd had a
car wreck, been thrown into the mud, found
myself trapped in a plastic bubble, flown
across town in a four-wheel drive, and had
a heart-to-heart with the world's hunkiest
ghost, was a whole lot of washing.

My spectral visitor promised me that

Midge and Bettina and the others didn't have the skill to manage brainwashing a flea, but they thought they did and I should play along.

"My daughter needs me," I told him, struggling to push back my bitter disappointment. "And I need to save her."

He said he understood but I wasn't sure he really did. I wasn't sure about much of anything. All I knew was that I was starting to feel like a bystander in my own life, unable to do anything more than watch as random fate made all the decisions for me.

I was a nurse. A trauma nurse, for God's sake. I had skills, important ones. I knew what to do in an emergency. I was the one you wanted on your side when things went bad. I was clearheaded, not prone to panic. At the hospital I had been the alpha in the pack, the one everyone else turned to for guidance.

And now here I was, curled up in the fetal position in a darkened room, in a strange house, while I waited for a ghost—a ghost!—to tell me what to do next.

I had believed Midge and Bettina and the others when they told me they would help me reach Steffie. I had opened my heart to them, allowed myself to be vulnerable in a way I hadn't since my baby died, and for what? For nothing. It had all been a lie, a trick to get my mind open so they could wipe away the last few days and protect their precious status quo.

Then again, how could I be sure that golden-haired ghost was telling the truth? I didn't even know his name. For all I knew, he was some kind of illusion meant to keep me docile, conjured up by the merry little band of paranormals who had brought me to the Inn in the first place.

I wasn't sure how long I'd been there, but judging by the light seeping through the closed blinds, it had to be at least a couple of hours. Where were Luke and Chloe? Why weren't they looking for me? Sugar Maple was the size of a good sneeze. How hard could it be to find a skinny, freckled, red-haired human in a town filled with magical movie stars and supermodels?

I heard footsteps moving along the hallway, and I closed my eyes and leaned back against the pillows.

"All she does is sleep," Midge complained as they paused outside my room. "Is that one of the side effects?"

"Do I look like a scientist?" the one named Verna said.

"This quibbling isn't doing us any good," Bettina said in a soothing tone. "We followed the instructions to the letter. There's no reason it shouldn't work. It just takes time."

The door squeaked open and they stepped inside. I willed myself to relax.

"She's such a teensy little thing," Midge said. "I want to take her home and give her a good meal."

"Pack her a lunch to go," Verna said. "All I want is for her to forget any of this ever happened."

Soft hands touched my forehead and cheeks, and I felt a deep sense of peace flood through my body, followed by a series of quick sharp stings over my left temple.

And then I felt nothing.

LUKE

The door to Sticks & Strings was wide-open. A half-empty cup of tea rested on the worktable next to one of Chloe's hundreds of socks-in-progress. I tossed my stack of handwritten notes and printouts on the table.

I didn't have a good feeling.

"Chloe!" I moved quickly toward the back of the store. "Are you in here?"

I flung open the door to the storeroom, looked behind six-foot-high stacks of boxes. This was one time when I was glad I didn't find anything.

"Chloe!" I shouted, louder this time.

I banged on the closed door to the bathroom. Again there was no answer. I didn't wait for an invitation. The door hit the wall and boomeranged back at me. No sign of Chloe.

I checked the alley behind the store. Everything was quiet.

Where the hell was she?

Penny the cat meowed loudly, then suddenly appeared in front of me, back arched, tail twitching. I don't know a whole lot about cats but that didn't seem like a good thing to me.

"What's wrong, Pen?" I bent down to scratch her behind the left ear but she backed away.

She emitted a series of noises that

almost sounded like human speech. Coupled with the fact that she and Chloe shared the same amazing golden eyes, the effect was unsettling.

Hell, it was more than unsettling. The hackles on the back of my neck stood up straight.

Maybe I was missing something. I looked under the table, in the storage closets. I broke into a cold sweat. I told myself that she had probably gone searching through the Book of Spells for some help finding Karen but I wasn't buying it.

I phoned Janice. She hadn't seen Chloe since this morning at Fully Caffeinated. Lynette said the same thing. I stepped out onto the sidewalk and scanned the street. No sign of her anywhere. No sign of anyone.

I unleashed a stream of curses as I stepped back inside the shop. Penny gave me a "stupid human" look, then leaped back into her basket of unspun yarn. Nothing like being shot down by a fat black cat in need of portion control.

I'd been a homicide detective for a long time. I'd been a cop even longer. And if there was one thing I knew, it was that no crime got solved without a hell of a lot of help from a hell of a lot of people. All those rookie cops and beat reporters and ordinary citizens who went out there and gathered up the puzzle pieces for the lead detective to put together into a whole that was definitely more impressive than the sum of its parts.

I'd found the mother of all puzzle pieces over there in the library, but without Chloe's input, I was still spinning my goddamn wheels. What good was it to know when something was going to happen if you didn't know where?

I looked down at the notes scattered across the worktable. Charts on Saturn's orbit. Timelines cross-referenced with anecdotal evidence of Fae attempts to co-opt the town.

"Damn," I muttered. That slice of decorated birch from some three-hundred-year-old canoe had gotten mixed in with my notes. I'd better get that back to Lilith ASAP before Penny decided to use it as a scratching post.

I wasn't a big fan of folk art, but there was

something eye-catching about the simple drawings. Something familiar. Representations of the sun, the moon, a waterfall.

I pushed the pages of notes aside and took a long look at the rug or whatever it was Janice had used as a table covering last night. Lots of trees and leaves. The sun and moon. The waterfall surrounded by craggy rocks and sharp-angled cliffs. A squiggle in the center of the waterfall pulled me closer. It looked like a variation on the symbol for infinity.

I spread the piece of canoe bark down next to it.

Lots of trees and leaves. The sun and moon. An eagle with wings outstretched.

And the infinity symbol in the same position at the center of the waterfall.

A rush of adrenaline hit my bloodstream hard.

Symbols were important in Sugar Maple. The Sticks & Strings logo was the symbol of a beautiful woman holding aloft a glowing sun. Chloe's parents' graves were marked by simple stones engraved with another glowing sun and a crescent moon. Isadora's son Dane had burned a star into the bark of an ancient sugar maple near Snow Lake to commemorate the murder of my friend Suzanne.

I shot over to the library and caught Lilith as she was getting ready to close for the day.

"I took this by mistake." I carefully smoothed out the piece of bark.

"Oh, Luke, thank you but that could have waited until tomorrow." She caught herself and winced. "I guess none of us knows what tomorrow will bring, do we?"

"I need your help again." I pointed to the infinity symbol at the center of the waterfall. "Chloe has a piece of needlework with the same symbol."

"Her tapestry." Lilith nodded. "I've seen it. If you look closely, you'll see the symbol for witches who fled Salem, were-clans— we're all represented."

I was fixated on just one thing. "That symbol in the waterfall. Does it have any significance?"

The answer was on the tlp of her tongue. "It's the symbol for New England Fae."

The adrenaline rush escalated. This was it. This was the puzzle piece I needed. Had Chloe already figured it out and was on her way there or had she found Karen?

I didn't know. Not knowing is hell to a cop. We want the solid, the real, the concrete. The only surprises we liked were the ones that came gift-wrapped at Christmas and birthdays.

The time for thinking was over.

It was time to act.

27

⁄

CHLOE

I'd lived in Sugar Maple all my life, but until Gunnar told me, I'd never heard a word about a series of tunnels that started near one of the logging roads south of town and terminated beneath the Inn. Apparently they had been used during the French and Indian War as a sanctuary for the native peoples and townspeople under siege.

Everything was exactly where he said it would be. I found the marker for the opening with no trouble and eased myself down the frayed rope ladder to the ground. The tunnel smelled like the dead groundhog

we found under my front porch last month
and the smell sent me racing for the other
end.

I hauled myself up another worn rope
ladder and popped up in the Weavers'
basement. My eyes had adjusted to the
pitch-black darkness of the tunnel so I was
quickly able to zero in on the shelves of
canned goods, jars of pickles and olives
and hot peppers, huge bins of flour and
sugar necessary to run a four-star restaurant.

Now the question was how to get from
the basement to the third floor, where
Karen was—I hoped—still locked in the
honeymoon suite. The Weavers and their
children assumed human dimension when
dealing with the outside world, but the rest
of the time they were pure Fae. I knew that
Renate and Colm had their own suite of
rooms under the windowsill in the parlor.
Their teenage daughters hid away beneath the first-floor staircase while the
married Weaver children and their families
maintained homes under floorboards, and
behind the dieffenbachia in the garden
room. And that didn't take into account the
enormous staff of itinerant Fae and house

sprites who kept the Inn running smoothly or the constantly changing parade of guest spirits who passed through on a daily basis.

Before I set out, I had armed myself with as many protective charms as I could conjure up, but I was still the pink elephant in the room. There was no way an almost-six-foot-tall half-human sorceress could blend in with the crowd.

Gunnar had promised he would help me if he could, but the forces of interdimensional communication were beyond our control. For the most part, I was on my own.

Fortunately I knew the layout of the Inn like the back of my hand. As a teenager I'd worked in the kitchen, the garden, and as an occasional chambermaid, which gave me a pretty thorough knowledge of how the enormous structure was laid out.

Unfortunately I also knew that the odds were against me.

The back staircase wasn't used half as much as the others. It went only as high as the second floor, but if I made it that far, just try and stop me.

I hugged the wall as I started up the first

flight with minimal squeakage. So far, so good. I rounded the bend and was halfway to the second floor landing when it happened.

"Chloe?" Paul Griggs, wielding a menacing-looking wrench, stepped out of the darkness. "What the hell are you doing here?"

KAREN

The golden-haired ghost had made me promise I would stay put until he came back or materialized or whatever it was ghosts did, but that was hours ago. Even Midge and Verna and Bettina had stopped popping in to monitor my lack of progress.

Most important of all, there were no more calls from Steffie.

I guess I'd been holding on to the hope that Chloe and Luke would come bursting through the door to tell me that the problem had been solved and Steffie's spirit was safely on its way to eternal happiness, but by the time darkness fell, I knew it wasn't going to happen.

I had to get out of there. Lying here on

this squishy mattress pretending to be communing with some New Age source of light was getting old. This was my problem too. Steffie was my daughter. She had reached out to me for help. I wasn't going to abandon her now.

There was a knock at the door and I leaped back onto the bed and closed my eyes. I heard the squeak as someone opened it a crack.

"Karen?" The male voice was unfamiliar.

I opened my eyes. He was tall, dark, and hairy. "Yes?"

He opened it wider and Chloe slipped inside. "I won't forget you for this, Paul," she said. "I owe you."

The door closed quietly behind him.

"He's Verna's husband," she said as we heard his footsteps recede down the hallway. "He was repairing the boiler in the basement."

"How did you find me?"

"It's a long story," she said. "Let's just say I had help."

"The ghost with the blond hair. He said he was going to find you."

"You *saw* Gunnar?"

"He didn't tell me his name."

She grabbed my hand. "How did he look? How did he get in here? Tell me everything you know."

"I blinked and he was sitting on the bed. I could see right through him but he was still the most gorgeous man I've ever seen in my life."

"That's Gunnar," she said and tears filled her eyes. "He was my best friend and he's the reason Luke is still alive."

"Is Luke here?" I asked.

She shook her head. "Just me."

"How are we going to get out of here?" I asked. "Can you magick us out?"

"The Weavers are a powerful Fae family. When it comes to security, they have this place rigged up pretty good. We'll have to go out the way I came in." She told me about the system of tunnels that ran beneath key points in Sugar Maple. "They're old and nobody thinks about them anymore. Lucky for us, the Weavers forgot to arm the entrance."

"Shh," I whispered. "Someone's coming."

Chloe ducked into the adjacent bathroom. I leaped back into bed as the door squeaked open and the usual suspects walked in.

"This should work," Bettina said. "I ran the probes over to the Falls to have them energized."

"Energized?" Midge sounded puzzled. "You mean like Lilith does with her crystals?"

"It's a Fae thing," Bettina said. "You wouldn't understand."

"You and your Falls," Verna said with a laugh in her voice. "It's just a big Shower Massage, honey. Nothing more."

I held my breath as Bettina's gentle hands inscribed tiny circles on my forehead, my temples, across my cheekbones. *Please don't work . . . Keep those energized crystals or probes or whatever they are away from me . . .*

I was about to slap Bettina's hands away when the bed started to shake and I had to force myself not to grip the edges of the mattress to keep from rolling off.

"Oh crap!" Midge said in her cartoon-girl voice.

"It's started." Verna sounded like the voice-over to a horror movie.

"Isadora," Bettina whispered. "She's flexing her muscles."

They were gone in an instant, hurrying

along the hallway, then clattering downstairs in their noisy clogs.

Chloe popped out of the bathroom, eyes wide. "What the hell was that?"

I sat up and tugged my clothes back into position. "It felt like an earthquake."

"We don't have earthquakes in northern Vermont."

"I think you just did."

We heard the sound of voices floating up from the street below. We took turns peeking through a crack in the blinds. Apparently everyone else in town thought it was an earthquake because villagers were pouring out of their houses and gathering across from the Inn.

"They're all out there," Chloe said, moving away from the window. "Let's go while we still can."

A surge of panic erupted in my chest. "That was an *earthquake*," I reminded her. "You want to run through a tunnel after an earthquake?"

"We don't have a choice."

She was right. We didn't.

She led me along the dimly lit hallway to the back staircase. It was narrow and steep and I had to concentrate to keep from breaking my neck. The twists and turns made my head spin.

"How many flights?" I asked, starting to breathe hard.

"Two more," she said. "Don't look down. It will only make you dizzy."

Outside, the crowd was growing louder. I was able to make out some of what they were talking about and I didn't like it.

"Isadora?" I asked Chloe as we rounded the landing and began to make our way down the flight of steps that led to the basement. "Do you think she caused the earthquake?"

"Most likely."

"That's crazy. You said her powers were limited."

She shot me a look over her shoulder. "They are. Imagine what she could do if we set her free."

The prospect was terrifying and went far beyond the Sugar Maple town limits.

"Now here's the really scary part," Chloe said when we finally reached the basement. "How do you feel about rope ladders?"

"About the same way I feel about the dentist."

She gave my hand a squeeze. "I knew I liked you."

Our eyes met and the insanity of the last few days vanished. For a second we were two women, both knitters, who probably could have become good friends if the circumstances had been different.

But they weren't, and right now I had a rope ladder with my name on it waiting for me.

28

CHLOE

We both made it down the shaky rope ladder with no trouble, then began moving
through the pitch-black tunnel toward the
opposite end. We gripped hands and that
connection with another person helped
keep my panic level from going over the
top.

"Claustrophobic?" she asked as the tunnel narrowed, then widened again.

"How did you guess?"

"Sweaty palms."

"Swell," I said. "Now you know all my secrets."

She laughed softly and I grinned into the darkness.

"I'm afraid of spiders," she said. "If a spider landed on me right now, I'd be able to tunnel up to the surface with my bare hands in three seconds flat."

I opened my mouth to speak but the deep rumbling freight train sound coming from the ground below our feet stopped me cold.

"Oh God," Karen said. "Not again."

Add fear of earthquakes to our list.

"Crouch down and cover your head." It was the only thing I could think of. "We'll ride it out."

I sounded so confident, so in control, that even I almost believed we would, but when you're afraid the ground beneath your feet was going to split apart like the Grand Canyon and take you with it, it was hard to believe in much of anything.

After what seemed like an eternity, the rumbling stopped and we cautiously stood up.

I carefully ran my fingers along the flimsy wooden supports overhead. "We'd better make a run for it," I said. "I'm not sure these supports can take another temblor."

"Great," Karen said. "Just when I thought we'd run out of things to worry about."

No such luck.

"Why aren't we moving?" she asked. "What's wrong?"

"Nothing," I lied. "It's just—" I cleared my throat. "I think we got ourselves turned around when we stopped."

"We're lost?" Her voice rose with each word. "We're in a tunnel. How can you get lost in a tunnel?"

Good question.

"I'd flip a coin," she said, "but it's too dark to tell if it's heads or tails."

Which for some strange reason struck us both as hysterically funny, and we laughed until we were hanging on to each other for support.

The laughter stopped the second the earth started to move.

"It's the third time," Karen said, her voice rising in agitation. "The *third* time!"

"I heard you the first time."

"We'd better run for the exit."

"We don't know which way the exit is."

"It doesn't matter. We'd be better off in the Inn than under it."

She had a point. We were in big trouble and there was only one way out.

"Hang on!" I yelled. "We're going for a ride."

I grabbed Karen's hand and tried hard to ignore the way the ground beneath us was swaying. "Clear your mind," I told her. "Focus on getting out of here in one piece."

"Not a problem," she said.

"Don't be scared," I warned her. "It might get a little bumpy."

"Okay," she said. "Anytime you're ready."

I didn't want to tell her that I'd been ready for at least two minutes and had invoked the spell that should have transported us to safety.

The ex was smart, though. She caught on.

"Are you sure you know what you're doing, Chloe?"

"Of course I do." I paused. "Theoretically I do." Oh crap. She might as well know the truth. "Actually I've never done this before."

"You mean you've never transported yourself out of an earthquake-rattled tunnel before, not that you've never transported anyone at all, right?"

The poor woman sounded so hopeful I hated to burst her bubble, but it wasn't like I hadn't done it before.

"I've transported other people—usually Luke and not deliberately—but this is the first time I've ever transported myself and not just myself but a second person along with me. It seems to take more power than I figured it would."

"Maybe you should talk to Bettina. She takes her crystals to some waterfall to charge them up."

I grabbed her arm and I swear I could suddenly see through the darkness. "What did you say?"

"Ouch. You're hurting me."

I didn't let go. "Tell me what you said again. Slowly. Word for word."

She did.

The waterfalls! Suddenly it all made sense. The legends. The air of mystery about the place. The sense of unease, dread almost, that I felt every time I went there. The mist that seemed to hover over everything.

Janice's talk about portals came rushing

back at me. The answer had been staring me in the face practically since the day I was born and I hadn't even suspected until now.

The irony that it had taken a full-blood human to point it out wasn't lost on me.

"When this is over," I said, grabbing Karen's hand one more time, "you can have your weight in cashmere and quiviut."

I centered myself, dove deep inside my consciousness, and suddenly we were moving through the earth like it was chocolate pudding, faster and faster with Karen next to me screaming. Or maybe I was screaming. I can't say for sure. I was too busy praying my newly impressive powers held on long enough to get us to the Falls in one piece.

The way I figured it, if we survived the landing, we had a good chance to survive whatever Isadora had in store for us.

If we were lucky.

LUKE

Without a flashlight, reading the signs carved into the trees was damn near impossible. The faint moonlight that filtered through the thicket of evergreens and budding maples was barely enough for me to see my hand in front of my face.

And those temblors weren't helping either. What next? Plague and pestilence?

I ended up following the sound and smell of rushing water, which ultimately led me to the Falls. The sheer magnitude of the cliffs surrounding the waterfall hit me like a kick to the gut. No wonder the Abenaki tribe had revered this as a sacred place. If someone had told me the ground I was standing on was the center of the earth, at that moment I would have believed it.

The roar of falling water filled my head. And there was something else, a low-pitched hum that moved along my nerve endings like an electrical current.

The portal to the world of the Fae was here. This was where Isadora recharged her powers.

This was where she was holding Steffie captive.

But where was Chloe? I was a good cop. Sometimes even a great cop. But I wasn't a fool. Without Chloe I was a dead man.

Come on, Chloe . . . Use your magic . . . The waterfall . . . I'm at the waterfall . . .

I heard a sound like breaking glass, a high-pitched yelp, and then something slammed into my back and sent me flying.

". . . ohmigodohmigodohmigod . . ." Karen was sprawled on top of me. Her entire body was shaking. "Am I dead?"

"No," I said as she climbed off me. "It just feels that way. Transport's a bitch on humans."

She stood up and tugged her sweater into place. "Where's Chloe?"

"I'm the one who should be asking you that."

"We were in the tunnel—"

"What tunnel?"

"The tunnel beneath the Inn and—"

"There's a tunnel beneath the Inn?"

"Luke, do you want to hear the story or don't you? We were in the tunnel when the earthquake started up again. Chloe grabbed my hand, told me to hang on, and the next thing I knew we were somersaulting our way through what seemed like one of those bouncy rooms they use at kids' birthday parties, and my hand slipped and—" She met my eyes. "I don't know what happened to Chloe."

"She's okay. She's probably on the other side of the waterfall and working her way over here now."

I believed it. I *had* to believe it. There was no way I wanted to live in this world or any other without Chloe Hobbs.

"Now what?" Karen asked as I stood up and brushed myself off.

"We wait," I said.

"How long?"

I looked at my watch. "Not long." It was almost nine o'clock. Witching hour when Saturn would pass closest to earth was ten forty-two. By ten forty-three it would be all over.

"I'd kill for a cigarette."

"I hear you."

She kept her eyes focused on the waterfall. "It wasn't just you."

I looked over at her but said nothing.

"Steffie had a mind of her own. She slipped out on me too, Luke."

I still said nothing.

"Once she got that bike, there was no stopping her. It could have happened on my watch."

"But it didn't."

"But it could have."

"Why are you telling me his now?"

She shrugged. "Because I can. I wanted you to hurt as much as I was hurting and that was the best weapon I had."

Our eyes met. "I was a lousy husband."

"You were," she agreed. "Good cop, lousy husband."

"I never screwed around on you."

"I know that." She patted my arm. "That might have been easier to understand."

"I'm sorry, Karen." I refused to drop my gaze. "Really sorry."

She nodded. "So am I."

We stood there in silence for what seemed like an hour. I looked at my watch again but only ten minutes had passed.

"She'll be here," Karen said.

"I know."

She lowered her voice. "I feel like we're being watched."

"We probably are."

"And you're okay with it?"

"I was," I said. "Not so much anymore."

"I don't think she'll ever leave here."

"This is her home."

"Is it yours?"

I was torn between telling her it wasn't any of her goddamn business and telling her I'd finally found the love of my life and was scared shitless I wouldn't be able to give her the happy ending she deserved.

But the sight of Chloe walking out of the woods toward us saved me.

In more ways than one.

29

CHLOE

It was like something from one of those sappy romantic movies I loved. I saw Luke. He saw me. I saw Karen too and was glad she had made it through her first transport in one piece but I'll be honest. At that moment only Luke mattered.

We started moving toward each other in slow motion until we were in each other's arms pledging eternal devotion.

At least that was the way it worked out in the movies. We weren't quite so lucky.

The second we reached each other, the

mist rising off the water turned oily and took on the scent of dying roses and lavender.

"Together again at last." Isadora's voice seemed to flow from the cliffs towering over us. "It's been too long."

I gestured for Luke and Karen to step back and let me be Isadora's focal point. I guess we were hoping my magick would act like a bulletproof vest and keep me safe.

"We're here for Steffie's spirit." No point beating around the bush.

"You're more direct than your mother," Isadora observed. "It must be your human blood speaking."

"Steffie's spirit," I repeated. "No negotiation. No compromise. Release her now."

"Free me from banishment," Isadora said, her voice spilling over the rocks like the rushing water. "Then I'll release the child."

"This isn't up for negotiation," I said again. "Release Steffie's spirit now."

"Free me and the child's spirit will be released." She turned her gaze to Karen. "Aren't you tired of the lies, Mrs. MacKenzie? Your daughter's soul or an insignificant town. It hardly seems difficult to decide."

Karen moved closer to me. Luke reached

for her arm, but she brushed him away with her hand.

"Why should I believe you'll free Steffie if I undo the banishment?" I asked Isadora.

"Because you have no other options."

I turned my back to the waterfall, a clear dismissal of her plea.

I was glad to see Luke's cop face had snapped into place. Karen looked vulnerable enough for all three of us, and like a heat-seeking missile, Isadora homed in on her.

"We're both mothers," she crooned. "We know how it feels to love a child. I wouldn't harm your baby's spirit any more than I would harm one of my sons."

Karen took another step forward. "Listen to her," she whispered in my ear. "I think she's telling the truth."

"She's a liar," I whispered back. "She'll say anything to bring you over to her side."

"I don't care about taking sides. I only care about Steffie."

"Karen." Luke's voice was low in warning. "Chloe knows what she's doing."

Did I? I hoped he was right.

I turned back toward the waterfall and

stifled a gasp. Steffie was looking out at us from behind a curtain of water.

It was more than Karen could bear. She called out, "Mommy's here, sweetheart. Everything's going to be fine," then started rushing toward her daughter.

"No!" Steffie screamed. "No!"

Luke and I saw the lightning bolt at the same time she did. Before I could react, Luke hurtled himself through the air, tackled Karen, and knocked her to the ground. The lightning bolt careened off his back, then disappeared.

"What the hell is wrong with you?" I screamed at Isadora. "I'm the one you hate. She's done nothing to you."

"Still standing up for your human blood," Isadora said with an amused smile. "Loyalty is an admirable trait, no matter how misplaced. If more of your kind had felt that way, perhaps there would have been hope."

Luke, looking more angry than hurt, picked himself up from the ground. The back of his sweater had a large tear and some scary scorch marks but somehow he had managed to avoid major injury. He held out a hand to Karen and she struggled to her feet, looking dazed and more than a little confused.

What was wrong with me? I felt like I was working my way through cold oatmeal. Why hadn't I thrown a protective shield over them the second I joined them? I quickly remedied that omission but my own inadequacy stung badly. Was I ever going to get this whole sorcerer thing right?

I have to admit I felt no remorse as I unleashed a barrage of fiery daggers in Isadora's direction. My aim was dead-on but bounced off the banishment spell and headed back toward us.

"Look out!" I screamed as the daggers flew past us before burning themselves out.

"What the hell?" Luke met my eyes. "They bounced right off her."

I didn't have time to explain the physics behind banishment spells. Isadora had managed to create openings from the inside that enabled her to reach out and wreak havoc in my dimension. I needed to find those openings and return the favor.

Unfortunately there was only one way I could do that and the idea scared the hell out of me. I needed to remove the banishment long enough to expose both Isadora and Sugar Maple.

Then I had to make sure I was the one who fired the first shot.

Luke's cop face was still in place, but pain was clearly visible around his mouth and in his eyes. Lightning bolts weren't any fun. Not even when they just side-swiped you. I was reminded again of the basic fragility of the human body, and the knowledge terrified me.

Karen was a lot tougher than her tiny frame suggested, but seeing her daughter had turned Karen's judgment inside out. "You had no right to stop me," she screamed at Luke. "I could have rescued Steffie."

"He saved your life," I snapped. "You should be thanking him. That lightning bolt Isadora threw would've split you in two."

"You don't understand. That's my baby we're talking about. I have to—"

"Mommy?" Steffie's voice seemed to fill the air. "Mommy!"

"Don't react, Karen," Luke warned her. "Isadora's trying to bait you. You don't know what you're up against—"

"Listen to me, Mrs. MacKenzie." Isadora rose up from the water and floated ten feet above the surface. "I'm the only one who understands."

"Isadora will say anything," I whispered to Karen. "She knows how to push your buttons. Don't let her know she's upsetting you."

"My freedom for your child's freedom," Isadora said. "It seems a fair exchange. You wouldn't want to lose her a second time, would you?"

This time Isadora went too far.

"Why are you doing this?" The words seemed to rip from Karen's throat. "What kind of sick, twisted woman are you?"

"Silence!" The word literally spooled out from Isadora's mouth, whipped around, then threw Karen to the ground. "I'm bored with human games." I could feel the heat rise as she turned her focus to me. "Undo the banishment now or suffer the consequences."

Apparently she'd swiped her syntax from bad costume dramas on Turner Movie Channel.

My mind was racing full-speed. My options were limited. I knew there would be no second chance to get it right.

"I'll do it." I ignored the shock in Luke's

eyes. I was feeling a little shell-shocked myself.

"I'm waiting," Isadora said.

"I'm still new at this. I need time. I wove multiple spells around you, Isadora, and they need to be unwoven in order."

"Three minutes," she said. "Not a second more."

"What the hell are you thinking?" Luke demanded as I turned toward him. "She's not going to release Steffie. The second you release her, it's over for us."

I inscribed a circle of protection around us, then quickly explained the problem. "As long as the banishment's in place, she can't be hurt by anything I throw at her."

"I'm not following."

"She thinks I'm giving up, but what I'm really doing is creating an opportunity."

I waited while it sank in. "You're taking a hell of a chance," he said finally.

"What choice do I have? The banishment protects her from anything I might send her way. Right now Isadora holds all the cards."

"Maybe not."

He quickly sketched out what he'd uncovered at the library. Something about

Saturn and its orbit and other things I'd never even heard about, much less considered. So the ticking clock was counting down the minutes for Isadora's chances too. If we could keep Sugar Maple safe until ten forty-three, we'd be safe for another thirty years.

"One minute," Isadora announced.

"Hurry," Karen urged, sounding desperate. "Please hurry!" "Thirty seconds," Isadora called out.

"Another minute," I pleaded. *Saturn . . . orbits . . . Saturn . . . orbits . . .* There was something else there, something important that was dangling just beyond my reach.

Isadora's laughter rang out across the clearing. "Do you actually believe I don't know what you're doing?"

The hiss began as a gentle sibilance, an almost subliminal promise of things to come. And then, at the moment I became aware of it, the hissing grew louder and I realized it was the sound of a dark purple gaseous substance slowly filling the air around us.

"What the hell?" Luke edged in front of me.

"Oh God." Karen groaned. "Not again."

The heavy purple gas was coalescing over the boulders at the base of the falls, drifting slowly into a long shape that reminded me of a felled tree or light pole or—

"Shit," Luke muttered. "What the hell is she doing with a battering ram?"

On cue, the battering ram upended itself, sailed fifty feet or higher above the highest treetop, then slammed into the earth, sending Luke, Karen, and me flying like crumpled pieces of newspaper.

Luke knew how to brace his body against impact but poor Karen hit the ground hard. She lay there gasping for breath, and for a moment I was afraid she wasn't going to get up at all.

It was time to make my move.

"That's it," I said. "I can't deal with this anymore." I pulled myself to my feet and looked up at Isadora, who seemed to fill the horizon with her presence. "You're right. I was trying to find a way out but there isn't one. I'll reverse the banishment."

"You'll do it now."

"Yes," I said, suitably chastened. "The reversal is in three parts. The banishment spells will reverse from last to first."

"You're making a mistake," Luke said. "Don't do it."

"It's the right thing, Chloe," Karen urged. "I'll be in your debt forever."

Shut up . . . shut up . . . shut up.

I couldn't listen to them. I couldn't listen to anything but my own instincts. Once the banishment spells fell away, I would have minutes, maybe only seconds, to strike, and this time I couldn't miss.

Her powers were awe-inspiring. I could see why her place among the Fae was supreme. If I hesitated for an instant, I would lose. The moment she entered our dimension, I had to be ready to summon up everything I'd learned from the Book of Spells and Sorcha and Janice and Lynette and Luke and everyone else who was important in my life, and turn it against Isadora before she took me out.

Because that was where this was leading. I wasn't just fighting for Sugar Maple anymore.

I was fighting for my life.

30

e

KAREN

I couldn't believe it was finally happening. I wanted to shout with joy. After all the talk about her responsibility to the township, the debt she owed the villagers, Chloe had come down on the side of freeing Isadora and saving my daughter.

I watched as she closed her eyes and started chanting. It was a combination of English and a language I'd never heard before, a strange rhythmic string of words that seemed to float in the air in front of me. I couldn't actually see them, but I swear to you I could feel their presence.

Luke was standing stock-still to Chloe's right. He was wearing jeans and a sweater Chloe had knitted for him, but he might as well have been her knight in shining armor. It was clear he would lay down his life for her, and I felt a twinge of jealousy. We had loved each other but not with that kind of "across time" passion. I wasn't sure I would have known what to do with it if we had.

Maybe we hadn't really gone wrong. Maybe this was the destiny he had been searching for all his life, and I was surprised to discover I was honestly happy he had found it.

My last gasp of bitterness evaporated on the cool spring air, and I felt happy for the first time in years.

Luke was motionless. Chloe's lips barely moved as she continued the chanting. The vision of Isadora—or illusion or manifestation or whatever term you want to use— still blanketed the horizon. My Steffie still looked out at us from her prison within the waterfall.

And me? I was barely breathing.

It seemed too good to be true. Chloe had been so adamant about her position. This sudden change of heart seemed out of character for her. But then, when you see the man you love struck down by a bolt of magic lightning, a woman might change her mind.

I wanted magic powers of my own so I could push time forward to the moment when my little girl's spirit would be freed and I could tell her what was in my heart. I longed to touch her, to brush her hair, to inhale the smell of her skin right after her bath, to listen to her laugh, to watch her grow up into a beautiful young woman, to be there when she fell in love and started a family of her own.

I knew it could never happen. I knew it was only a dream. But my heart, my soul, yearned for my child, and that yearning made it hard to pull breath into my lungs.

I'd heard all the warnings. Stay back. Let Chloe do her thing, whatever exactly that meant. Don't draw Isadora's attention. Remember it was all illusion, that none of this was real. The Isadora I saw was nothing more than special effects from a Hollywood movie. Even Steffie's spirit was only random particles of memory and dreams reconstructed for our human eyes.

What was most real in this world (or any other, I suspected) remained invisible.

"That's it," Chloe announced. "The banishment should be gone."

"What happens next?" Luke asked.

"I don't know," she said. "I've never done this before."

At first nothing changed. We stood there at the edge of the pool of water created by the Falls and we waited. Would there be fireworks? An explosion? Shooting stars zooming through the night sky? This was Sugar Maple, where even I knew anything was possible.

I could feel the tension coiled in both Chloe's and Luke's bodies. For me it was more anticipation. Strangely my fear of Isadora and her dark powers had vanished, and in its place was nothing but gratitude to Chloe for making this happen.

I wasn't crazy or any of the other things people had whispered behind my back. I was just a mother who loved her daughter more than life. There was an explanation for the phone calls, the dreams, the visions.

Steffie *had* been trying to contact me. She did have a quest to complete. She needed our help, and this time we had managed to be there for her.

"She's disappearing," I said, pointing toward the waterfall. "Both of them are!"

Isadora no longer filled the sky. She was shrinking, narrowing, growing smaller and smaller until she was nothing more than a point of light that flickered, then went out, taking Steffie with her.

"No!" The scream ripped my throat. "Steffie, no!"

"Over there," Luke said, pointing to an outcropping of rock on the western side of the Falls. "It's happening."

The center rock began to glow, first silver, then golden, then a rich, deep royal purple that seemed almost iridescent. A narrow band of pure white light bisected it vertically, then widened into a child-sized opening, then lengthened into an entrance fit for a Fae warrior.

As breathtaking as Isadora had seemed to me before, the sight of her in the flesh as she stepped from her world to ours was overwhelming. Her beauty was like another presence in the room. It wiped out everything else and made it impossible for me to glance away.

This was the creature that held my daughter's eternity in her graceful hands. I had to keep reminding myself that she was the personification of evil, not Mother Teresa in an embroidered velvet cloak.

"You're a woman of your word," Isadora said, nodding in Chloe's direction.

"Now it's your turn," Chloe said. "Release the child's spirit."

Isadora lifted her arms and instantly Steffie reappeared, floating above the jagged rocks.

"Release her," Chloe said in a calm and even tone of voice.

Isadora's teeth gleamed in the glittering light like the finest pearls but she said nothing.

"Now, Isadora." Who would've guessed there was steel in the supermodel? But it was there. I could see it.

Isadora's smile didn't waver. She raised her arms above her head and moved them in a circular motion, and as she did, the bottom of the cage dropped out and went spiraling down into the pool of water below. Steffie screamed and grabbed the edge of the enclosure just before it slipped beyond her reach. I knew those soft baby hands couldn't hang on for long.

"A terrible fate for a child," Isadora said with a delighted laugh as Steffie swung in space like a rag doll. "And it will only get worse."

Just in case we didn't understand, Isadora made sure that scenes of horror and cruelty beyond imagination flashed in front of us. Steffie screaming as she fell through space . . . Steffie's body slamming against the jagged rocks . . . over and over until I thought I was going to go crazy with rage and despair.

Isadora should have known there was a lion in every mother and that night the lion in me was ready to break free. Maybe it was adrenaline. Maybe it was a kind of magic born of love. I don't know. All I knew was that nothing short of death would stop me from saving my baby from the hell that bitch had in store for her.

31

CHLOE

Karen cried out and I grabbed her wrist and held tight. Her love for her daughter was blinding her to the very real danger we were all in.

Not that I was doing any better. I was drowning in Steffie's fear and loneliness, drowning in Luke's rage and Karen's terror. My human bloodline registered everything they were feeling and multiplied it tenfold.

I had to block them out, pretend they

didn't exist, that nothing existed but Isadora and the need to stop her once and for all.

I had been close, so close, to figuring out the last part of the banishment equation, but now my brain was nothing but a jumbled mass of neurons and impulses.

Magick was still new to me. I didn't know how to turn my back on almost thirty years of being human. I had lived my entire life as a mortal woman, and letting my past drop away from me felt like my heart was being ripped from my chest. A heart that right now was too filled with emotion for my own good.

I glanced at Luke's watch. Five minutes from now Saturn would swing close to Earth and the portal between dimensions would open wide enough to allow an entire town to slip through. Six minutes from now Saturn would begin to move away and I could breathe easy for another thirty years.

It was time.

I took a step forward and that must have triggered some Fae warning system because suddenly a pair of strong hands encircled my throat, slender fingers pressing hard but not too hard against my windpipe, just enough to choke off most of my air. I was lifted off my feet and whipped side to side like a rabbit in the jaws of a wolf, and I was having trouble remembering my name, much less any of the dozen banishment spells I knew like the back of my hand.

Luke sprang into motion and there was nothing I could do to stop him. Isadora removed one of her hands from my throat for a second and flung her arm against Luke, a careless gesture that sent him hurtling into the moss-covered rocks halfway up the hill.

I saw him clearly in my mind's eye. I heard the crack of his ribs breaking. I felt his pain as he lost his grip on the slick mossy rock and shot down the Falls into the pool below.

And then I was the one who was falling into a mocking darkness, fully aware yet powerless. It seemed like the story of my life.

Was this the way I was going to end my time in this dimension? Strangled to death by a powerful Fae leader who thought so little of my abilities that she didn't bother to use her magick against me? What pathetic star had I been born under? What once-in-a-lifetime conjunction of planets had—

That was it. The transit of planets. The birth of stars. Those mighty astronomical and astrological forces that changed worlds and shaped lives. The Fae understood the importance of those celestial patterns. They got the deeper meaning only a handful of humans had ever understood.

Suddenly I knew exactly what I had to do, and I had Luke to thank.

It had taken the very human man I loved to make me see what had been in front of my eyes all this time.

I could link a hundred banishment spells together but they wouldn't be able to contain Isadora permanently. They were temporary fixes, nothing more. But the stars and the planets were forever. The Fae understood that. I needed to link my strongest banishment spell with an astronomical event in the vastly distant future that was so devastating it would wipe the cosmic slate clean.

Isadora loosened her grip for a second and oxygen flooded my screaming lungs and swept clarity in with it.

My heart pounded in my ears. Pulse points in my wrists and throat throbbed as adrenaline pushed blood through my veins and the answer swam into focus.

The death of the sun.

This would give us a few billion years to figure out a way to live together in harmony.

The way I saw it, we would need every single one.

Right now Isadora was toying with me but that wouldn't last much longer. I had to put the final banishment in motion before she tired of the game and finished the job.

I wished I'd paid more attention to the old *Kung Fu* reruns on Nick at Nite. There were probably any number of nifty moves that would break a choke hold and look great in the replay.

But never underestimate the power of passive resistance. It wasn't flashy but it worked.

I went limp. The surprise of one hundred fifteen pounds of sagging deadweight knocked Isadora off balance and sent us crashing to the ground.

"A small triumph," she said, looking up at me. "Enjoy it while you can."

The human-sized portal in the waterfall

was expanding, growing wider and taller with every second.

"It's over," she said. "In the name of my ancestors, I claim final victory."

I scrambled to my feet and started the chant, calling upon my own ancestors and every force for goodness that had ever walked the earth and all its dimensions.

Her laughter rang out. "This is absurd."

". . . fortress against evil . . ."

"You're a child. Your powers are insignificant."

". . . unbreakable . . . inviolable . . ."

"Nothing but words. You know I'll find my way out."

". . . through time and space until the sun—"

"Stop!" Isadora commanded. "Stop talking!"

". . . moves from red giant to white dwarf . . ."

"No!" Her cry made the earth tremble. *"Noo!"*

". . . to blackness and all life follows."

Our eyes locked. The air between us shimmered with heat. I was aware of Luke and Karen standing a few feet away and wondered if they felt the same pulsing of energy coming off the Fae ruler. Did they have any idea of the magnitude of what was happening here?

I had attained the unattainable: I had beaten Isadora at her own game. My reputation as a sorcerer, as the rightful heir to all that Aerynn had built, had been made tonight. I was euphoric and I didn't try to hide that from the Fae leader.

"There are many ways to win, Chloe," Isadora said as she began to fade. "Remember that after I'm gone."

I laughed out loud. She was finished here. I didn't need any of her lofty pronouncements meant to strike terror in my half-human heart. I had evolved past that. I was a leader now.

I heard the choking sound of sobs from Karen and looked at her with confusion. We were barreling toward an unexpectedly happy ending. Isadora was about to disappear, Sugar Maple hadn't been pulled beyond the mist, Steffie would be free, and we were all still standing.

I followed Karen's gaze and saw Steffie still imprisoned, still terrified, still alone.

I had misplayed my hand, trusted someone who was inherently untrustworthy.

Only the rankest novice, the most self-obsessed fool of a sorcerer-in-training, would ever have made a mistake like this, and now Steffie's spirit would pay the price.

"You lied," Karen said to Isadora, her voice filled with inexpressible pain. "You said you would release my daughter but you lied."

"A small oversight," Isadora said with a cold smile. She was little more than a shadow now. "It could have happened to anyone."

Karen gave her a pitying look. "I can't believe Gunnar is your son. He's good and kind and decent."

Stop while you're still ahead, Karen. This isn't going to end well.

Isadora was little more than an afterglow, but she had one final trick up her sleeve. A high-pitched wail sounded in the distance. We glanced around but saw nothing. It sounded again and I found myself wishing there were some place to hide. It was the sound of evil unleashed.

The sound grew closer, then suddenly the sky lit up and fire-breathing winged creatures with bloodred eyes and claws like grappling hooks appeared over the horizon. Their hide was plated like the hide of a rhino, and it glistened iridescent blue in the moonlight. Still screaming, they swooped in on Steffie, nudging her with their flat and fiery snouts, tearing at her white dress with their claws, tossing her around like a soccer ball while she screamed for her mother.

With a guttural cry, Luke launched himself in Steffie's direction but his injured ribs brought him to his knees.

Karen ducked around him and took off full speed toward her daughter. Her fate and her daughter's were inextricably linked and always had been. She was where she was meant to be. This was her moment.

Protect them, Aerynn, I beseeched my ancestor. *See them to safety in the name of all mothers and daughters.*

Steffie's spirit was falling fast. Karen gathered speed, and just when she was about to hurl herself into space in an attempt to somehow save her child from eternal agony, a jagged bolt of lightning pierced the sky and headed straight for her.

She was gone, vaporized before the image reached our retinas. Only Steffie, eternally tortured, remained. Falling and falling—

"Look!" Luke's voice was hoarse with emotion as he pointed toward the spot where Karen had been struck.

A shadowy human form appeared, lingered for a moment, then rose into the spring night, moving slowly toward Steffie.

"It's Karen," I said. "Her spirit is—" I couldn't speak over the huge lump in my throat.

Steffie stopped her endless tumble into darkness. "Mommy?" she whispered as a joyous smile lit up her face. That one word held everything that was good about the world, everything that we could ever hope to be.

Luke and I clasped hands, holding tightly to each other, as Karen opened her arms and Steffie ran into her embrace. The familiar silver and gold fireworks melted into the night. I would have given almost anything to share a moment like that with my own mother, but that wasn't my destiny. Helping Karen and Steffie find each other again ran a pretty close second.

Steffie met Luke's eyes over her mother's shoulder and she smiled at him, the smile of a little girl whose world was exactly the way it should be. The guilt and sorrow he had carried around for so long melted away like the spring thaw.

I pressed my face against his warm, strong shoulder and started to cry.

You always were a sucker for a happy ending.

"Gunnar?"

"What?" Luke asked.

He can't hear me. Only you can.

"You did this, didn't you? You brought them together."

"Who are you talking to?" Luke asked.

We're confusing him. He's still only human, Chloe. Be kind.

"Why did you do it?" I asked Gunnar.

Forever is a long time, Hobbs. Those two deserved better than they got.

"Things are going to be great now. You'll see. Sugar Maple's problems are a thing of the past. Maybe you could—"

He was there for an instant. Or at least I thought he was. Maybe it was only that I missed my old friend so much that I conjured him up, but it was so wonderful to see his face again that—

"Gunnar?" Luke said. "What the hell?"

"You saw him too?"

"Over there," he said, pointing toward Steffie and Karen. "He's with Karen and Steffie."

I caught a glimpse of them as mist rose up from the pool at the base of the waterfall, rising higher and higher until it enveloped all three of them in a thick cloud, then evaporated, leaving behind nothing but the faint shimmer of Gunnar's silvery-blue glitterprint.

"Don't worry," I said to Luke through happy tears. "They're going to be all right."

32

LUKE

"It looks like nothing happened," Chloe said as we gazed out at the waterfall by moonlight. "Everything is just the way it was before."

The portal to beyond the mist was gone. Isadora was finally banished for good. Karen had found peace at last with our daughter, and unless I missed my guess, Gunnar would be watching over them the same way he watched over Chloe. The Falls, the pool of water beneath it, the trees surrounding it, they all looked the same as they had before.

But I knew that was another illusion because nothing would ever be the same again.

Including Chloe and me.

She had claimed her place in the world tonight, and now I had to do the same.

I sucked in as much air as the cracked ribs would allow and swung for the stands.

"A couple nights ago you asked me a question."

Next to me, she went very still. "About staying on as chief."

"And I didn't answer you."

"I remember."

"I want to answer you now."

She let go of my hand and wrapped her arms around her chest. "I think I know the answer."

"I don't think you do."

She turned slightly and met my eyes. "The last couple of days have pretty much been hell."

"No argument here."

"So don't say it. Tomorrow you can tell me but not tonight."

"My answer won't change."

"I know," she whispered. "Just give us tonight, Luke."

"I'm staying."

"What did you say?"

"I said I'm staying."

Her beautiful golden eyes widened in surprise. "Are you crazy? After everything that happened?"

"You're here," I said. "That's all I need to know."

"Your family," she said as a loopy smile lit up her face. "Boston. Your friends. Our life will be here, Luke. This is my destiny."

"Trying to change my mind?"

"Trying to make sure you understand what you're saying."

"I understood it the first time you turned me into a Ken Doll." I tried to pull her into my arms, but the broken ribs had other ideas. We settled for linking hands. "We'll have a lifetime to figure it out."

Sometimes the future is so clear, so obvious, that you wonder why it took you so long to see what had been in front of your face all along. I belonged here. Maybe not in the same way Chloe and the rest of the villagers did, but this was where I was meant to be. One day they'll understand. I'll still be here when they do.

There were no fireworks overhead. I didn't get down on one knee and offer up a sparkling diamond. We were both battered, bruised, broken in ways big and small, muddy and exhausted, but none of it mattered. This was where we had been headed since I first saw her through the window of the old church and fell in love with a knitter who just happened to be a sorceress-in-training.

Sometimes even a cop had to quit asking why and just roll with it. All the logic in the world, all the reasons why this could never work, none of it mattered. Logic didn't stand a chance against that feeling deep inside your heart every time you thought of her.

When that happily-ever-after ending comes knocking at your door, you answer. It was that simple.

Someday your grandkids will thank you for it.

EPILOGUE

Chloe

Did you ever have the feeling you were exactly where you were meant to be? I'd lost that feeling for a while, but now it was back and the future seemed ours for the taking.

I'd knitted my boyfriend a sweater and we'd lived to love another day. If that wasn't magick, I didn't know what was.

"I think I can repair the damage to your sweater," I said as we slowly followed the path away from the waterfall.

"Or you could knit me another one."

"There's an idea," I said. I'd knit him a thousand sweaters, each with a strand of my hair knitted in if it meant we'd be together forever.

I didn't have the energy left to transport us back to town and Luke didn't have the strength to withstand it. I worked a little magick along his rib cage to dull the pain but I wasn't a healer. We would need Lilith for that and maybe one of Janice's tisanes to help him sleep.

There would be problems ahead. We were still a divided town. But at least now we would have the luxury of time to work out our differences. Despite all that had happened these last few days, I felt happier and more hopeful about the future than I ever had before.

Isadora knew me well. She knew where I was weakest. She understood in her own way the loneliness I'd carried with me all my life.

She had found the best way to break me but she hadn't counted on love.

She hadn't counted on Luke.

And I guess up until tonight, neither had I.

But he was still here, still standing next

to me, still willing to stand up to whatever forces were unleashed against us.

"We'll get through this," he said and I nodded my head, unable to speak over the rush of love inside my chest. "You'll win the town back to your side. You're not alone anymore."

He reached for my hand across the darkness, and I held on tight as we stepped into the clearing near the cemetery.

"I can't wait to get home," I said, looking over my shoulder at Luke. "We'll get you cleaned up. I'll make us a big breakfast and then—"

He stopped and the expression in his eyes almost made my knees buckle.

"You're hurt," I said, my heart pounding. "Don't go all guy on me and start pretending everything's okay. Sit down on that bench over there and—"

"Chloe." It was there in his voice, his eyes, the way he reached for my hand across the darkness and I knew before I turned around that Isadora had the last laugh after all.

Sugar Maple was gone.

AUTHOR'S NOTE

There are many reasons why I wish I could talk to my mother one more time. Every day I find myself wishing I could pick up the phone and share some silly piece of gossip or get her take on what's happening in this fractured world of ours. Lately, however, I've been wishing I could sit down with her and talk about The Argyle Sock.

I found the sock in her tiny sewing basket a few months after she died. The sock is perfect. I remember sitting on the edge of the bed and peering at the stitches through my tears. The construction of it was beyond me. All of those tiny stitches.

Those toothpick-tiny double points. Little bobbins of thread-thin yarn. And the instruction booklet circa 1952! What treasures. The sock represented magic to me. A home kind of magic, which is really the only kind that's important.

Why hadn't I ever asked her to teach me how to use double points? Why did she drop sock knitting? My father was just a few weeks away from his own end at that point, and all he could remember was that he loved the homemade socks and wore out pair after pair of argyles. He seemed to remember commenting that the spots where she darned the heels gave him blisters and she tossed a ball of yarn in his general direction and quit sock knitting then and there.

It wasn't until I ventured back into knitting in August 2003 that I began to look at The Argyle Sock with a critical—and more knowledgeable—eye. The cuff and leg were done flat! Who knew? The red diagonal line was duplicate stitch! How did I miss that the first time around? The rest is clearly circular knitting. What even stitches she created. I couldn't find a slip or mistake anywhere.

I always was awed by my mother's knitting, both her approach to it and the finished results. She wasn't a slave to patterns. If an improvement or design change occurred to her, she gave it a shot. If it didn't work, she ripped it out and started all over again. No angst. No fears. (Meaning, not at all like her hyper daughter who lived in fear of public knitting humiliation.) I remember most clearly the gorgeous Aran fisherman's cardigan she made for me when I was maybe nine or ten. It took her all summer and was ready to wear on the first day of school. I loved it so much I wore it despite the 80-degree weather that day! A big gorgeous ivory-colored sweater with front patch pockets and bone buttons. I loved it more than any other article of clothing before or since and even incorporated it into some of my books along the way. (I guess that was my way of holding on to it even though it's long gone.)

The funny thing is I'm not sure I ever told her, really told her, how much I loved that sweater she made for me. She read the books with the references in them. She knew that I held every single item she ever knitted or crocheted or embroidered or hooked for me in the highest esteem. But did I ever tell her how I felt about that sweater? How I can still see it in front of me, feel the stitches beneath my fingers, all these years later?

I hope so.

NANCY HERKNESS'S
WHAT (VERY LITTLE) I KNOW
ABOUT KNITTING LACE

1. A lace knitting project is a great antidote to the terror of flying. It seems to trigger the rational part of your brain that quotes all the statistics about airplane safety while drowning out the irrational part that screams, "This giant tube of metal overloaded with people and baggage can't possibly stay thirty thousand feet up in thin air." I know this because I have that brain.

2. "Life-lines" are critical to retaining your sanity while knitting lace. It's a simple concept: every X number of rows, use a tapestry needle to thread a length of dental floss through all the loops on your needle, and leave it there until you have threaded the next life-line. This allows you to rip out sections you

have messed up (because messing up is almost inevitable in knitting lace) back to the nearest life-line, where you can easily pick up all the stitches in the right position. Dental floss is the best material for this because it's thin and slippery, and therefore easy to pull out when you are ready to move it to its new position in your lace.

3. "Life-lines" are also important if you are taking your knitting on an airplane (see Item 1), just in case an overzealous security guard decides your knitting needles look like a weapon of mass destruction and refuses to let you take them on the plane. Then you can take the needle out of the lace and the life-line will save your project. Note: I have never once had a problem getting my bamboo knitting needles on an airplane but there are reports of folks who have. They recommend taking a preaddressed and stamped mailing envelope if you want to save your needles; you just pop them in the envelope and drop them in the nearest mailbox.

Nancy Herkness is a knitter and award-winning romance novelist. She's also a member of the merry band of knitter-writers at the *Romancing the Yarn* blog. You can visit her website at www.NancyHerkness.com.

FRAN BAKER'S TWIG STITCH THROW

This is an easy casual throw to knit and is reversible.

Materials
Medium worsted weight yarn:
    Variegated: 4–6 balls
    Coordinating color: 4–6 balls
Circular knitting needle, size 15 (10mm)

Note: Throw is made holding one strand of variegated and one strand of coordinating color together.

Twig Stitch Pattern:
K3, *K1, YO, k2tog; repeat from * to last 3 stitches, K3

Stitch Guide:
K = Knit, YO = Yarn Over, k2tog = Knit 2 Together

Instructions

Cast on 90 stitches

K 4 rows

Row 5 and all rows in pattern: K3, *K1, YO, k2tog; repeat from * to last 3 stitches, K3

Continue in this pattern until length suits

K 4 rows

Bind off in knit

If you wish to make throw wider or narrower, do so in units of 3 and purchase yarn accordingly.

Fran Baker is a bestselling author who also owns her own small press. Readers are invited to visit her websites at www.FranBaker.com and www.DelphiBooks.us.

CAROLINE LEAVITT'S KNITTING WRONG COULD BE VERY RIGHT

I was making my first-ever designed cardigan, which had open work leaves on it and fancy buttons. I must have spent months on it, and when it was finished, to my horror, I found one side was about three inches shorter than the other. Defeated, I threw it in the trash, and then fished it out the next day and tried it on solely for the purpose of seeing if I had sized it right. Guess what? The three-inch difference actually looked really, really cool! Since then, I have worn the sweater constantly, and people always ask me (admiringly, I might add), "How did you think to get one side shorter than the other? I want to try that!"

Caroline Leavitt is an award-winning screenwriter and author of eight novels. Her ninth novel, *Breathe*, will be published by Algon-

quin Books of Chapel Hill in Spring 2010. Her website can be found at www.carolineleavitt.com. Read her blog at carolineleavittville.blogspot.com.

CINDI MYERS'S CONNECTING THREADS

For me, knitting has always been about connections—the connection of loops of fiber to form useful and beautiful items, certainly—but even more the connections that knitters make with one another and with those who receive or admire their work. While knitting may seem a solitary pursuit, once one picks up needles and yarn, one becomes a part of the knitting community. When my fourth-grade teacher taught me to knit, she wasn't merely passing on a useful skill to occupy my fingers and mind. She also made me part of a community that transcends location and time.

Whenever I take my knitting with me to while away the time before the beginning of a concert or to make more bearable the wait at a doctor's or dentist's office, I never fail to meet others who knit. When I step through the door of my local yarn store or log on to a favorite knitting blog, I am assured of an instant connection with others who gather there. The people who receive a pair or socks, a sweater, or a humble dishcloth that I have knitted become part of that community as well. When they wear or use the gifted item, they will think of me, but they also will probably think of a friend, a grandmother, or a favorite aunt who also knitted. Knitting connects past and present, creator and created-for, in the most lovely web of artistry, thoughtfulness, and understanding.

Cindi Myers is an avid knitter and prolific author of more than three dozen romance and women's fiction novels. Find out more about her at www.CindiMyers.com.

RACHAEL HERRON'S
FAVORITE TRICKS FOR KNITTING

The prettiest left-slanting decrease to pair against the right-slanting k2tog is a beautifully modified SSK (slip, slip, knit). Slip one as if to knit, slip one as if to purl, then knit both together through the back loop.

A long-tail cast-on can be used for just about everything, always.

No one else will ever notice your mistakes. They won't notice the miscrossed cable because they'll be so impressed with the sweater itself.

Knitting and wine go together well, but combining knitting and whiskey is usually ill-advised.

When traveling, take only socks-in-progress. You'll be too interested in everything around you to pay real attention to any other kind of pattern. Sock yarn takes up very little room in your carry-on, leaving you space to buy souvenir yarn to bring home.

Rachael Herron lives in Oakland with her love, three dogs, four cats, many spinning wheels, and even more old-time instruments. She writes for Yarnagogo.com and is known as simply The Knitter to her friends.

BARBARA BRETTON'S
TEN ORGANIZATIONS THAT
CAN USE YOUR KNITTING

There's no question that knitters (and crocheters) are among the most generous crafters on the planet, and their generosity isn't limited to tax-deductible monetary donations. Knitters give their time and talents (not to mention thousands of FOs) to a multitude of organizations. Here are some of the ones I know and love:

1. **H4HA**—www.h4ha.org/snuggles—knitted or crocheted cage blankets for shelter animals.

2. **Bear Booties**—twistedpdx.com/download/BearBooties.pdf—mittens for bear paws.

3. **Knit 4 Children (K4C)**—knit4children.tripod.com—supplies baby blankets, caps, booties, lap throws for seniors,

etc., for a number of American hospitals.

4. **Children in Common (CIC)**—www.adoptionstogether.org/common/index.asp—primarily woolen socks for orphanages in Eastern Europe.

5. **Project Linus**—projectlinus.org—"security" blankets for sick kids.

6. **Seamen's Scarves**—www.seamenschurch.org/484.asp—long-standing charity based in New York City.

7. **Warm Up America**—warmupamerica.com—afghans and blankets for families in need.

8. **Afghans for Afghans**—www.afghansforafghans.org—an international effort.

9. **Veterans Hospitals**—www.nationalww2museum.org/media/press-releases/knit-your-bit-the-national-1.html—scarves for Vets a small way to say thank you.

10. **Red Scarf Project**—orphan.org/index.php?id=40—scarves for kids

who have aged out of the foster care system.

Barbara Bretton wrote the book you just finished reading. You can find her at www.bar barabretton.com or at bmafb.blogspot.com or especially at romancingtheyarn.blogspot .com.

MARY ANNE MOHANRAJ'S MOSSY DREAMS OF SQUARES AND BOBBLES

This modern scarf is appropriate for crochet beginners; if you can sc (single crochet), dc (double crochet), tr (treble crochet), you can do this. The only new stitch is the cluster stitch, described in detail below. It's also very fast to make! The scarf is basically worked in three blocks: an open squares block, a cluster block (which I only used near the ends), and a solid block. In my version, I alternated open squares and solid for the body of the scarf, but you can vary the blocks to your taste. This took me just over two skeins of bulky-weight yarn, but of course that's dependent on how long you want your finished scarf. If you do it in the recommended insanely soft alpaca, you'll enjoy a luscious crocheting experience.

Level: Beginner

Yarn: Misti Alpaca Bulky

Hook: G

Cluster stitch
* yo, insert hook in stitch, yo and pull up a loop, yo and draw through 2 loops on hook; repeat from * 3 times more, yo and draw through all 5 loops on hook

Stitch Guide
ch-chain, sk-skip, sc-single crochet, dc-double crochet, tr-treble crochet, yo-yarn over

Instructions
Row 1: ch 19
Row 2: ch 4 (first tr of row), tr 18

Open Squares Block
Row 3: ch 4, * ch 2, sk 2, tr, repeat from * 6 times (forming 6 open squares)
Rows 4–5: repeat row 3

Clusters Block
Row 6: ch 2, sc 18

Row 7: ch 4, tr 18
Row 8: ch 4, tr, cluster (*yo, insert hook in stitch, yo and pull up a loop, yo and draw through 2 loops on hook; repeat from * 3 times more, yo and draw and through all 5 loops on hook), tr 6, cluster, tr 6, cluster, tr 2
Row 9: dc 18
Row 10: repeat row 8
Row 11: ch 4, tr 18
Row 12: ch 2, sc 18

Open Squares Block
Row 13: ch 4, * ch 2, sk 2, tr, repeat from * 6 times (forming 6 open squares)
Rows 14–15: repeat row 3

Solid Block
Row 16: ch 3, dc 18
Rows 17–19: ch 4, dc 18
Row 20: ch 3, dc 18
Rows 21–onward: repeat open squares and solid blocks until desired length is reached, ending with an open square, and leaving length for one more cluster block, open square block. Finish with a row of tr and a row of sc. You're done!

Mary Anne Mohanraj is the author of Bodies in Motion, Sri Lankan–American linked stories (HarperCollins) and nine other titles. Bodies in Motion was a finalist for the Asian-American Book Awards and has been translated into six languages. Her other books include A Taste of Serendib (a Sri Lankan cookbook), and The Poet's Journey (an illustrated children's book). She teaches creative writing, Asian-American literature, and post-colonial literature at the University of Illinois. Visit her website at www.maryannemohanraj.com.